The Skylarks' War

Hilary McKay

Margaret K. McElderry Books

New York   London   Toronto   Sydney   New Delhi

"So in the morn there fell new tidings and
other adventures."

For Kevin, with love

MARGARET K. McELDERRY BOOKS
An imprint of Simon & Schuster Children's Publishing Division
1230 Avenue of the Americas, New York, New York 10020
This book is a work of fiction. Any references to historical events, real people, or real places are used fictitiously. Other names, characters, places, and events are products of the author's imagination, and any resemblance to actual events or places or persons, living or dead, is entirely coincidental.
Text copyright © 2018 by Hilary McKay
Originally published by Margaret K. McElderry Books in 2018 as
Love to Everyone
Cover illustrations copyright © 2018 by Dawn Cooper
Interior illustration copyright © 2018 by Rebecca Green
All rights reserved, including the right of reproduction in whole or in part in any form.
MARGARET K. McELDERRY BOOKS is a trademark of Simon & Schuster, Inc.
For information about special discounts for bulk purchases, please contact Simon & Schuster Special Sales at 1-866-506-1949 or business@simonandschuster.com.
The Simon & Schuster Speakers Bureau can bring authors to your live event. For more information or to book an event, contact the Simon & Schuster Speakers Bureau at 1-866-248-3049 or visit our website at www.simonspeakers.com.
Also available in a Margaret K. McElderry Books hardcover edition
Book design by Irene Metaxatos
The text for this book was set in Minion Pro.
Manufactured in the United States of America
0819 OFF
First Margaret K. McElderry Books paperback edition September 2019
10 9 8 7 6 5 4 3 2 1
CIP data for this book is available from the Library of Congress.
ISBN 978-1-5344-6004-1
ISBN 978-1-5344-2711-2 (pbk)
ISBN 978-1-5344-2712-9 (eBook)

PRAISE FOR *The Skylarks' War*

★"Buoyant with the warmth of family love and friendship, and especially with McKay's witty, incisive style."—*Horn Book*, starred review

★"McKay manages a near-miraculous balance of light and joyous touch with sometimes serious and even heartbreaking material."
—*Bulletin of the Center for Children's Books*, starred review

★"Though love, pain, and loss shape this emotionally resonant story of coming of age in turbulent times, the ending is quietly hopeful and wholly satisfying."
—*Booklist*, starred review

"Vivid, hilarious, and heartbreaking, Hilary McKay's radiant characters touch my heart like real people, friends and loved ones I know well. Possibly the finest writer of our time."—ELIZABETH WEIN, *New York Times* bestselling author of *Code Name Verity* and *The Pearl Thief*

"I thoroughly loved *The Skylarks' War*. The story is at once intimate and sweeping."—KIMBERLY BRUBAKER BRADLEY, #1 *New York Times* bestselling author of *The War That Saved My Life*

"I LOVED *The Skylarks' War*. Hilary McKay is a genius. It's the best children's book I've read this year."—KATHERINE RUNDELL,
Boston Globe–Horn Book Award–winning author of *Cartwheeling in Thunderstorms*

"Hilary McKay is a genius. This beautiful book is so many things simultaneously. . . . I never wanted it to end."—BONNIE-SUE HITCHCOCK, author of William A. Morris Award finalist *The Smell of Other People's Houses*

"I laughed, I cried, and I wanted all the characters to be my best friend."
—NATASHA FARRANT, author of *The Children of Castle Rock* and
Lydia: The Wild Girl of Pride and Prejudice

"McKay is incapable of writing an uninteresting character or a dull scene. . . .
I loved it." —MARY HOFFMAN, *New York Times* bestselling author of
Stravaganza and *Amazing Grace*

Also by Hilary McKay

One

MORE THAN ONE HUNDRED YEARS AGO, IN THE time of gas lamps and candlelight, when shops had wooden counters and the streets were full of horses, a baby girl was born. Nobody was pl eased about this except the baby's mother. The baby's father did not like children, not even his own. Peter, the baby's brother, was only three years old and did not understand the need for any extra people in his world.

But the baby's mother was pleased. She named the baby Clarissa, after her own lost mother. "'Clear and bright,'" she whispered to the baby. "That's what your name means. 'Clear and bright.' Clarry."

Clarry was three days old when her mother died. Many things were said about this great calamity, and some of them were regretted later, when people had calmed down and there were fewer tears and more worried frowns in the narrow stone house where the baby had so inconsiderately arrived and her mother had so inconveniently departed. For it was, as the baby's father remarked (in no one's presence unless a week-old baby counted), a blasted nuisance. And if it had to happen, and she had to die, the father added bitterly, then it was a pity that the baby had not also . . .

Luckily at this point, Peter stamped into the room, and stopped the awful words that might have come next. Peter was kinder than his father. He merely gripped the bars of the cot and screamed.

"Go away, go away," screamed Peter to the quiet baby. "Mumma, Mumma, Mumma, Mumma, Mumma!"

Poor Peter's voice was hoarse with shrieking; he had been protesting in this way for what seemed to him a lifetime, but he did not give up. Long after his fingers had been unpeeled one by one from the bars, and he had been hauled downstairs and handed to his grandmother, he kept up his lament.

"It is all completely beyond me," said Peter's father truthfully. He was a man who believed in escaping inconveniences and in his opinion there was no inconvenience worse than a newborn baby. After Clarry's arrival he took refuge in his office in town. There, he did who-knew-what in blissful peace for as long as he could make the hours stretch. He never came home willingly.

The children's Cornish grandmother was not there willingly either. She already had one unrequested child living with her, her grandson Rupert, whose parents were in India. Rupert had been left behind in Cornwall when she had hurried to take charge at Peter and Clarry's home.

"I expect the best thing would be to take the boy and the . . . er . . . the other one . . . back with you when you leave," said the children's father hopefully as he sidled toward the door. "And then all three could be brought up together. Nicer," he added, although he did not say for whom.

The children's grandmother had been expecting this proposal and had prepared a reply. She said very decisively that she would not dream of depriving Clarry and Peter of their father's company.

"Even if," she added, "at my great age, I felt able to cope with bringing up three such very young children. "

"Sixty-five is nothing these days," protested her panic-stricken son.

"I have my heart and my knees," his mother said firmly. "Your poor father has his chest. However," she added (since a look of imminent orphanages was appearing in the panicking one's eyes), "for the present I will stay here and help as best I can."

To make it possible for Clarry and Peter's grandmother to stay with them, Rupert was packed off to boarding school. Then, for the next year or so, the children's grandmother juggled the interviewing of servants, the demands of her abandoned husband, Peter's rages, Clarry's teething, and their father's total lack of interest.

"He's grieving," suggested Miss Vane, who lived across the road.

"No, he isn't," said the children's grandmother robustly.

"Then the poor man is still in shock."

"Selfish," said the children's grandmother. "Also spoiled. I spoiled both my boys and now I suffer the consequences."

"Mrs. Penrose!" exclaimed Miss Vane.

"Spoiled, selfish, immature, and irresponsible," continued the children's grandmother.

Miss Vane laughed nervously and said that dear Mrs. Penrose had a very droll sense of humor.

"If you insist," said the children's grandmother, as she wiped Clarry's chin for the hundredth time that afternoon and removed Peter from the coal scuttle. She considered it a great relief when a few days later she heard that her abandoned husband had caught pneumonia.

"He has no one in Cornwall capable of nursing him," she

told the children's father. "Clarry is walking and almost talking. Peter is quite able to manage by himself. I have found you an excellent general servant who is fond of children, and I absolutely must go home!"

Then, despite Clarry's startled eyes, Peter's wails of "Come back! Come back! Gramma, Gramma, Gramma, Gramma!" and their father's outraged disbelief, she hurried off to Cornwall, by way of horse-drawn cab, steam train, and pony trap.

Fortunately for Peter and Clarry and their despairing parent, in those days almost everybody either was a servant or employed servants themselves. They were a part of life. Over the next few years the children were cared for by one after another of a long stream of grumbling, hurrying, short tempered, tired, and underpaid women, who trundled, stomped, tiptoed, and bustled through the house. They swept carpets with brooms, boiled puddings in saucepans, washed their charges' hands with hard yellow soap and their faces with the corners of aprons, carried coals, cleared ashes, fried chops, mopped tiles, polished shoes, chased away cats and pigeons, jerked hairbrushes through tangles, made stale bread and milk suppers, shook dust from rugs, sat down with sighs and rose with groans, irritated the children's father with every breath they took, and left as soon as they possibly could to find work that wasn't so hard.

Inside the narrow house, the wallpaper faded and the

furniture became shabby, but the children grew. Peter became such a nuisance that he was sent to a day school. There, he was discovered to be extremely clever, which probably accounted for his shocking temper. Clarry was not a nuisance; she was brown haired and round faced and more or less happy. Miss Vane popped over the road to invite her to join her Sunday school class.

"She doesn't believe in God," said nine-year-old Peter, who had answered the door. "I've told her it's not true, haven't I, Clarry?"

Clarry, who had pushed under his arm to smile at Miss Vane, nodded in agreement.

"I think I would prefer to talk about this with your father," said Miss Vane.

"Father wouldn't listen," said Peter, and then Mrs. Morgan, by far the most long lasting servant, came hurrying over, extinguished Peter with a bat from a damp dishcloth, removed Clarry's thumb from her mouth, ordered, "Upstairs, the pair of you, you're forever where you're not wanted!" and told Miss Vane that she was sure Mr. Penrose would be very pleased to have Clarry out of mischief for an hour or so on Sundays, and they'd send her across in something clean or as best as could be managed.

And this happened, and was the beginning of Miss Vane's Good Deed and Christian Duty of Keeping an Eye on the

Family, which was sometimes helpful, and sometimes not, and often made Peter growl.

"I daresay she's one of those people who need to make themselves feel useful," said the children's father to Mrs. Morgan. "She's offered to help sort out whatever it is the . . . Clarry wears. Her grandmother can't be relied on, since she still insists on living in Cornwall. Miss Vane is harmless enough. I can't see why anyone should find the arrangement a problem."

"She stands too close and she smells of cats," said Peter, after a particularly dreary Miss Vane afternoon.

"Cat *food*," said Clarry fairly. "Liver. She boils it. She was boiling it when I went there for her to pin up the hem on my dress." Clarry sighed. Already she was suffering far more than Peter from their neighbor's helpfulness. Miss Vane took her for long, chilly walks, murmuring instructions about pleasant behavior. She had knitted her an itchy striped scarf. When Clarry's winter dress was scorched beyond repair by Mrs. Morgan drying it over the kitchen fire, Miss Vane had made a brand-new one in hideous green and mustard tartan. Clarry had had to stand on a chair while Miss Vane jerked and pulled and stuck in dozens of pins.

"The joins don't match and those brown buttons look awful," Peter had remarked the first time she wore it. "But I don't suppose anyone will care."

"She's knitting you a scarf too," Clarry told him.

"Let her," said Peter. "I'll drop it in the river."

"You couldn't drop a scarf that a poor old lady had knitted for you into the river," said Clarry, very shocked.

"I could. She's not poor either. She's not even that old."

But to six-year-old Clarry, Miss Vane was very ancient indeed, and so were all Miss Vane's friends. Two of them ran a school for girls at the top of yet another tall bare house. They were called the Miss Pinkses.

"The what?" asked Clarry's father.

"The Miss Pinkses," repeated Miss Vane earnestly. "I do agree, it is quaint. As is the school. Old-fashioned values. I mention it because it is just around the corner. I believe the girls start at about Clarry's age."

"Her grandmother was saying that it was time I found her a school," admitted Clarry's father, and the next thing Clarry knew she was climbing the three flights of stairs to the Miss Pinkses' schoolrooms.

The first of many climbs, year after year.

At the Miss Pinkses', the light was dim, the street felt very far away, and there were always dead bluebottles lying upside down on the windowsills. By midafternoon the suffocating fumes from the oil stoves that warmed the rooms made heads ache and eyes blur, so that it was hard to stay awake.

But at least, as her father said, even if she didn't learn anything, she was out of the house.

Two

RIGHT FROM HER YOUNGEST DAYS, CLARRY HAD understood that all the uncomfortable difficulties of their lives—Miss Vane and the itchy knitting, the uncertain cooking of Mrs. Morgan and her kind, the remote unhappiness of her father, the increasing shabbiness of the house, the bread and milk suppers, and the desperate fierceness of Peter's temper— were because she, Clarry, had been born and her mother had died. Nobody ever said it quite as plainly as that, but if they had, Clarry would have bowed her head and agreed that it was true.

Nevertheless, she hummed when she was drawing. She skipped downstairs in long airy jumps, she stopped to speak to cats and horses, and she was never frightened by Peter's moods.

"You don't want to put up with him bossing you around," advised Mrs. Morgan, as they peeled potatoes together. "You've no cause to go running every time he shouts. What's he wanting now?"

"Homework," said Clarry, already half out of the kitchen.

"Tell him he must manage without you!"

"No, no, no," exclaimed Clarry, and left before Mrs. Morgan could make any more ridiculous suggestions. Homework with Peter had begun the day he started school. Ever since, every evening, he had demanded that she understand and help with whatever he brought home. It didn't matter to Peter that she was a girl and three years younger. Doggedly he shoved and nagged her through math, history, Latin vocabulary, science, geography, and all his current obsessions. Clarry never questioned the use of being able to locate on a map the Roman roads of England, or to know what went on inside the hall clock.

Or any of the rest. "Where would you find the nearest black rat if you had to find one right now?" Peter would demand over his shoulder as he left for school. "The nearest golden oriole? Basking shark? Wild peacock?" Clarry didn't know, but she learned how to find out. The two dusty shelves of the *Encyclopaedia Britannica* that once lived in the sitting room had long since been relocated to the middle of her bedroom floor.

This evening Clarry found Peter at the foot of the stairs, carefully unpacking something from his bag. "Where've you been for so long?" he demanded. "We've math and some stupid Shakespeare to learn and I've got this book to borrow. Look!"

It was called *The Story of the Heavens* and bound in dark blue and cream. There was a pattern of gold rings on the front. *Halos,* thought Clarry, and opened it, expecting to see angels. Instead she found herself looking at an engraving of a lens as it gathered and made visible the light from a star.

"Look!" cried Clarry. "It's all about stars! It's showing you how a telescope works!"

"Of course," said Peter.

"And there's a comet!" Clarry looked again at the cover of the book. The halos turned out to be the orbits of planets. There were gold-edged pages, and constellations embossed on the spine. She had never seen anything so beautiful and so new.

"Where did you get it from?" she asked, touching the stars.

"It'd just come into the library. We can keep it for two weeks."

Clarry glowed at the "we."

"It's exactly the sort of book I'm going to write!" she said admiringly, and then they both heard their father's dry, impatient "Oh, please!" as he came through the door behind them.

"I could," said Clarry, rather hurt. "Don't you think it would be nice?"

"What I think would be nice," said her father, "would be to not have your brother continually encouraging you to imitate everything he says and does and thinks! It'll be a very good thing when . . ." He paused, took a deep breath, and shrugged.

"When what?" asked Peter, looking at him with extreme suspicion.

"Nothing. Excuse me, please, both of you. I'm in a rush. Peter, shouldn't you be getting on with homework? And Clarry, surely you might be helping Mrs. Morgan?"

"I was. I will. I just . . ."

"Off you go, then."

"Yes," said Clarry, and turned back to the door behind the stairs which led to the part of the house her father had not visited for years: the kitchen, scullery, and low dank cellars that were beyond his geography.

"Wait!" ordered Peter, pushing past his father to reach her before she vanished. "Here's the book! Take it. Read it."

"That is exactly the sort of thing I wish you would not take it upon yourself to do!" snapped his father, but Clarry was gone, and Peter turned away as if he had not heard.

"Well!" said Mrs. Morgan, looking up as Clarry came in. "I was listening! Them two squabbling as usual, and you in the middle of it!"

"It was only about a book," said Clarry. "This one. Peter brought it home from the library. It's about the moon and stars and planets."

"Fortune-telling!" said Mrs. Morgan, sniffing. "I'm not surprised your father wasn't pleased!"

"No, no, telescopes and things!" said Clarry. "Science!"

"I can't see your father caring for telescopes either," said Mrs. Morgan. "Never mind, sit down and read me a bit while I get these greens washed."

Clarry sat down, flicked through the pages, and read:

"'Who is there that has not watched, with ad . . . with admiration, the beautiful series of changes through which the moon passes every month? We first see her as an ex . . . as an exquis . . . exquisite crescent. . . .'"

"Gray," remarked Mrs. Morgan, hacking at cabbage with a blunt knife. "Gray and patchy it looks! Piled up with dust! Go on!"

"'An exquisite crescent of pale light in the western sky . . .'"

"Exquisite indeed!" said Mrs. Morgan. "Washed out, more like. Always looks washed out to me, does the moon. Like that father of yours!"

"Father? Washed out?"

"Fearful, you might call it," said Mrs. Morgan. "Afraid of the world. Then when he snaps at you, that's just his fear coming out. Now don't you stare at me like that, madam! I've made up my mind to say a few words and I'm telling you for your own comfort. So as you don't let him upset you so often as he does."

Clarry turned her face away.

"Now, my father," said Mrs. Morgan, sweeping a heap of cabbage into her saucepan and beginning on another pile of wrinkled green leaves, "took a belt to me! Regular!"

"A belt!" exclaimed Clarry, horrified. "Why?"

"Well, for what I got up to. Cheeking him. Climbing out of my bedroom window to go off with the boys. Going away with his horse to get to the fair. Took it out of the shafts of the cart, I did, while my father stood outside the cottage and never noticed till I'd gone! Too busy staring at the chimney!"

"What was the matter with the chimney?"

"It was afire," said Mrs. Morgan placidly. "I was bound I'd get to the fair that year, so I'd stoked up the hearth good and hot inside, and put on a bundle of straw. I'd missed the fair the time before, you see. I was out all night, and me only fourteen! What a performance when I got back the next day!"

Clarry gazed at Mrs. Morgan in complete admiration, all her troubles forgotten.

"Oh, he was a very determined man, my father!" said Mrs. Morgan, nodding. "Now, yours is a gentleman, whatever his temper. Is that enough greens?"

"Yes," said Clarry, who was not fond of cabbage. "Thank you, Mrs. Morgan."

Three

IT WAS STRANGE HOW MRS. MORGAN'S REMARKS about fathers helped Clarry. She did not completely agree with them, and she could not help wondering how hot tempered her own father would have become, if she had behaved anything like Mrs. Morgan had as a girl. Still, it was comforting to know that other people had difficult relations too.

There were other reasons for cheerfulness in Clarry's world. The long cold winter was passing. The light grew brighter, even in the Miss Pinkses' fume-filled classrooms. The air was wet and salt-tanged from the sea. There were birds above the chimney pots and daffodils to be spotted on

Miss Vane's chilly walks, and it was spring, with summer on the horizon.

Summer was shining bliss. Summer was opals and topaz and lapis and diamonds flung down from the sky. Summer was Cornwall.

Every summer they were there, for weeks and weeks, for an endless time, for so long that when they were little they forgot that one day they would have to go home. There was never a day of winter that Clarry did not count as one day closer to summer. When the time before leaving for Cornwall could be counted in days rather than weeks, there was no sadness that could touch her. At the beginning, when she and Peter were very small, their father had been forced to travel with them, but since Peter was ten they had been judged old enough to manage the journey alone. They were dispatched at one end by their father, and collected four or five hours later at the other by whichever grandparent happened to be about. When Miss Vane first heard of this careless arrangement she had been so horrified she offered to take them herself.

"Er," their father had said. "Why? What could happen to them?"

Miss Vane suggested missed stations, robbery, and kidnapping. Unmoved, the children's father said he generally gave a shilling or two to the guard and so far this had not happened. That was no guarantee of the future, said Miss Vane.

"Er," said the children's father, and most unusually, asked Peter's opinion.

"What?" cried Peter in horror, and added that he would rather be robbed, kidnapped, and walk the whole distance than sit in a railway carriage with Miss Vane all the way to Cornwall. Clarry, hovering anxiously on one foot in the background, did not disagree.

"Well, er . . . ," said their father, "very well. As I thought."

So the children continued to travel alone, unrobbed, unkidnapped, and correctly delivered.

The summer that Peter was thirteen and Clarry was nearly ten, things were different. As the date for departure came closer, happiness fizzed in bright bubbles through Clarry's days and nights, but it was not the same for Peter. There was a tension in the air between Peter and his father that made any mention of the future a perilous thing. Cornwall was never the pure joy for Peter that it was for Clarry anyway. For a start, there was the journey to be got through. This began, every time, with the parting at the station and their father's annual summer speech, made always in jerky sentences, with his pipe clamped in his teeth.

"It's very good of your grandparents . . . every summer . . .

make an effort, for heaven's sake, not to be . . . trouble to them. . . ."

Peter's expression was entirely blank, but his eyes rolled sideways.

"We're never any trouble," Clarry assured him. "They hardly see us most days. And we do help. Last year we mowed the grass quite often, and posted letters and things."

"Er . . . good. Excellent. Oh, Clarry, your birthday . . ."

Clarry blushed with embarrassment. He had remembered. Sometimes he didn't. Sometimes he did. She never knew whether to be glad or sorry, but she was always ashamed.

"To celebrate."

A coin in her hand. Small, but heavy. Ominous.

"Oh no, oh no! Father, you needn't! It doesn't matter."

She and her mother had overlapped each other in time for only a very short while. Less than a week. Three days. How could any birthday be celebrated if that was the case?

"Choose a treat!"

"Oh, thank you, thank you, but . . ."

Clarry looked around for help from Peter and found he had vanished. Far down the tracks appeared a great cloud of steam. The platform stirred like a rock pool at the turn of the tide. It was the moment of farewell.

Clarry's father took his pipe from his mouth. He dipped his head. Clarry kissed a patch of air somewhere near his left ear. His hand touched her shoulder briefly. They both sighed with relief and the racket of the arriving train shook them into their separate worlds again.

"Here we are, then. Where's your brother?"

Peter was back, shaking hands with his father (anything to avoid the horror of a hug), clutching his bag, rigid.

"Postcard," said their father, pipe in place, straightening his shoulders as if putting down a load.

"Yes, yes," said Peter impatiently.

"Might you come and see us?" asked Clarry. "You could, couldn't you? Perhaps?"

"Er . . . well . . . no. Now then, off you go."

Their bags were on the train, heaved up by Peter with their father hovering behind.

"Behave, and so on!"

"Don't be lonely!" said Clarry, leaning out of the window. She caught a glimpse of his face unguarded, and saw that he could not wait for them to go.

Oh, Father. Oh, thank goodness, the guard was beginning to pace the length of the train, closing carriages. On the platform, a crowd of people surged between them. The doors slammed. There was a pause of quietness and then a shrill whistle, an eruption of noise, a great deal of steam, a smell in the air like winter fires in summer, and the train was moving.

At the last moment, Clarry stretched out of the window to scream, "I love you! I *do* love you!"

"Sit down!" growled Peter, but Clarry waved until the station was out of sight. Then she retreated to a seat opposite her brother and unclamped her fingers from her birthday present.

It was a gold sovereign, the first she had ever held. Clarry gasped out loud and Peter glanced over.

"For my birthday," Clarry told him. "He remembered."

Peter refrained from saying, *I reminded him.*

"Do you think he can afford it?"

"Of course."

"I'll give you half."

"No thanks. I've got money."

Unlike Clarry, Peter had a godfather. A useful one too. He lived in Scotland and did not communicate in any way, but on the first Monday of every month he sent to Peter a postal order for five shillings. On the first Tuesday of every month Peter posted back to him a message of thanks on a postcard: *Thank you very much. P. Penrose.*

It was like, Clarry sometimes thought, having a very small private gold mine.

But postal orders were only printed paper. This was actual gold. Heavy. The king on one side. Saint George and his dragon on the other. Clarry bent to study it. The dragon was not yet slain. It was putting up a good fight. One twist, and it could slip aside, spin round, and come at Saint George from behind. That was a sovereign, such a thing of beauty to Clarry that she thought she might keep it forever. The next minute, though, she had begun a list of all that it might buy. What was Peter's heart's desire? What would make her father smile? What would please her cousin Rupert?

The future sparkled with possibilities and the sun came out and illuminated the carriage's stale gray air. Soot and pollen and the dust of humanity that rose in clouds from the itchy horsehair seats, all glittered as if newly enchanted.

Could Peter see the glimmering air? Clarry looked across at him.

No. He couldn't. He couldn't see anything. His eyes were clenched tight shut, his face was white, his hands gripped together into a bunch of bony knuckles. He was fighting a battle. Peter suffered from travel sickness. The journey to Cornwall was more than four hours long.

"Peter," whispered Clarry.

"Shut up."

"We're nearly halfway through the first hour already."

He gave a small moan.

Clarry had with her a secret store of strong brown paper bags supplied by Miss Vane. She had six. Last year she had brought two, which had not been enough.

"Drop them discreetly from the window after use," Miss Vane had instructed. Clarry had dropped them, but not discreetly. Discreetly was not easy with other people in the carriage. Another problem was that the bags had to be invisible until the moment of crisis. It was fatal for Peter to catch sight of them a second too soon. It was all very difficult indeed, the bag hiding, the swift producing at the critical moment, the scarlet-cheeked endurance of their indignant fellow passengers while the bags were in use, the collection, the wobbly steps across the carriage, the one-handed tugging down of the window, the drop.

I must be careful not to let go of my sovereign by mistake, thought Clarry suddenly, and that was such a dreadful idea that she jumped up to stow it away.

"What are you doing?" hissed Peter, as she climbed on the seat beside him to retrieve her case from the saggy string luggage rack overhead.

"I'm putting my money in the little pocket in my case," whispered Clarry. "I won't get it down. I just need to get the strap off. . . ."

"You're bouncing the seat!"

"Sorry! Wait!"

"Stop it," moaned Peter. "Oh no! Oh no!"

Clarry glanced down and dropped both open case and sovereign as she leaped to the rescue. A cascade of clothes tumbled onto the floor, together with Clarry's beloved paint box, the sovereign went rolling away, but she managed to push the bag into Peter's hands before the worst happened.

"Phew!" said Clarry.

"Well done!" cried a grinning youth from the seats opposite.

"Good girl!" agreed an elderly man, smiling with approval, and lifted his toe to show her the sovereign, caught before it rolled out of sight. A thin, bright-faced woman was already collecting and folding the tumbled clothes. "Happens to the best of us," she said, passing them to Clarry, and there was a murmur of agreement that changed to loud polite conversation about the view from the window, while Peter suffered again, although as privately as his fellow travelers could manage.

"Thank you," said Clarry, overwhelmed at all this kindness. "Thank you, he can't help it, he'll be better soon, and anyway, I have five more bags. . . ."

"Shut up!" moaned Peter, bending again, but after a few ghastly moments he was well enough to ignore Clarry's helpful hand and stagger to the window.

"There you go!" said the grinning youth, who yanked it down for him and afterward gave him his seat. "Better facing forward," he said, and this turned out to be true. So they got through the rest of the journey with three bags to spare, and it was all worth it, because at the end was Cornwall.

Four

CORNWALL WAS THEIRS FOR THE SUMMER, AND the best part of all—better than the turquoise sea, the white gulls, and the gold and purple moor, better than the tangled garden, the scutter of rabbits in the early morning, and their dark footprints in the silver dew, better than the bounty of the Cornish kitchen (apple dumplings, brown eggs, saffron cake, and raspberry tart), better even than Lucy their grandmother's pony who pulled the pony trap—was that in Cornwall was Rupert. Rupert. Rupe. Nearly seven years older than Clarry, three and a half years older than Peter. Their cousin, their fathers were brothers. Clarry and Peter had never met Rupert's parents, last seen waving to three-year-old

Rupert from the boat train, now (according to Grandfather) in Calcutta, drinking themselves to death. Rupert spent his holidays in Cornwall and termtimes away at boarding school. Having endured the desertion of his parents, a Cornish winter when a gale was so strong it blew him off the cliff, a Christmas of scarlet fever, and innumerable years of compulsory education, he was assumed to be indestructible and allowed to do what he liked.

Rupert had a curving smile and lazy green gold eyes, completely unlike Peter's wary gray glance. His jokes were the best, his tennis balls flew the highest, his stories charmed the most listeners, cats strolled over and sat beside him, dogs regarded him with comradely affection, the sunlight tanned him apricot gold, and rain rolled off him in silver drops. He was recklessly kind. For Clarry he was the center of summer, the light on the water, the warmth in the wind, the contented bee-humming of the moor.

Rupert was on the platform when they arrived, and a moment later Clarry had jumped down to be swept into her annual hug of greeting. Rupert hugged Peter too, which Clarry was never allowed to do.

"Get off," said Peter grumpily. He considered himself far too old for hugs, and he was not feeling very fond of his cousin that summer. In the last few weeks his father's mutters and hints had resolved into a family conspiracy to send him away

to school. To Rupert's boarding school, which, as Peter's grandparents had pointed out, had been "the making of his cousin."

"I don't need making!" Peter had protested, but his father
clearly thought he was wrong. He had actually invited him
for a walk to talk over the matter, in the longest conversation he had ever attempted with his son. Peter had been
marched up and down windy streets, listening to the tale of
how Rupert had begun school as a miserable seven-year-old
and become, through the influence of education, the success-
ful and confident person he was now.

"I'm not going and you can't make me," Peter had said,
every time he had a chance to speak. These words had had
the good effect of making his father walk twice as fast, and
at a speed where it was impossible to talk. Unfortunately, as
soon as he calmed down a little he began once more.

"I'm not going and you can't make me," Peter had repeated
mutinously in the next available pause, and off they would go
again. This continued for nearly two hours, and then quite
suddenly Peter's father had spun round, turned into a side
street, and without another glance, vanished.

Peter had arrived home to find Clarry alone in the house,
hovering by the front door and worrying.

"Where is he?"

"Who cares?" asked Peter, pushing past her and stomping inside.

"What did he want?"

"To get rid of me." Peter marched up the stairs to his bedroom, and slammed the door very hard. He had been in a slamming mood ever since, ignoring his father, snubbing Clarry, hunched and miserable on the train. He blamed at least half of his boarding school troubles on his cousin, who had survived far too long and well. Now here was Rupert himself, behaving as if it was none of his fault.

"Sick much?" asked Rupert kindly, ignoring Peter's growls.

"No."

"Three bags," said Clarry cheerfully. "None on the floor this time. Who's coming to meet us?"

"Grandfather," said Rupert, as he led the way out of the station. "But we have to wait for a bit. He dropped me off and went on into town. He'll be back in a few minutes to collect you."

"Is he all right?" asked Clarry. "And are Grandmother and Lucy?"

"Of course they are."

"And are you as well?"

"Don't I look all right?" asked Rupert.

Clarry nodded, not wanting to say anything that would make Peter even more cross, but her eyes shone so brightly she might as well have spoken.

"You should just stay here in Cornwall with Rupert if you like him so much," said Peter, sour with jealousy. "I don't suppose Father would care."

"You would, though!" said Rupert, laughing. "You couldn't manage without Clarry! What about if I come and live at your house instead?"

"Could you?" asked Clarry.

"Of course. You wait and see. I'll turn up one day and bash on the door and you'll all hide behind the curtains and pretend to be out, like Grandmother does when the vicar's wife comes here."

Clarry laughed. Grandmother and the vicar's wife were old enemies. Church on Sundays was brightened by their after-service battles. Even Peter usually enjoyed the duels in front of the altar vases, the nodding hats and the vicious retweakings of each other's lilies and ferns. Today, however, Peter wasn't in the mood for family jokes. He stayed sulking until their grandfather arrived. He had his camera with him and insisted on taking photographs, with many orders such as "Clarry, please look at the camera, not Lucy!" "Rupert! Good heavens! Not quite such a buffoon!" "Stand up straight, Peter! Very well, if that's how you want to appear. . . . Clarry, you're squinting!"

But at last he was satisfied and they were allowed to climb into the pony trap, and there was the long road out of town ahead of them, and then their grandparents' granite house between the moorland and the sea, and they had arrived.

"Now, don't go rushing off," said their grandfather. "If your grandmother is down from her nap, I'm sure she'll want a word."

Peter groaned. Grandmother's words were sometimes difficult to bear. She told the truth, no matter how painful. That was all very amusing when she was telling the vicar's wife that her roses were half dead and the vases smelled like a duck pond. The vicar's wife was a tough old lady, and would point out with equal truth that Grandmother's sweet peas were crawling with greenflies. It was less funny when she remarked that Rupert's parents had probably forgotten he existed, or she hoped Peter actually was brighter than he looked. She also had a way of gazing at Clarry and sighing that made Clarry hang her head. Yet, in her way, she was fond of them all, and now here she was, smiling in welcome, taking Peter's hand, stooping to kiss Clarry.

"*Here* you are again! *How* quickly the summers come around! Well, you know where your beds are and your supper is already waiting for you in the morning room. Keep out of the kitchen, please—they asked me to remind you that they really don't want you in there! Clarry dear, your dress! Don't let me see it again! Straight up to the bathroom, please. You'll find fresh towels and new soap! And then put something suitable on and don't forget to brush that hair! Off you go! Wait, please, Peter!"

Peter, who had got half out of the door after Clarry, paused, glaring.

"A decision has been made about school for you, Peter, for your own good entirely, by the people who care about you most."

"I'm not . . ."

Clarry, in the same dress, with her hair still unbrushed, and clearly having not yet found the soap, fell through the door and flung her arms round Peter. "He's been very ill on the train!" she said fiercely. "You're not to tell him off!"

"Stop it, Clarry!" said Peter, disentangling himself. "Don't fuss! Go and get clean, like Grandmother told you. I don't mind where I go to school. I used to do, but I don't now. I expect I will enjoy it!"

"Good man!" exclaimed Grandfather, smiling like a harbor seal, but Clarry retreated backward across the room, and then went to find Rupert.

"He's pretending he doesn't mind," she told him.

"He might as well," said Rupert unhelpfully. "They won't let him off, so why fight it?"

"He used to say he would die if he had to go. People don't die at boarding school, do they?"

"Never," said Rupert. "Well, hardly ever. Stop worrying

about it! Come on, we'll go and catch Lucy and you can see how long you can stay on!"

Clarry fell off Lucy several times and cheered up. After all, they were back in Cornwall with summer all before them. The swallows' nest was where it had always been, her bedroom floor still dipped and rose like the deck of a ship, and the secret treasure box she had hidden up the chimney was still intact. Clarry counted her hoard: twelve pale pink cowrie shells, a lock of Lucy's mane, a rock containing crystals of gold, and a very small penknife with a pearly handle and a blade that didn't cut. Before she went to bed she added the gold birthday sovereign, and a white heart-shaped stone that Rupert had produced, saying, "Look what I found on the beach for you!"

"That's nice," the new unknown Peter had remarked (he who would previously have said, "That's quartz") and then he had gone to ask his Grandfather if he needed any help with putting away the pony trap for the night. Clarry had looked after him, absolutely baffled.

In church the next day Peter's transformation continued. Clarry observed him praying as if he meant it, putting a whole precious shilling in the collection plate (she was so shocked she took it out again and smuggled it back into his pocket), and asking the vicar about the age of the font, which turned out to be sixteenth century.

"I thought it might be," said Peter.

"M'second grandson," said Grandfather to the vicar, his hand on Peter's back. "Very promising scholar!"

"Thank you, sir," said Peter, steady as a rock. (He had taken to calling his grandfather "sir." It was delightful to hear him.)

"He can't possibly keep it up," whispered Rupert to Clarry, but at Sunday lunch, the once-a-week meal with the grandparents, Peter showed no sign of flagging. During the course of roast beef and jam sponge he correctly identified a landscape Grandmother had painted in her youth, demonstrated an intelligent knowledge of the headlines in the day's papers, retrieved Clarry's napkin from underneath the table, and said at the end, "Come on Rupert, we'll take the plates out to the kitchen!" After that he vanished until Clarry tracked him down reading under the apple trees. He smiled when he saw her and called, "Hullo! Coming to join me? That'll be nice!"

"Peter, Peter, please stop it!"

"Stop what?"

"Being so nice and kind."

"I'm sorry. Aren't I usually nice and kind?"

"OF COURSE you're not!" said Clarry, beating him with her fists.

Peter flopped on his back laughing and said, "You know what? This tree would be a really good place for a hammock."

"A hammock!"

"You could stretch it right across between those two big branches. Or would it damage the apples? I don't see why it should if we were careful. I'll ask Rupert what he thinks. Would you use it, Clarry, if I fixed one up for you?"

"No, I wouldn't!" shouted Clarry, and ran sobbing into the house and collided straight into her grandfather, who said, "Hey, hey, what's this?"

"Nothing. Peter."

"What about Peter?"

"He said the big apple tree would be a really good place for a hammock . . . ," said Clarry rather damply.

"Yes. Go on."

"If it didn't damage the apples."

"I fail to see cause for tears," said her grandfather. "However, I'm too old for tree climbing. Tell him to ask Rupert to give him a hand."

"He *is* asking Rupert."

"Beyond me what the problem is, then," said her grandfather. "Unless you are ill? Are you not feeling well? You'd better go and have a word with your grandmother."

Clarry shook her head, but later she overheard him having a word himself.

"Surprised it's not the girl who causes all the problems we hear about at home! The boy's no trouble at all. If you ask me his father has no idea how to handle him. Great improvement on last year! Perfectly charming."

Peter was perfectly charming all the next day too.

It's being here, thought Clarry, trying to explain it to herself, *and not arguing all the time with Father, and having so much space outside.*

Outside was limitless, garden and fields, moorland and sea. There were no rules, only consequences. The year before, Rupert had picked up an adder which had bitten him and left him with a very sore arm for a week. They had all three regretted eating the mushrooms that they had so confidently gathered. Clarry once freed a dozen trapped bullocks that were pushing at a gate and then could not prevent them following her home.

"You were lucky not to be trampled," said the farmer who came to collect them from the remains of the front lawn.

"I know," said Clarry, still trembling.

"How else can they learn?" asked their grandparents, after all these happenings. "Can we follow them about the countryside saying, 'Don't touch the snake! Leave the bullocks! Those are toadstools, you foolish child!'? At our age? No!" Whichever it was, the freedom or the peace, Peter's transformation continued. On the third day of his new personality, he asked to borrow his grandfather's binoculars to watch kestrels over the moors.

"If you break them I'll flog you," said his grandfather, but he handed them over quite cheerfully, Peter being his new favorite person.

"Thank you, sir," said Peter.

"Would you like my bike too?" asked Rupert, but Peter said no, he'd probably be walking most of the time.

This did not happen.

Five

WHAT PETER DID, AFTER SETTING OUT WITH HIS grandfather's binoculars and his wonderful new manners, was buy a shilling ticket for the branch line train that ran through the valley at the bottom of the grandparents' garden, and step off it as it rattled and puffed its way across the moor.

Nobody knew this for ages and ages, not until the return train went past, and someone happened to notice him lying by the track.

"I thought he was dead until he raised his arm," said the passenger, explaining afterward. "Lying there, half buried in the bracken, white as a sheet. Whatever happened?"

No one could answer that. Peter was retrieved by

stretcher, transported to the nearest town by train, hurried to the local hospital, diagnosed with bruises, shock, and multiple fractures of the left leg, knocked out with chloroform, woken (screaming), dosed with morphine, and very luckily identified by his grandfather's name inside the binocular case. When he finally came round and was well enough to talk, he said he couldn't remember anything after leaving the house.

Two days afterward he recalled getting on the train, and as the days passed, more of the journey came back to him.

"I remember standing up," he said cautiously. "And then I think I opened a door to look at something."

He was home now, after nearly a week in hospital, propped up in bed with his leg in plaster from heel to hip and his bruises as purple as plums.

"You might have died," said Clarry. "Then what?"

"Died!" said Peter scornfully. "I didn't even break the binoculars!"

"And you hate trains! Why did you go on one when you didn't have to do?"

"I found a shilling in my pocket and I thought I might as well."

"Oh, Peter!" wailed Clarry.

"What?"

"I put it there! After church, that first Sunday."

"Well, then, stop blaming me for everything! It's half your fault!"

Rupert, who was leaning against the doorframe, looking thoughtfully at Peter, said, "Oi!"

"Why did you have to open the train door?" persisted Clarry. "Couldn't you have just opened the window if you weren't feeling well?"

"Look!" snapped Peter, for since he had so illogically opened the door of a moving train, his perpetual irritation with the world had returned as if it had never been lost. "Who said I wasn't feeling well? I was on a train! I got off a train! The end!"

"But the train was *going*!"

"Not very fast."

"And you just stepped off *on purpose*?"

"It was much higher above the track than I realized."

"What was it you saw, anyway?"

Peter did not reply, and Clarry saw that his eyes were closed. He had turned his face toward his bedroom wall and she noticed how shabby his old striped pajamas looked, how limp the thin brown hair. "Are you hot?" she asked, reaching out a hand to check his forehead. The doctors had told them that he mustn't be hot; it meant infection from the broken bones.

"No!" Peter pushed her hand away. "I'm just tired. Clear

off, and leave me alone. I'm supposed to be resting. I didn't get much sleep last night." He yawned a large fake yawn, and closed his eyes.

"You're an awful actor," said Rupert, grinning.

"Just get out!" howled Peter, sitting up furiously. "Aaaaah, no! I've yanked it again! Clear off with your rotten questions! It's your fault! It's all your blasted fault! Hell."

He pulled a pillow over his face, but not before Clarry had glimpsed a glitter of tears.

"Peter . . . ," she began, but from under the pillow came a tremendous angry growl.

"Pete, we're going," said Rupert, reaching out for Clarry and steering her toward the door. "Leaving you in peace. I'll be back in a while in case you need anything. Come on, Clarry!"

"But . . ."

"Let him rest."

Out in the garden, Clarry said, "Poor, poor Peter. I don't believe he saw anything special from the train. I expect he was just sick, like always, and couldn't get the window down, and then he must have fallen."

"Yes, perhaps," agreed Rupert.

"And now he's miserable and his whole summer is spoiled."

"Do you always worry about him this much?" asked Rupert, amused.

"Yes, of course I do."

"Well, don't. He'll soon be able to get around a bit, and then he'll cheer up. Stop fussing him, though. No more questions! We'll find something ordinary to talk about. What does he like to do at home? Does he paint things, like you do?"

"No." Clarry shook her head. "He likes looking things up in books," she added, after some thought.

"We'll find him some things to look up, then. We'll go foraging for mysteries! Now then, I'll fetch my bike and you can ride on the crossbar and we'll whiz into town for ice cream!"

"And bring some back for Peter?" asked Clarry.

"It would melt," said Rupert, and then, seeing her disappointed face, added, "We'll bring lemons, to make him lemonade," and watched it shine again.

Clarry took the lemons to the kitchen and was shooed away while the lemonade was made. To pass the time she went hunting outside. Very soon she found a great number of things that could be looked up in books, including a two-headed dandelion, a crystal of pink quartz, a miniature wasp's nest, light as a paper shell, and a metallic blue feather, barred with black.

"I found something too!" said Rupert, and held up a yellowing sheep's skull with gray teeth still intact.

"Yuck!" said Clarry.

"Nonsense, he'll love it! The teeth are loose. He can pull them out and stare into the holes!"

"It's horrible," said Clarry, but Rupert was right and Peter did love it, so much that he inspired Rupert to search for more excitements.

"We could start a museum," Rupert said, emptying a pocketful of stones and seashells onto Peter's bed, and Peter, who liked nothing better than organizing things into straight lines and lists, began cataloging at once.

This was how Peter's recovery began, although the doctors explained that he would be on crutches for months. Even after that, they told him, his left leg would never straighten properly at his knee, and would be at least an inch shorter than his right.

"I don't suppose that will matter much," said Clarry hopefully, when she heard this news. "Nobody will notice."

"They say I'll need to wear a special shoe," said Peter. "Built up. And do exercises. They said they nearly took it off!"

"Peter!"

"So I suppose I've been lucky."

He was so calm about it that his grandfather said gruffly, "Good lad." The grandparents treated the whole affair in much the same way as they had the misadventures of the past. Clarry had learned to leave field gates closed, and

Rupert no longer picked up snakes. Mushrooms were gathered with caution. In future Peter would be more careful with train doors.

Peter did not complain very much. The pain became less, until it was just an uncomfortable stiffness and a mostly ignorable ache. Quite early on in the summer it was decided that he could not be sent to boarding school with Rupert that September.

"What a pity," said Rupert blandly.

"Yes," agreed Peter.

Six

"AND WHAT WILL YOU DO WITH YOURSELF WHILE your brother's laid up?" Clarry's grandfather asked her.

"I thought I might learn to swim," said Clarry, and he burst out laughing and said, "Ha, ha, very good!" and later told her grandmother that she was "quite a little character!" as if she had proposed to take up golf or arranging the flowers in church.

However, Clarry was quite serious. For a long time she had envied the boys their swimming. They went almost every day.

"Well, you're a girl and they are boys," Clarry's grandmother had said when Clarry first mentioned it, a year or two before, and at the time Clarry had nodded, disappointed but accepting. There were a lot of things to accept, she found, about the differences between girls and boys. That boys had pocket money and girls didn't. That boys needed to learn things at school but girls just had to be quietly occupied. That Peter had a bicycle and could ride all over town, but that her own boundaries were school (two minutes' walk away) and Miss Vane's house (across the road).

And most of all, that the boys knew best. And boys were best. It was fact. It was life. It was natural history.

Rupert had learned to swim when he was eight, in the con-crete tank at boarding school (unheated gray water, six feet deep, straight in and no shrieking). Every boy in the school learned to swim; it was the only sensible thing to do, the alternative being to drown.

After the school swimming tank, the buoyant blue and green waters off the Cornish coast were easy. A foaming translucent element of liquid airy joy.

Rupert, on a hot summer's day, would leave his grand-parents' house to run across field and moor, racing along narrow fox paths between bramble and gorse, and galloping quaggy stretches of bog. Not pausing for thorns, nor the fiery patches his sandshoes rubbed on his heels, shoving aside fat sheep, to where the cliff dipped down to the sea. Here, high tide or low, there was always water. In the last few yards of his race, he shed shirt and shoes, and when he reached the edge he leaped without pausing. Each time it was the best moment of life. One element to another. One world to another. Escape.

It was not the same for Peter. Even before he broke his leg, he wasn't much of a runner. The first time he saw Rupert leap from the cliff he assumed his cousin would drown. He shuffled to the edge and peered over, down into the blue water. There was Rupert, only a few feet below him, laughing and blowing like a human porpoise.

"Come on!" called Rupert.

Every now and then Peter was struck by a mood of reckless madness. It hit him then. He also dragged off his clothes and, in a skinny tangle of shoulders and shinbones, hit the rocking water. Peter could swim too; twice a week in summer term the boys from his day school were marched down to the town pool. In water Peter was as agile as Rupert. He could dive as well. He was the first to take off from the cliff in a swooping header, but it was Rupert who had said, the year before, "We should bring Clarry."

"She can't swim," said Peter.

"She'd soon learn, like we did."

Clarry, when asked, said, "Yes! Yes, please! But how could I? What would I wear?"

They looked blank.

"What do you wear?"

"Bathing suits or we don't bother."

"I can't not bother and I haven't got a bathing suit," said Clarry.

"Ask Grandmother," suggested Rupert, but that was no use. Clarry's grandmother said that little girls paddled. They paddled in their summer dresses carefully at the water's edge, having left their shoes and stockings neatly on a rock. This behavior entirely prevented any risk of drowning, said Clarry's grandmother, and closed the sitting-room door.

Clarry (in private) contemplated her reflection in her knickers and her liberty bodice. It was awful. She tried on Peter's old bathing suit and it hung in great black loops from her shoulders to her knees. And so she gave up hope of swimming with the boys that year, although she often sat on the cliff above, watching as they dived and porpoised through the blue and green water.

And then the next summer, there was the sovereign!

It was agony to part with, but she did it, and for ten shillings bought a black bathing suit from a dismal little shop near the marketplace. It was made of wool, rather rubbed up because it was not new, baggy around her knees, and gathered with large bright blue bows at the shoulders. Clarry didn't like the bows, but the bathing suit was the lightest thing she had ever worn. She put it on and pranced into Peter's room, saying, "Look! Look! Look!"

Peter was lying on his bed, reading and resting his aching leg. He put down his book and peered at her. He said, "It's the worst thing I've ever seen you wearing."

"Oh," said Clarry. "It can't be!"

"It is. Can you get that blue ribbon muck off?"

"The bows? They're what hold it on."

"Well, it's awful," said Peter, picking up his book again. "Wait till Rupe sees it. He'll tell you."

"What'll I tell her?" asked Rupert, coming in just then. "Oh . . . CRIKEY, Clarry!"

"What?" demanded Clarry.

"Did you make it yourself?"

"I bought it," said Clarry. "With my own money. Some of my birthday sovereign."

"From a shop?" asked Rupert incredulously, and then, seeing Clarry's face and remembering his manners, added, "Well done! Good for you! Superb!"

"Are you mad?" asked Peter. "Look at her!"

"I only wanted to learn to swim," said Clarry humbly. "I'm tired of just paddling. I know it's not a very nice swimming suit."

"It's just right," said Rupert. "Come on, then! Put something on top and we'll try it out. We'll run across the moor."

Clarry cheered up tremendously, pulled a dress on top of the bathing suit, hugged Peter good-bye, and scampered after Rupert so quickly that in less than twenty minutes they were at the cliff edge, looking down.

"Now what?" asked Clarry.

"Jump!"

"Straight in, not round by the rocks?"

"No, no, of course not! You said you were tired of paddling!"

"Is that what you did the first time you went swimming? Jump straight in?"

"Yes. Straight in, and no screaming at the cold or else detention in the gym!"

"And then you just started swimming, as easily as that?"

"Of course," said Rupert, and he honestly believed it was true.

"It's not far down, is it?"

"Hardly a step," said Rupert. "In you go and you'll come up swimming like a duckling. Even Pete did. I'll count you down, shall I?"

Clarry wavered on the brink, nearly overbalancing.

"Three . . . two . . . don't try diving. Diving needs practice. Do it the safe way, feet first, just to start with. Now then, one!"

The safe way, Rupert had said, and Clarry shut her eyes, stepped into nothingness, flailed in sudden panic, and then found herself plunging, down and down below the slapping green waves, into such coldness that she gasped in great panicky gulps, not air, but salt water.

Everything ended then, the whole warm lovely world gone in a moment. There was no direction to reach for, and no air to breathe.

There was an icy grip, disbelief, and then blackness.

Rupert, smiling, waited for her to bob up.

This did not happen. Nothing happened. The green glass sea swung and rippled, quite undisturbed. Rupert shaded his eyes and craned sideways to see if she was climbing up by the rocks, and as he did so, he caught sight of a small black shadow rocking in the depths.

Sheet lightning fear flashed from the water, blinding Rupert as he dived. Even so, he found her, weightless as a shadow, dragged her to the surface, towed her to the rocks, rolled her over, and hit her between her shoulders.

Water poured from Clarry in streams and rivers and fountains. She was fish cold and gray granite pale.

"Clarry!" bellowed Rupert, and turned her upside down and shook her. She retched and came alive but her eyes didn't open.

Rupert picked her up, hung her over his shoulder, staggered across the rocks, up the steep sandy path, and lowered her onto the turf. He wrapped his shirt round her, rubbed her back, and shouted at her. When he propped her up she slid sideways, heavy now, and limp as a jellyfish.

"Oh, God, Clarry," moaned Rupert, and saw her reach out a hand to comfort him.

After a few minutes, she began shaking and then crying silently, yet more salt water pouring down her cold cheeks.

"Why didn't you swim?" demanded Rupert, suddenly angry, but she only shivered and cried even more.

"Poor little duckling," said Rupert, and at last Clarry sat up and wiped her eyes.

It took him ages to get her home. She kept stopping to lean on things. When they finally arrived he left her in the hall and knocked on the sitting-room door.

This time, the grandparents were not so calm as usual. Twice in one summer was too much. First Peter, now this. It beggared belief. Every year their grandchildren were met at the station, provided with beds, and catered for with astonishing quantities of food. There was sea and moorland, a town, a garden, and a pony. What more could be expected? Where was their common sense? Why on earth couldn't Rupert be trusted to take care of Clarry?

"It wasn't his fault," croaked Clarry, the first words she had spoken.

"Never heard such nonsense!" growled her grandfather, and Rupert was sent off to fetch the doctor while Clarry was hustled up to bed in the room next to Peter's, piled with blankets, and scolded.

"What's happened? What's happened? What's happened?" demanded Peter. They closed his bedroom door tight shut because they had enough to deal with as it was, and then they opened it again because he was thumping on the wall. With the help of his crutches, Peter dragged himself out of bed and went to join the turmoil in the room next door.

"She might have drowned!" fumed her grandfather. "A nice job for me, that would have been, telling her father she'd drowned!"

Peter snorted and said something so outrageous that he was ordered to get out. The doctor arrived, with Rupert in tow. Clarry fell unhelpfully asleep in the middle of him listening to her lungs. She slept for hours and hours. When she woke up her grandmother was sitting beside her looking terribly bored.

"I'm sorry," said Clarry.

Her grandmother looked down at her.

"I shouldn't have jumped. I guessed that really. I just thought . . . I thought . . ."

"Rupert must know best," finished her grandmother.

Clarry nodded.

Now you know he didn't, said her grandmother, not in words, but with an eloquent sniff. She gave another sniff as she picked up the sodden bundle of Clarry's bathing suit from the washstand. "Is that what you spent your birthday money on? What a dreadful-looking garment!"

"It didn't take all the money," said Clarry. "Don't throw it away. I need it."

"I can't imagine what for."

"I'm still going to learn to swim."

"Oh, are you?"

"Yes, and I heard what Peter said. Father *would* have minded if I'd drowned!"

"Everyone would have minded, Peter most of all," said her grandmother sharply. She got up to go then, but hesitated at the door, and then suddenly came back, stooped, and kissed the top of Clarry's head.

"You should go to sleep again now."

Clarry dropped off almost at once, but she woke in the night gasping with fear and groping blindly into the blackness surrounding her. For a day or two, it hurt her chest to breathe. It rained, and she stayed in her room, reading Sherlock Holmes adventures in faded blue paper-covered copies of the *Strand Magazine*. Her grandfather had produced them, silent proof that he too was glad she had not drowned. On the third day she felt better, the sun came out, and her grandmother handed her the bathing suit, dried out and transformed. The saggy legs had been shortened and edged with neat black bands, the blue bows on the shoulders replaced with black and white ruffles, and all the seams taken in. Most surprising of all, her grandmother had news for her. She said, "I have been asking my friends. I find that one of them has a grown-up daughter who swims. Also she tells me that there is a part of the bay that is roped off for safe bathing. Would you like me to arrange for you to meet?"

So in time Clarry learned to swim after all, and later to dive, not like a duckling but like a slim black seal. Rupert said, "See! I knew you could do it!" and Peter said, "You shouldn't have panicked. Swimming is obvious."

"Swimming is not obvious!" said Clarry. "Not unless you're a fish. Or frog. Otherwise it's a lot of puffing and managing. Arms as well as legs. And hair in your eyes and being absolutely drenched. Not just wet, absolutely . . . oh, well, it doesn't matter. I can do it now anyway."

The boys were moderately pleased with her. They were never very good at admitting they were wrong, but she carried on adoring them just the same.

Seven

THAT AUTUMN PETER WENT BACK TO HIS DAY school, limping slowly away each morning and returning with remedial exercises to do at night. This meant that Clarry had another year of being raced through his homework. Mrs. Morgan said, "Amazing how some folks get their own way!"

"It wasn't a bit like that!" said Clarry loyally.

"Oh, wasn't it?" said Mrs. Morgan. "Well, he couldn't have had much of a summer, I don't suppose. And what did you get up to while His Majesty was lying around in bed?"

"I learned to swim," said Clarry proudly.

"You never did!" exclaimed Mrs. Morgan, looking impressed at last. "That's something I can't do. But then, I never had nobody to show me. Your cousin Rupert teach you, did he?"

"It was his idea," said Clarry, after hesitating for a moment. "His and Peter's."

"Them two's your heroes!" said Mrs. Morgan amiably. "Can't do no wrong nor ever could. I was never like that with my brother."

"Weren't you?"

"I was not! I used to think, well, I'm as strong as him. Stronger! I'm as hard a worker. Harder! I've got as good a brain as him. Better by a long way. I'm just as good as him, for all he's a boy. So I used to think things out for myself."

Mrs. Morgan gave Clarry a very significant nod, as if to say, *And so should you!*

Clarry ignored it. She already was beginning to think things out for herself.

It was the great falling away of illusions that was the start of growing up.

A year passed.

In the autumn of 1913, Peter was sent to boarding school, white faced, sulking, and beset by black-hearted rage. He did not expect to survive. It made no difference that Rupert had been there for years, or that there had hardly ever been a boy who did not survive. (Appendicitis not reported soon enough, and the loose guttering on the chapel roof, which never should have been climbed. Could the school be blamed for that? No.)

Already Peter was much later to go than he should have been; the direct result of stepping off a moving train. It had saved him for a year, but it could do no more. It was not, as Rupert had once remarked, an escape route that could be taken twice. Anyway, Peter had brains, he should go to university, and for that he would need a scholarship. His day school was not the sort of place that got university scholarships. This boarding school was. And so an old trunk was dragged down from the attic and packed with school uniform, a lot of it passed on from Rupert. Clarry and Miss Vane filled a tuck box with gingerbread, peppermints, pots of jam, and potted meat. Mrs. Morgan brought him a tub of eucalyptus ointment to rub on his chest. His father gave him a leather purse containing four half crowns, five silver shillings, and ten sixpences.

"At least you're being paid!" said Clarry, when she saw it.

A train ticket was bought, and that was that. There was nothing left that Clarry could do for him except stuff his pockets with brown paper bags. Peter, limping (one shoe built up to make his bad leg long enough to match the other, stiff at the knee, and twisted at the ankle), climbed onto the train and entered another world.

This was school, and everything he'd feared. Barren, jarring, stale, always lonely and never alone. He had known it would be bad, and it was.

For the first few weeks Peter existed in a state of numb isolation. Rupert could not help him. Clarry's letters were collected but unopened. It was the longest and most intense sulk of his life, but finally he began to notice people. First, the small blond boy in the next bed. They even had a conversation. At the end of it the blond boy asked Peter a question:

"Where would you run away to," he demanded, "if you were running away?"

"Cornwall," said Peter.

Even Peter, who hardly noticed anything, noticed the swift, intense glance the blond boy gave him then. It was the last time he saw him; he disappeared the very same day. Peter did not tell anyone about their conversation, but all the same, he wondered. Had the boy made it to Cornwall? Was he happy there? If he wasn't, would he come back?

Peter found himself wishing that he would. He thought of questions he would ask him if he did. He regretted not having taken more notice of the blond boy.

Thinking like this, Peter felt his numbness begin to wear off, a painful process. He longed for it back, but it would not come. He felt very exposed now, and took to scuffling around, like a small animal under a big sky.

After a few more days had passed, a new person was given the blond boy's bed. Bonnington. The boys called him Bonners, shortened to Bones, as they called Peter "Penrose," shortened, though he did not know it, to Penny (Rupert being Rosy). Peter privately labeled Bonners "the Bony One" in his head. The Bony One was tall and thin. He had either more bones than most people or bigger ones, or both. It showed especially around his eyes, and in his enormous hands that looked like bundles of shaking firewood.

Despite the Bony One's extra bones he was not tough. He said to Peter, "I hate Games. Hate it."

"So would I," said Peter.

"Mud. Football boots. Training on the Big Field. Showers in the Hut. You escape. You're lucky."

It was true, Peter knew it, he was lucky. He did escape. He couldn't play football or rugby or cricket. He couldn't join in the long, sodden cross-country runs and he couldn't climb ropes in the gym. He spent the times when other people were taking part in these activities huddled beside the lukewarm radiator pipes in the hardly visited library, together with the boy with the dicky heart and the one with asthma.

"What do you do, while we're out there doing Games?"

"I go to the library."

"What, on your own?"

Peter told him about the bad heart, and the asthma, and

the Bony One looked at him with eyes like those of a hungry dog. He said, "I suppose you have to be born with a bad heart?"

"S'pose so," agreed Peter.

"Asthma's not catching, is it?"

"No."

The Bony One looked at Peter's leg and the built-up shoe.

"It's not that wonderful, being out of Games," said Peter defensively. "It's nothing special, hanging around a cold library."

"Yes, it is," said the Bony One.

He became silent then, but the next morning he brought the subject up again. He said, "It hurts. Football hurts. Rugby really hurts. Cross-country is agony. How'd you break your leg so bad?"

"Jumped off a train."

"A moving train? Or a standing train?"

"Moving."

"Did it hurt?"

"Of course."

"Even so," said the Bony One, "it would only hurt once. You'd just have to shut your eyes and do it."

He seemed, thought Peter, to be preoccupied with pain.

"And if you changed your mind and didn't want to," the Bony One continued, "you could always go on to the next station and get off."

The bell for chapel rang, and the conversation ended, but Peter found himself concerned. He made up his mind that the next time he saw the Bony One he would make something plain. He would tell him that he wished he had not jumped off the train. And also that it hurt. In fact, it never stopped hurting. Jumping off the train had been a mistake. He would tell the Bony One this at bedtime, and make sure he understood.

However this plan turned out to be impossible because that night the Bony One's bed was empty. Peter, who, since the blond boy, had become sensitive to empty beds, noticed it at once.

He was alarmed. So alarmed that he slid out of bed (forbidden), crept out of the dormitory (banned), nipped down the back stairs (out of bounds), made his way along to the darkened junior common room (where no one was allowed after nine o'clock), and there was the Bony One halfway out of the window.

At first the Bony One would not say where he was going, or be persuaded to come back in. He said he needed fresh air, he said he was interested in astronomy, he said he was going to look for a book he had accidentally left outside, and he said he thought he'd heard owls.

"I don't believe you," said Peter.

"Don't, then," said the Bony One. "It's all right for you!"

and he looked bitterly and jealously down at Peter's leg, and Peter looked at it too.

"It hurts. It hurts all the time. They pinned it with steel plates to hold it together. I can feel the steel. It hurts to walk and it hurts to keep still. I have to wear a weird shoe. It's rubbish."

"You didn't tell me any of that before," said the Bony One accusingly.

Peter shrugged.

"Why did you do it?"

"I was a coward."

"Why did you come after me?"

"Why'd you think?"

"To save me," said the Bony One, and climbed back down from the windowsill.

Eight

SO IT WAS THAT THE TWO OF THEM BECAME FRIENDS, and when Simon (for that was the Bony One's first name) had his family visit a week later he introduced Peter as the boy who had persuaded him not to jump from a moving train. Peter was taken out to dinner, forgiven for being sick in the car, and introduced to Simon's sister, Vanessa. In Simon he seemed to have found someone as completely unsuited to school as himself. He and Simon did not talk much, but it was nice to have someone to sit beside at mealtimes, or to stomp across the quad with when the bell clanged for morning chapel. They shared letters from home now and then. Vanessa sent postcards to Simon. Clarry painted butterflies for Peter:

careful paper models to add to the collection he had started in Cornwall.

In chapel their friendship blossomed. They discovered the knack of fitting their own words to the rhythm and melody of the hymns. If anyone in the past had told Peter he would enjoy singing in chapel he would have dismissed them as insane, but Peter was changing.

> *Oh, God, our help in ages past,*
> *I did not do that math*
> *He set us all for prep last night*
> *So could I copy yours?*

> *Yes, if you want I do not care,*
> *I'm sick of everything,*
> *The whole east wing is stinking of*
> *That fish we had last night.*

> *I know, it must have been weeks old,*
> *The breakfast eggs were green,*
> *I've got some biscuits if you like*
> *From our eternal home.*

They both could sing well, clear and in tune, but occasionally tears of silent laughter would roll down Simon's

nose and cause him to snort and gasp. This never happened
to Peter. He took pride in maintaining an expression of perfect, blank-eyed calm. He enjoyed his friend's snorts however, and wrote about them to Clarry, which made a change
for her from his usual list of commands and grumbles. He
mentioned other things too, that he had not thought worth
recording before, such as the problem of the common-room
fire, which blew smoke down the chimney until people's eyes
watered and they went early to bed.

Clarry wrote back:

*You remember Mr. King, the rag-and-bone man
who bought our old fish-smelling piano for one shilling
and a pink geranium? Father is still complaining and
Miss Vane says I should not talk to such people. But I do,
because he is perfectly nice and so is his black and white
horse, Jester. (Mr. King is very proud of Jester because he
came all the way from Devon by train.) Well, I saw him
yesterday and he stopped Jester to say, "All right, missy,
I hope?"*

*"Yes, thank you," I said. "What are you collecting
today?"*

*"Worthless brass and copper," he said. "Terrible
heavy old stuff that nobody wants but if you can't do
a kindness now and then, where would we be? I'm too*

softhearted, as my friends do like to say. I takes it off folks' hands and leave them a flower to remember me by. Saucepans, stair rods, candlesticks, old brass coal scuttles, pile them on my cart, missy, and I'll have them out of your way. But you'll have to be quick because I've a terrible smoky chimney to sort."

"How do you sort a terrible smoky chimney?" I asked him, and he said, "Oh, that is a trick worth knowing but if you've nothing for the cart I must be moving on at once."

So I remembered that awful Indian table with the brass top that snags you every time you pass and it was so heavy he had to come and help me. But he told me about chimneys while we dragged it down the hall. Miss Vane came to the front door just as we reached it with the table and she was not happy. She made us put it down.

"I am shocked," she said. "First that valuable piano, spirited away without a by-your-leave, and now this beautiful table!"

"But it has such sharp edges," I said.

"Sharp edges or not, I'm not taking no risks!" said Mr. King, walking very quickly backward down the steps toward his cart. "Not in this house twice! You must mind your poor old granny, miss, and I must be off!"

Then he jumped into his cart and shouted "Lively, Jester!" to his horse, and Jester did go, very lively, clattering down the street, and Mr. King blew kisses as they left.

"That man is an impertinent scoundrel!" exclaimed Miss Vane. "Really, Clarry, you should NOT let him into the house!"

Then she looked anxiously in the hall mirror.

"I suppose I am getting old," she said very quietly, and she dabbed her eyes with one of her small hankies, the ones with heather in the corner that she bought from the church bazaar.

"Angus would not know me now," she said.

"Of course he would," I said. "You're not old! Mr. King was just being awful because he wanted the table."

She shook her head and sniffed.

"Who was Angus, anyway?" I asked.

"When I was eighteen I danced with him at a party in London. A Christmas party. The last one I ever went to. I always remember how the snow drifted down in the lamplight outside the windows. Oh, well."

I told her it sounded like a party in a story.

"It was like that, Clarry," said Miss Vane.

"Did you dance with him just once?" I asked her, because she seemed to want to go on talking.

"Three times," said Miss Vane proudly. "A country dance and two waltzes, and then we stood by the windows and watched the falling snow."

"Then what happened?" I asked.

"He was Scottish. He went back to Scotland. I believe he married a very nice Edinburgh girl," said Miss Vane, and then she started pushing the brass-topped table back down the hall.

I have drawn a picture of the way the rag-and-bone man said to clear the chimney and I don't see why a fireworks rocket wouldn't work instead. They have them in the shops just now.

Very much love from,

Clarry

P.S. It would be perfect if you were expelled.

Peter was very scornful to Simon about Miss Vane and her lost Scottish Angus but the fireworks rocket idea appealed to them both. They followed Clarry's instructions and became rather pleased with themselves. Rupert, to whom Clarry had given the almost impossible task of taking care of Peter without him noticing, saw that his cousin looked happier and was interested.

"Introduce me to your friend!" he said, meeting them one evening as they hurried down a corridor.

"Oh," said Peter. "Well, he's Bonnington. Bonners. Simon, or something. And this is my cousin. Rupert. Penrose. Rosy. Sixth form."

Simon's ears went scarlet but he managed to say, "I know . . . I mean, I've seen . . . oh, God . . ."

"So where are you both rushing off to?" inquired Rupert, more to put an end to the Bony One's agony than because he was interested.

"Double detention," said Peter. "Because of mucking up the common room. If you must know."

"'Course I must! Aren't I a prefect? Both of you? What'd you do?"

"Cleared the chimney," said Peter. "The smoke kept blowing back down."

"It always did," agreed Rupert, grinning. "How'd you clear it, then? Send up the skinniest first year?"

"Fireworks rockets. Three."

"Ah!" said Rupert. "I noticed you both had a grayish look, but I didn't like to mention it. Double detention! How ungrateful of them! What's a bit of soot?"

"More than a bit," said Peter.

"Generations," said Simon, and did one of his snorts, stumbled over nothing standing still, as he sometimes did in moments of crisis, and turned an even darker red.

"Well, I think you showed great public spirit," said Rupert, kindly ignoring these antics. "Congratulations to whichever of you thought of it first!"

"It was his sister," said Simon.

"What, Clarry?" exclaimed Rupert. "Brilliant! I might have guessed! I'm going to write and congratulate her tonight!"

Rupert drew a picture for Clarry of rooftops and chimneys, lit by an explosion of red and green stars.

Clarry, you are a genius! he wrote underneath.

Clarry was so pleased she stuck it up on the sitting-room mantelpiece, and it was still there when Peter came home at Christmas.

"You should have seen the Bony One jump when the rocket went off," he said. "He doesn't like bangs."

"I wish I had seen," said Clarry. "What's his real name?"

"I keep forgetting . . . Simon! Simon Bonnington. Bonners. He lives quite near here, in this town, anyway, not that far away. He said to bring you over. He's got a sister."

"You told me. Vanessa."

"That's right. A bit older than him."

"What is she like? What does she look like?"

"I don't know! Tallish. Hair."

"Of course she has hair!"

"Long, and very bright, like leaves."

"Not green?" said Clarry, laughing.

"No, no! Fall leaves, and she's got weird ideas. She wants to go and live in Paris."

"I think that's a brilliant idea!"

"I don't know why," said Peter, rather grumpily. "I can't imagine you in Paris. Anyway, I said we'd go tomorrow."

"Good. I couldn't go now. I'm busy!"

"You! Busy! Doing what?"

"Decorating for Christmas," said Clarry. "I've made miles of paper chains. They're up in my bedroom, waiting to be hung. And we've got a Christmas tree coming. A friend of mine is bringing it."

"That rag-and-bone man!" guessed Peter.

"Yes."

"What did you give him?"

"A Sunday school prize. One of those awful books they give you. About doing good and dying, that sort of book."

"I suppose it's one way to get rid of them," agreed Peter. "I don't know why you want a Christmas tree, though."

"Because last year Christmas was so empty. Not one Christmassy thing except church in the morning, and you and Father wouldn't come. Don't you remember?"

"I remember that you tried to cook a chicken with the insides still in," said Peter.

"I've learned to do it properly this year," said Clarry. "And there'll be a real Christmas pudding and something else too."

"What?"

"I'll tell you later. Miss Vane gave me the idea. Come and help hang up my paper chains."

Peter was so glad to be away from school that he came and helped fairly willingly, and the next day set off across town with Clarry to visit the Bonningtons. There, Vanessa and Clarry made friends instantly, completely, and for life.

"Come to our Christmas party," begged Clarry, as they left.

"What Christmas party?" demanded Peter. "Don't be stupid, Clarry."

"We're having a party on Christmas Eve. I'm arranging it all. Father said I could do as I liked so long as he wasn't involved. There'll be ten people, if Vanessa and Simon come. Ten is enough for a really good party!"

"Ten?" asked Peter. "Father'll never let ten people into the house at once!"

"He will. You and me. Mrs. Morgan and Mr. Morgan with their little grandson Christopher, who they're looking after that night. Him. Vanessa and Simon. Miss Vane. There'll be music too, because Miss Vane is bringing her gramophone and Mr. Morgan his Spanish guitar. . . ."

"That's only nine," said Peter, keeping count.

"And Rupert!"

"Rupert?"

"Yes, and he's staying all Christmas Day! The grandparents said he could. Vanessa, you will love him!"

"Will I?" asked Vanessa. "Do you?"

"Of course I do," said Clarry.

At Clarry's party there was a Christmas tree with silver paper stars and red candles and paper cones filled with sugar mice and toffees. Presents hung amongst the branches, bought by Clarry with the long-hoarded remains of her sovereign. There were two gold paper roses for Miss Vane and Mrs. Morgan, a tin trumpet for Christopher, a guitar duster for Mr. Morgan, a red handkerchief with holly printed on it for her father, Bengal matches for the boys, and a pink bead necklace for Vanessa. When Vanessa saw these presents she took off her silver bangle, borrowed a pencil, found a scrap of paper, labeled it with Clarry's name, and hung it with the stars.

Miss Vane was sure the tree would catch fire, and said so several dozen times. Christopher choked on a sugar mouse and had to be turned upside down. Mr. Morgan made his duster into a hat and played his guitar much too willingly for most people. Peter, to the barely concealed wrath of his father, stoked the fire to a cherry red blaze. The children's father gave sherry to the guests but drank whisky himself and constantly deserted them all to stalk into the street and check that the chimney had not caught fire.

None of these things in any way spoiled Clarry's party. They ate gingerbread hearts brought by Vanessa, mince pies from Miss Vane, miniature sandwiches made by Clarry and Mrs. Morgan, grapes and nuts and figs, and tangerines wrapped in silver paper. They played hide the thimble, oranges and lemons, forfeits, and blindman's buff. Then the furniture was pushed back to the walls, the children's father vanished in disgust, Peter operated the gramophone, and they danced colliding polkas in the living room and gallops up and down the icy hall.

Miss Vane and Rupert: "Not so fast! Oh, my goodness! Oh, do take care of the Christmas tree!"

Vanessa and Mr. Morgan: "What a brilliant party! I do like your hat!"

Mrs. Morgan and Simon: "Come on, young man!" Mrs. Morgan ordered that petrified and bony one as she hauled him to his feet.

Clarry and Christopher: "This is my best spinning round!" "Wonderful, Christopher, it's my best too!"

Afterward they sang "The Holly and the Ivy," "I Saw Three Ships," and "God Rest Ye Merry Gentlemen" with a lot of guitar strumming between verses. To finish, Rupert called, "Come on, Clarry!"

So Rupert was Good King Wenceslas and Clarry his loyal page, while Vanessa dreamed on the hearthrug, and Peter paused his fire stoking, and Christopher's eyes were lollipop round, and the grown-ups were quiet, remembering other Christmases. And Simon the Bony One gazed in silence from the dusty folds and shadows of the faded scarlet curtains.

Nine

RUPERT STAYED FOR FIVE NIGHTS. SIX DAYS, thought Clarry, not whole days of course, but nevertheless, six days with Rupert in them. It was as if summer had arrived midwinter. She had only really known him in Cornwall before. There, in the sunlight, with the sea glitter and the enormous light skies, he had blended into the brightness. Here, in winter, in the bare damp house, he shone like a warm lamp. He was always humming. He laughed out loud. On Boxing Day he swung Clarry into a few steps of dance, twirled her round, glanced into her face, and read her mind.

"You're worrying!"

"I'm not."

"About me."

"Not really."

"*Is Rupe bored? Is he cold? Does he mind the way Miss Vane appears so often? Is the food too awful? Does he understand about Father? Might he wish he hadn't come? What will we do all day and will Peter sulk?* Admit I'm right!"

"A bit."

"I love Miss Vane. After a thousand years at boarding school I'm never cold and no food is awful. My father is worse than yours. I love being here, I hardly ever see you. I think we should always do Christmases like this. We're going to the theater this afternoon! It's going to be wonderful and silly."

"Are we? Are we?"

"I went to the box office and got tickets this morning."

"But what about Father?"

"Do you think he would like *Columbine*? Vanessa and Simon are meeting us there. It's all arranged! Smile! Say, 'Rupert, you're my favorite cousin!'"

"You're my only cousin."

"But if you had a hundred?"

"I've never been to the theater! Yes! Even if I had a hundred!"

Peter said, not unadmiringly, "Rupert does as he likes here. Father can only just about bear it."

Rupert bought bacon and cooked it for breakfast. He fixed the terrible creak on the landing. When Clarry got drenched feeding carrots to Jester he hung her rain-soaked coat to dry before the living-room fire. He ran up the stairs two at a time and came down them in jumps. He sang. He vaulted over the banisters, hung by his hands, and dropped into the hall. He fed sugar lumps to horses he met in the street. He said "Whoops!" when he bowled Miss Vane into the coat stand, straightened her up, and apologized so seriously that she went straight home and baked him a treacle tart. Vanessa and Simon came over every single day, causing Clarry's father to remark that the house was becoming worse than Piccadilly Circus.

"Do you like him?" Clarry asked Vanessa proudly.

"Well," said Vanessa. "I suppose."

On the last day that they were all together, the conversation turned to school. Vanessa described the girls' high school, with its clubs and homework and lists of rules and hats like pale giant mushrooms. Simon made a few bleak remarks about mud, wind, football pitches, and frostbite. Peter said it wasn't much better inside and even the classrooms were so cold you could see your breath like smoke. Rupert said that he'd once tried a cross-country shortcut and got so lost he'd been out till after dark. He told them he'd found his way back by the northern lights, so arctic cold was the night. Vanessa described how at the high school all the top windows were kept open, even when the inkwells froze. Then it was Clarry's turn to tell an icy school story.

"Where do you go to school, Clarry?" asked Vanessa.

Clarry mumbled that it wasn't very interesting.

"Clarry goes to the Miss Pinkses' Academy for Young Ladies," said Peter.

"The what?" demanded Simon.

"It's two old bats in an attic," said Peter. "You ought to see it. You can, it's just round the corner. Come on! I'll show you!"

With that, Peter, who usually never showed anyone anything, led the whole group out to see the front view of the Miss Pinkses' Academy for Young Ladies, which looked like any other house on the street, bare walls, shabby paint, and dark windows.

"It's those three rooms at the top," said Clarry's suddenly ruthless brother, pointing (while Clarry lurked miserably behind). "She's been going there for years, ever since she was six, and she has never learned a single useful thing. Sewing handkerchief cases, that's all she did last term!"

"We did other things too!" said Clarry, scarlet cheeked, but she had to admit, the handkerchief cases had been the main event of the term. They had been embroidered with pink and blue daisies at the two creaky tables where the Miss Pinkses' young ladies also sat to copy faded maps, to add farthings and pennies and shillings into pounds, to draw shaky sketches of suitable subjects (A Winter Posy, A Quiet View), and to learn psalms from the Bible. The varnish of those tables was always slightly sticky and the air smelled of the paraffin stoves that heated the rooms from September to May.

There were no open windows or icy breezes in the Miss Pinkses' establishment. Quite the reverse: by midafternoon the combination of boredom, fumes, and stuffiness was so overwhelming it was all the young ladies could do to stay awake. Often Clarry drifted into a headachy sleep on the sticky tables.

Peter was right, it was an awful school.

"Since I went away she's done absolutely nothing," said Peter.

"She sent you all those letters," observed Simon, "and those two butterflies!"

"I mean nothing *intelligent*. . . ."

"Those butterflies were really clever," said Simon, warming up his defense when he saw Rupert's approving grin. "I couldn't have made them in a million years. And you liked them! You kept getting them out and looking at them!"

"Yes, yes, yes!" said Peter impatiently. "But I meant she

hasn't *learned* anything. Before I went away, I used to teach her—"

"You didn't!" interrupted Clarry indignantly. "I helped you! I helped you with your homework! Stop grinning like that! Vanessa, Simon, stop it! I did help him! And I didn't choose to go to the Miss Pinkses'! You needn't think I like it, because I don't."

"Then why do you go?" asked Vanessa.

"Because she's too lazy to make Father send her somewhere better!" answered Peter.

"I am not!" stormed Clarry. "And how could I, anyway? How can I make Father do anything?"

"Of course you can't," said Rupert, putting an arm around her. "Shut up, all of you! Leave her alone! Clarry can do as she likes. Not everyone wants to go prancing off to Paris. Or boil their brains at university. I wish they'd let me into the Miss Pinkses'! They'd never get me out!"

Vanessa and her brother laughed and Peter snorted in disgust, but Rupert took no notice and led Clarry away.

"I've got to go back to Cornwall tomorrow," he said, still with his arm around her. "Want to come with me?"

"Father would never let me," said Clarry.

"Run away, then! Back to the ancestral home in the west! I've got money for train tickets."

"Just me?"

"Just you."

"What about Peter?"

"What about blooming Peter? Come on, Clarry! You've never seen Cornwall in winter. Come and surprise the grandparents! You could stay till it was time to go back to your lovely Miss Pinkses'."

"I really couldn't."

"You really could!"

"Rupert?"

"Mmmm?"

"I don't want to go back to the Miss Pinkses'."

"Just because Peter teased you? 'Course you do! Where else would you go?"

"Vanessa's school."

"It's all rules and frozen inkwells, according to Vanessa. Anyway, I can't see you becoming a high school girl, stomping around in a mushroom hat."

"I wish you could," said Clarry.

Ten

RUPERT HAD GONE, CHRISTMAS WAS SUDDENLY over. All the brightness was being washed away by torrents of gray rain. Peter was exiled in his room with a sudden and ferocious cold. A new term with the Miss Pinkses was about to begin.

Clarry brushed her hair very carefully, put on her most tidy dress, sewed up a hole in the knee of a stocking, and went down to tackle her father.

"Oh, really, what now?" he demanded, as soon as she stopped hopping about from one leg to the other and pushed open the door. "I am a busy man, you know, Clarry!"

"I know," agreed Clarry. "But I need to ask you something very important. About schools."

"Has Peter put you up to this?" demanded her father explosively. "In any case, the answer is no! The subject is not up for discussion. Peter is staying where he is!"

"No, no, no," said Clarry, laying a hand on his arm. "Not Peter's school. Mine."

"Yours?" he repeated, sounding completely surprised.

"Yes," said Clarry, and then as best as she could she explained about the handkerchief cases and ancient maps, the headachy oil stoves and the psalms, and Vanessa's school, across the other side of town, where there were science labs and open windows and—

"I didn't particularly care for that girl Vanessa, as you call her," interrupted Clarry's father. "And why on earth would you want that sort of education, anyway?"

"To *learn* things!" explained Clarry.

"But what would be the *point*?" asked her truly baffled father.

"You don't mind Peter learning things."

"Peter is a boy."

"Girls can learn things too!" cried Clarry. "I used to learn a lot when Peter let me help him with his homework. In Cornwall I learned to swim. Why is it different for Peter?"

"Peter," said her father, "will one day have to earn his own living."

"Well, so will I!"

"Clarry, that's enough," said her father, getting up from his chair and beginning to fold his newspaper very carefully. "This conversation is quite unnecessary. Even if you do not marry, there will never be a need for you to live independently."

Clarry opened her mouth to protest, but her father was faster.

"I'm sure there will always be a home for you within the family. If not here, perhaps with your grandparents, or even with Peter. Someway or other you will be provided for! Now, off you go!"

He rolled his newspaper, patted her on the head with it in dismissal, twice, *bump, bump,* and was gone from the room before she could say another word.

Until then, Clarry had not thought much about the future. Year after year, she had lived in the storybook world of childhood, the glowing adventures of summer in Cornwall, the long dull chapters of life in between, bookmarked in the middle by Christmas. The illustrations for the stories had changed, it was true. Rupert grew taller, sometimes he even stepped out of the book completely. Peter went to boarding school, and when he came back he glanced around the old familiar pages of home as if they held new words. But all through the book Clarry hardly changed at all, and it never occurred to her to wonder, *What will happen in the end?*

Until her father's "Clarry, that's enough."

And there she was! Huge chunks of story turned over in wodges. Whole chapters skipped. Grown up, and nothing before her but other people's homes.

Clarry did not spend much time staring at this bleak last page. She rushed up the two flights of stairs to Peter's room and clattered in without knocking.

"God," said Peter unwelcomingly, rolling away in bed.

"How can I get away from the Miss Pinkses if Father won't help me?" demanded Clarry, shaking his back.

Peter groaned and hunched under the covers.

"You know what will happen to me if I don't," said Clarry.

"Nothing."

"Yes, nothing. Forever and ever and ever. Like Miss Vane."

Peter shrugged.

Clarry pulled away his pillow and his eiderdown and heaved at the thin mattress until it slid to the floor with Peter still on it. He seemed to be laughing, or shaking at least.

"It's not funny!"

"There'll be an exam," said Peter.

"What?"

"For that school Vanessa goes to."

"An exam?"

"It's miles away. Right across town, near their house. How would you even get there?"

"Perhaps there are buses," suggested Clarry. "Anyway, I could walk. Do you really think there's an exam?"

"I'm cold. I feel awful. Help me up."

Clarry helped him lift his mattress back, shook up his pillows, smoothed his eiderdown, fetched the blankets from her own bed, and piled them on top.

"Wait," she told him, and went down to the kitchen, boiled a kettle, and made tea. She stirred honey into it, wished for a lemon, and found one amongst the Christmas oranges. Mrs. Morgan was there doing vigorous things with a pile of onions and a very large knife. She asked, "What's to do?"

"Peter's got an awful cold. All shivery."

"Hot-water bottle," said Mrs. Morgan, groping in the dresser cupboard to find one.

"He hates them."

"Doesn't matter. Sweat it out. There you are, that'll warm him! Check the stopper and wrap it up in something soft. Father gone out?"

"I think he might have. He was a bit cross not long ago. What are you cooking, Mrs. Morgan?"

"Onion broth, with barley to soften it. There's a pair of chops for your father after, and you and His Majesty who doesn't like hot-water bottles can have eggs whenever."

"Thank you," said Clarry gratefully. Mrs. Morgan's cooking was unspectacular and only fairly reliable, but it had kept them alive for a long time now. "Soup will be just right for Peter. I liked cooking that chicken at Christmas. I should learn to cook properly."

"Whatever for?" asked Mrs. Morgan.

"Then you needn't always do it all by yourself. And we could make exciting things, like at Grandmother's house in Cornwall. Saffron buns and apple dumplings and—"

"I often make you a cake!" interrupted Mrs. Morgan, ponderously indignant.

Rough Cake Mrs. Morgan called it. "I'll make you a Rough Cake," she would say, and later it would appear, currants and raisins in a heavy fragrant slab with brown sugar sprinkled on top. Very sustaining. Delicious on hungry days.

"I love your cake, Mrs. Morgan," said Clarry. "It's just the sort of thing I wish I could cook."

"I'll show you, one of these days," said Mrs. Morgan. "Get off up to your brother now, before we have pneumonia on our hands."

Clarry collected her things and went, not fast enough for Peter, though, who complained, "You've been forever," as soon as she opened the door.

"Ten minutes. Less. I made you tea with lemon and

honey and you're to put this under the blankets. You've got to sweat it out, Mrs. Morgan said."

"What does she know?"

"Lots of things we don't. Peter, what about Vanessa's school? Do you think I could really go there?"

"You could if I helped you."

"Will you help me?"

"Yes. Leave me alone a bit to think."

Clarry went back to the kitchen and made a cake with Mrs. Morgan. They mixed it in the enamel basin usually used for washing dishes.

"Goodness," said Clarry, who had not expected that.

"Well," said Mrs. Morgan, "it's only a rough cake."

The Rough Cake was a success and neither smelled nor tasted of washing up. Clarry and Mrs. Morgan gazed at it with pride.

"What else can I learn?" asked Clarry.

Mrs. Morgan sighed and gave her a look. "I daresay Mr. Morgan would show you a bit on his guitar," she said.

"Oh," said Clarry. "Yes. One day that would be nice."

"For, you see," went on Mrs. Morgan, "if I was to learn you like the things you was saying, fancy work, saffron buns and dumplings and the like, then what?"

"What?"

"I'll tell you, my girl! You'd be down here making them!

You get too clever in this kitchen and you'll be landed with it!"

"Mrs. Morgan?"

"Yes, my dear?"

"It's not just cooking I want to learn."

"'Course it isn't. Nor was it with me."

"What did you want?"

"Blacksmithing!"

"BLACKSMITHING?"

"Time was, Clarry, I could have taught you to shoe a horse! My father had a forge, and there was just me and my brother, and he was much younger. And nothing did he care about it. I started off holding the horses' heads, and then I was on the bellows, and before I finished I could shoe a horse and what do you think of that?"

"I never knew girls could!" said Clarry, hugely impressed.

"Girls can do anything, but they're hardly ever let."

"Why did you stop shoeing horses? Because you married Mr. Morgan?"

"Because my brother got interested in the forge."

"Oh."

"And when my father died, it went to him, the forge and the cottage with the garden and the two pigs out the back and the old horse and the cart."

"How unfair!"

"And my brother drank it all away and I went scrubbing

and charring! But I've still a store of horseshoes, put away for special. Made them all myself."

Clarry flung herself into Mrs. Morgan's enormous arms and hugged her.

"Us girls must stick together," said Mrs. Morgan, hugging her back.

Peter's cold made his eyes and nose run, his head ache, his chest wheeze, and his temper frightful. Clarry dosed him with lemon and honey, Vanessa sent butterscotch for his sore throat, the Bony One appeared one afternoon and visited the kitchen to boil up hot black licorice water, and Mrs. Morgan cooked up vats of mutton soup, beef broth, stewed chicken, and gruel. Despite all this, he was still coughing when his new school term began.

"I'll tell Rupert how you are when I get back, shall I?" asked the Bony One, when it became clear that he would have to leave without Peter.

"Don't bother, he won't care," said Peter, and then, in a moment of humanity, seeing his friend's disappointed face, "Yes, all right, if you like," and started coughing again.

"Poor old Peter," said Clarry.

"You should be pleased I can't go," said Peter.

"Why?"

"That exam."

Clarry had asked Vanessa, and found that Peter had guessed right. There was an exam. Vanessa had said, "Oh, that exam! But you could do it, Clarry. History questions. Math. Some Shakespeare, *Twelfth Night*. It's always *Twelfth Night*, everyone says. Scripture. I think that was all. And there will be the forms to sign, of course."

"What sort of forms?"

"Entrance forms. For parents. I'll go to the office and get them for you, if you like."

Vanessa had done this the next day and made the trip across town to deliver them. Now Peter demanded to read them.

"I was going to show you when you were better," said Clarry.

"I'll have to go back to school when I'm better. Show me now."

"Father will have to sign them before I even begin."

"He never will. Give them to me!"

Peter signed the forms: *P. Penrose*, in his usual cramped handwriting.

"Shouldn't you even try and make it look like Father's?" asked Clarry.

"No. If you get in there'll be more forms to sign sometime or other. Easier not to start faking things. Come on, what's next? 'Employment of Father.' What'll we put? 'Dithers around'?"

"No!"

Insurance and banking, wrote Peter. *Mother deceased.*

They both hated looking at those two words so much they turned to the next problem.

"'Address for Correspondence,'" read Peter. "It'll have to be here. 'Date.' There, done it. You can post it. What about that exam?"

"Vanessa's going to help. She says *Twelfth Night* is full of jokes and we can read it together," said Clarry. "I'm learning all the kings and all their dates, that was Rupert's idea. I'll talk to Miss Vane about Scripture, without saying why. Simon said it was bound to be Saint Paul. He said examiners love Saint Paul."

"I've forgotten who he is," said Peter. "Don't try and tell me. I don't believe in any of them. The only thing that really matters is math."

Over the next few days, wrapped up in blankets and reeking of eucalyptus, Peter hurried Clarry through a refresher course of long division and multiplication, fractions, percentages, and angles of triangles. Unfortunately his father noticed how much he got better during this process. He was sent back to school before he had time to instruct Clarry on the areas of circles. As his train pulled out of the station he leaned from the window to shout last-minute advice:

"Find out about pi!"

꧁

"Pie?" asked Mrs. Morgan. "There's pork and there's apple and there's steak and kidney, and now and then there's rabbit, and when I was a girl there was rook!"

"Rook pie?" asked Clarry, aghast.

"Dark meat," said Mrs. Morgan.

"But what did it taste like?"

"Cat," said Mrs. Morgan. "It was very like cat and I didn't care for it."

I found out about pie from Mrs. Morgan, wrote Clarry to Peter, and Miss Vane was perfect for Scripture and Saint Paul. She said her father traced his journeys on a map and marked them all with different colored inks. She showed the map to me. Green and blue and purple. Red for Damascus and black for Rome. Miss Vane said her father was a man very like Saint Paul. They both wrote letters all the time and both were bald. But Miss Vane likes Saint Matthew best. She says he may have been a tax collector but he was the only one who took the trouble to write down what he heard at the Sermon on the Mount.

When Clarry eventually sat the exam for the high school, the Scripture question was the first she read: "Describe two saints, giving a brief summary of their lives and their contributions to Christianity."

Clarry was so thankful that she smiled.

Eleven

TWO WEEKS AFTER CLARRY SAT THE HIGH SCHOOL entrance exam, a letter arrived, addressed to her father. It said that his daughter had obtained a place and could begin after Easter.

Clarry's father was not a shouter, or a banger around. He was a sulker. His silent anger filled the air like a dark and clammy fog. He kept it up until Clarry was reduced to a hovering misery about the house and a whole week had passed. Then one evening, meeting her on the stairs, he looked at her directly for the first time for ages and said, "I was not consulted at any stage."

"Right at the beginning you were," replied Clarry bravely.

"I don't suppose for a moment you considered the extra expense."

"Vanessa said I can have her old books and her grown-out-of uniform," said Clarry, "and Grandmother has sent me ten pounds."

"Did you ask her for that?"

"No, of course not!"

"Why would she do it, then?"

"Rupert told her about me taking the exam. I think she was pleased. She helped me before once, when I wanted to learn to swim."

"So everyone knew, except me?"

Was he sad? He sounded terribly sad to Clarry. She could hardly bear it. "I truly don't think it will make any difference to you, Father," she told him earnestly. "I'll just have to leave a bit earlier in the morning and be back a bit later in the afternoon. Everything else will be just the same."

Her father sighed.

"And when I grow up," she added anxiously, "I'll be able to get a job and earn my own money and you won't have to work so hard."

"I hope I have never complained about that, Clarry."

"Of course you haven't!" she exclaimed.

"Well," he said, and sighed again. "Well, I suppose you must do as you please."

"Thank you," said Clarry. "Oh, thank you, thank you! Would you like to come and see it, Father?"

"See what?"

"The school. So you know where I am."

"Thank you. I do know the location as a matter of fact."

"Vanessa says there are concerts and things, when parents are invited."

"We'll see, Clarry."

"I didn't mean to make you angry."

"I'm not angry, just disappointed. However, you must tell me if there is anything you need."

There were many things Clarry needed, but nothing would have made her say that to her father just then. With Grandmother's ten pounds and Vanessa's help she gathered together the essentials: three school blouses, a pleated blue skirt that Vanessa had outgrown, and a mushroom hat with a gold and blue ribbon. She also became the owner of eleven brown-paper-covered textbooks which she carried to and from school each day, sometimes sparing a penny for a bus if the weather was dreadful, usually walking, often reading a book as she trudged. As time went by, it was as if she wore an invisible track across the town. She grew a little taller, the books changed, and the new ones were heavier than the old.

"Hmm," said Peter, inspecting them when he came home from his own school. "A bit different from the rubbish you were doing with those old bats in the attic."

"Yes," agreed Clarry.

"What does Father say about you being there now?"

"I don't think he really notices."

"I bet he never went to see it, did he?"

"Not yet."

"He never will," said Peter, and Clarry could understand why he was bitter. Their father had never visited Peter at his boarding school once. Not at the beginning when he had vanished into misery so deep that Clarry thought he must have died. Nor for the winter concert when (dressed in tissue paper kimonos) he, Rupert, and Simon astonished the whole school into wild applause with their performance of "Three Little Maids from School." Not even recently, when scarlet fever had raged through the classrooms and corridors, and Peter had been one of the victims.

"I don't mind Father not bothering about my new school," said Clarry. "I truly don't. It's better in a way. It saves him worrying too much."

"It saves him moaning too much, you mean," said Peter, grinning.

"No, I don't! Well, only partly. And it's more private this way."

Clarry had had private worlds before, but they had all been in her head. She had never had a private world with real live people in it. Now she had. At the new school she was not

Peter's nuisance sister, Rupert's little cousin, her grandparents' youngest grandchild, Mrs. Morgan's kitchen helper, Miss Vane's Good Deed, and her father's personal destruction.

At school she was Clarry Penrose.

People noticed her smile and her too-long skirt, her quietness, her chopped-off hair, and the speed with which she could climb a rope in the gym. She became a person who walked miles to school, could be asked about math, honestly loved Latin, would remove unwanted spiders, and never had any money. A bit of an oddity, but so were many others. It was a good school, and accepted oddities as long as they had brains.

It was in every way different from the Miss Pinkses'. There was a rose garden in the front; a graveled drive; long, light corridors; and bare, cold classrooms. There was a library with a polished floor and blue curtained windows that held window seats, a gym with wall bars and ropes, a chemistry lab with Bunsen burners and a whiff of sulfur and explosions, a biology room with a field mouse family in a tank.

Every morning began with assembly: one hymn, one Bible reading, one prayer, and a list of announcements. These covered everything from the correct place to store outdoor shoes to Those in Our Thoughts Today. Those in Our Thoughts Today only ever made the list once; the following day they were expected to have got over whatever it was that had caused their mention. The school motto was *"Quaere verum,"* which meant "Seek the Truth." It should have been "Do Not Fuss."

Not fussing was the basic expectation of every girl, and came in very useful when it was time for the midday meal. This was either mince and two boiled potatoes, fish and two boiled potatoes, or cold meat and two boiled potatoes, and was always followed by half a hard green apple and an optional portion of rice pudding. If you didn't eat your midday meal no fuss was made. You simply went to a little room by the gym and signed a book to say you were fasting. Fasting people were given a spoonful of cod-liver oil and a glass of lukewarm milk, a combination so appalling that people seldom signed the book twice. Clarry, ravenous after her hurried bread-and-butter breakfast, long walk, and five morning classes, managed her dinner with no problem at all.

She became friendly with a lot of people very quickly. Friendly, but not friends, except for Vanessa, much older and seldom seen beyond a cheerful wave now and then. Friends her own age at school meant more than Clarry could manage: tea at each other's houses, birthday presents, and shared outings at weekends. Even so, there were a lot of people to call "Hello, Clarry!" in the mornings, and "See you tomorrow!" at the end of the afternoon. "Yes, tomorrow!" Clarry would call back, as she turned toward home.

Somewhere along that hour-long trek, schoolgirl Clarry was left behind. She would enter the door of the tall stone house as quiet as a shadow, scuttle upstairs with her books and her mushroom hat squashed under her coat, and reemerge in her old blue dress, as if the long school day had never happened. She was often hovering on the stairs when her father came home, sometimes with a book, sometimes with the knitting Miss Vane had recently introduced to her Sunday school pupils. "It's a square for the Home Mission Blanket," she told her father once. "Miss Vane is collecting them and sewing them together. We have to hand in one a week."

"Excellent," said her father.

"When she has one hundred and sixty it will be a whole blanket for a poor family," said Clarry, encouraged by his approval. "We each have a color, but it has to be a dark color because of not showing the dirt. I'm maroon."

"Very nice."

"Mrs. Morgan made a stew this morning and I'm hotting it up for our supper and there's greens and some apple pie from yesterday. Do you think it would be nice to eat it in the kitchen? It's warmer there."

"Eat yours in the kitchen by all means," said her father cordially. "A very good idea! I will have mine in the dining room, as usual."

"Oh," said Clarry. "Oh. Would you rather I was . . . rather I stayed . . . would you like me to keep you company?"

"As a matter of fact, I have some thinking to do," said her

father. "Another day, though, I would be very pleased to have you."

It became a pattern that they both soon followed: Clarry in the kitchen with her dinner and a book. Her father in the chilly dining room with his thoughts. However, on Sundays they ate together, discussing with a strained sort of politeness knitting, the weather, the latest letter from Peter, whether Clarry was happy ("Yes, thank you, Father"), whether her father was happy ("Yes, thank you, Clarry"), and whether Peter was happy ("It really isn't relevant at this stage of his life").

Other more interesting topics introduced by Clarry, such as the acquisition of a kitten ("I don't think so") or what one would buy first should one acquire a million pounds ("I really don't have time for such silliness"), always resulted in Clarry's father leaving the table before pudding, saying, "Do carry on without me. I have a great deal to do." It might have been lonely for Clarry, but it wasn't because of the vast amount of homework school expected her to accomplish. No one could be lonely with Latin and French to translate, chemistry practicals to write up, literature to analyze, and endless quantities of math.

I am so glad I moved to the high school, wrote Clarry to Peter and Rupert.

I knew you would be, replied Peter smugly. *About time you started using your brain.*

Rupert also wrote back to her:

Congratulations on surviving so much education! The trick is knowing when to stop. My whole aim now is to ESCAPE!

He was eighteen, and finishing school just as Clarry was beginning. He had endured twelve years of it but the grand-parents had no intention of allowing him to escape. Oxford was their next plan for Rupert, Oxford University, whether he liked it or not, because it was a family tradition.

Count me out! wrote Rupert to Clarry. *Family tradition be blowed! I've done my share. Twelve chalk dust years of "Sit there and learn this!" Twelve years of clammy morning chapel! Twelve years of listening to inky men in flapping black gowns tell me what to do! TWELVE ENDLESS STULTIFYING YEARS AND THEY THINK THEY'LL MAKE ME GO TO UNIVERSITY! NO, THANK YOU!*

More and more, as she grew older, Clarry was the per-son to whom Rupert wrote with his dreams and schemes and startling ideas. Clarry tried hard to understand, even when she didn't agree, especially about school and university. After all, it was wholly her fault that Rupert had been sent away to boarding school when he was only seven.

I think Oxford would be wonderful, she wrote back, *but I do see what you mean, because sometimes I dream I am back at the Miss Pinkses' and in my dream I run away down the stairs, and down the stairs, and down the stairs, but I am always still there. The grandparents are furious with you, though. My father says you are the first in the family for three generations not to aim for university.*

"What, girls too?" I asked, and he said, "Obviously not counting the girls."

"I don't think obviously not counting the girls is fair," I said. "Why should the girls never go, even if they would like to do, and the boys always go, even if they would rather not?"

So Father went away.

Most of the time there is only Father and me in the house, me in my room right at the top and him in his room right at the bottom and all the empty rooms in between, but yesterday was lovely because Vanessa came and stayed the night. She said, "Give my love to Rupert whenever you write."

Mrs. Morgan says to tell you it's a load of nonsense to go to university. You'll have to be done learning one day, she says. She thinks you should be on the stage!

I have been thinking about our summers in Cornwall. The long rail journey, and the feeling of getting closer and closer. Then, toward evening, the train stopping at last at the little station and there you always were, waiting and waving. It was the best moment ever. Perhaps you might like to be a railway porter, Rupert. You're good at meeting trains.

I have other plans just now, replied Rupert, by way of a cheerful crumpled postcard. *However, one day I may be a railway porter, but only at one station and I will only meet one train, which no one will be allowed to travel on except Peter (perhaps) and you.*

Usually Clarry shared her messages from Rupert, but not this one. The breezy jokes were typical Rupert, but 'other plans'? She wondered, and put it away privately, under her pillow, where it gave her uneasy dreams.

At the end of Rupert's last term of school he didn't go back to Cornwall. He had a friend whose family lived in Ireland, a fiery-headed footballer named Michael who had won the Latin prize, and he went home with him instead.

"Is he nice?" Clarry asked Peter.

"I suppose so," admitted Peter grudgingly. "Everyone said he was a bit mad, but I think they say that about a lot of people. He was very brainy. So brainy he didn't get expelled when he stole a car."

"Stole a car? Whose car?"

"The Head's. The Old Fish's."

"What did he do with it?"

"Oh, just went off for a weekend. He brought it back all right."

"Well," said Clarry, "if Rupert has to go to university, at least he'll have someone good fun to go with."

"Perhaps," said Peter, but to Clarry's surprise he seemed suddenly worried.

"What's wrong?"

"Oh." Peter shook his head irritably, as if shaking away an annoying thought. "That chap's going into the army. Like his father. Silly fool."

"You just said he was very clever!"

"For goodness' SAKE!" snapped Peter. His mood was not improved by the arrival of a postcard that same afternoon.

Having a lovely time, wish you were here, wrote Rupert. *Lots of love, and DON'T WORRY!*

Clarry and Peter were not having a lovely time. It was summer, as gold and green and blue as any summer they had ever known, but this year they were not in Cornwall. The grandparents, exhausted by Rupert and his battles, had decided they had had enough of grandchildren. Vanessa had been whisked away by her mother to visit an aunt. Only Simon was about. He trudged across town every few days to ask, in the most roundabout way he could devise, for the latest news of Rupert, always beginning, "Vanessa said to ask . . ."

"He's having a lovely time," Clarry told him, the day after the postcard.

"Yes, I know that," said Simon petulantly. "Sailing on the lake and all those dances . . ."

"What?"

"Well, that's what he said, anyway. On a card that came for Vanessa . . ."

"A postcard?"

"Yes. Shamrock and a donkey. But it didn't say anything about what he was going to do next. That's what I . . . Vanessa . . . we . . . were wondering if you knew."

"Oh," said Clarry, so startled to hear about the postcard to Vanessa that she couldn't think what else to say. "No. No, sorry, Simon. He hasn't told us anything. Do you miss him?"

Simon stared down from his lonely bony height at Clarry and asked, "What do you mean?"

"I miss him," said Clarry. "So I thought you might too. Is Vanessa all right?"

"Yes. Staying with Mum at our great-aunt's cottage. Drawing things. Dresses. And she says they speak French to each other all day to practice for when she goes to Paris. I mean, if she goes. . . ."

Then Peter came down and he and Simon went off together, Peter with his hopping limp, and the Bony One with his bones, and Clarry returned to her books. In her high room at the top of the house she walked in private landscapes so vivid that the real world went almost unnoticed, except now and then, when very startling things happened.

"Rupert's joined the army," said Peter. "So has his stupid Irish friend. I knew they would. I guessed they would. The fools, the fools, the fools!"

Twelve

IT WAS 1914, BRITAIN WAS AT WAR WITH GERMANY, and Rupert had joined the army. The grandparents in Cornwall acted like it was the end of the world. Peter was appalled. For the first time in his life, he and his father were in agreement. When Clarry tried to argue he snapped, "You don't understand."

It was true; she didn't.

One day in August there was a great banging on the front door and calling in the street, "Come out! Come out! Wherever you are!" and there was Rupert, taller, broader, browner, eyes sparkling, laughing with delight at the sight of Peter staring from an upstairs window, at Miss Vane, hands clasped to her heart as she peeped through her curtains, at Mrs. Morgan's great bellowed "Ha!" and most of all at Clarry's flight to be the first to reach him. He swung her in a circle, kissed her on both cheeks, and said, "I've got two hours. Aren't you going to let me in?"

They let him in, and then they gazed at him. He was in uniform, khaki brown, brass buttons, pockets everywhere. A flat-peaked khaki cap was pushed way back on his head. He looked wonderful.

"I left my kit at the station," he said, as if it was the most natural thing in the world to have kit. "We're on our way to camp. Gosh, this is better than school!"

"Good thing Father's not home," said Peter, and Clarry said, "Yes," in thankful agreement, without taking her eyes off this new glowing Rupert.

"I know, I'm the family disgrace," he said, grinning. "Hurry up! Don't waste time! Where shall we go for lunch?"

"What?"

"I won't see you both for ages. Grab a jacket, Pete! Clarry, stop worrying!"

"But this dress . . ."

"It's fine. Blue. Is it blue? Quite all right."

"Shall I get my Sunday white? We've never . . . what do people wear for lunch? I've got a skirt Vanessa gave me."

"Clarry, you're fussing! Come on! Get a hat or something. Ready, Pete?"

"Money," mumbled Peter, his cheeks burning red with shame.

"I've got it. We'll grab a cab at the corner."

"A cab!" protested Clarry. Cabs were for going to the train station, when you had more luggage than you could carry, but still, willy-nilly, she found herself being driven down the street, with Rupert in front and Peter beside her, and soon they were seated in a large hotel, and she was confronted with a menu as big as an atlas.

"Hurrah, Cornish lobster!" said Rupert, reading over her shoulder. "Iced soup, lobster salad! Lemonade, Clarry? Ginger beer? Raspberry? Beer for me, what about you, Pete? A beer for you?"

"Yes, all right," said Peter, "but stop talking so loudly! And I don't like lobster. I'll have something plain."

"Ham?" suggested Rupert, and ordered iced soup, ham, hot rolls, lobster salad, deviled chicken, minted new potatoes, raspberry fizz, two cold beers, and Neapolitan ices with strawberries to follow.

"Are you sure you have enough money?" asked Clarry, as this appalling array of food was piled all around them. "What if you haven't?"

"We'll leave you to wash the dishes, and me and Pete'll

run for it," said Rupert cheerfully. "Come on, tell me the news! Have you had any more parties? Has Mr. Morgan taught you how to play his Spanish guitar? How is lovely Vanessa? Why aren't you in Cornwall? Did they miss me at school, Pete, when I wasn't there for speech day?"

But it was impossible to talk properly, impossible even to believe they were here, in this ridiculous hotel, and that here was Rupert, and that very soon, in less than an hour, he would be gone, and meanwhile he had bought them all this food, so how could they not eat it, and suddenly there was less than thirty minutes for him to catch his train, so here was another cab, lurching horribly at the bends, and Rupert would be leaving them at the station, and how could you say good-bye in a cab?

It was awful. He was gone. Clarry and Peter walked silently home together, parted without words, and spent the afternoon being clammily, privately sick.

Thirteen

CLARRY HAD TO KEEP REMINDING HERSELF THAT the thing that mattered most of all was that Rupert was happy. Every day, while her family complained, Clarry remembered the happiness of Rupert. The grandparents actually planned to visit him in his training camp, in an effort to intervene. They even demanded that Clarry's father should go along with them.

"I don't see what I could possibly be expected to do," he said petulantly to Clarry. "It's not as if we . . . the boy . . . Rupert and I . . . were close."

"No," agreed Clarry, and wrote to warn Rupert:

The grandparents and Father are coming to see you. They

think there still might be a way of getting you back.

"I think Rupert really loves being in camp with his friends," she said to her father. "Can't you tell the grandparents not to worry?"

"Not to worry about the waste of years and years of expensive education? Not to worry that there is a chance that their grandson will be at war? Of course he won't, he's not even trained and it will be over by Christmas, but even so . . . no, Clarry, I don't think I can tell them not to worry."

He went off with them a day or two later, and came back in a temper.

"Blasted boy turned up on a motorbike," he fumed. "Told us he was planning to buy a banjo! I didn't hear an intelligent remark from him all afternoon, let alone a word of apology to anyone. He sent you his love, for what it's worth."

"Did you give him that cake Mrs. Morgan and I made for him?" asked Clarry.

"I didn't go all that way to deliver cake!" snapped her father, and stamped grumpily away.

Grandfather has gone to London to see a friend who might help him, wrote Clarry to Rupert. *The friend is in the army. He still wants to get you out. What are you doing all this time in camp?*

Lots of things! wrote back Rupert. *Trick biking (I am getting really good at jumps). Cooking (once we roasted a whole pig), signaling with Morse code and field telephones, tremendous games of football, thirty players on each side, more sometimes, miles and miles of exploring. We make maps afterward of villages, and orchards, and where to find mushrooms, and pubs with warm fires.*

Clarry, who had no idea how much had been left out of this description, thought it sounded wonderful. Peter was back at school for the autumn term and so not able to share Rupert's letter, but Vanessa read it. Vanessa said, "That poor pig, but I do love cracklings! They did it on a spit, just like in the olden days."

"Did they?"

"Well, that's what it looked like. He drew a little picture in his letter to me. . . . I think he's enjoying himself. But what will he do next? Everyone except my dad says the war will be over by Christmas. . . . Clarry?"

"What?" Clarry jerked herself back from the last words she had noticed. *In his letter to me . . .*

"I know he wants to be sent abroad. . . ."

"Does he?"

"So he says. But there are awful casualties already. They bring them back on trains."

"Trains?"

"From France."

"But there's sea. How . . ."

"Oh, Clarry, of course they put them on ships in between! I might be a nurse. A VAD. The VAD is the Voluntary Aid Detachment. Think how wonderful I'd be!"

"But what about living in Paris, designing beautiful clothes?"

"Well, obviously that's off, until afterward at least. I'm leaving school, anyway."

"Vanessa!"

"Well, I'm a dunce, Clarry, let's face it! My dad's being recalled to active service in the navy. He was hardly retired for even a year. Simon's away at school. So Mum wants to close the house and go and stay with her aunt, my great-aunt that is. She lives in a village nine or ten miles out of town. And I'm bored with school, I'd rather do something real. I'd be a wonderful nurse, I can't bear sick people! I'd have them better in no time, just to stop them annoying me!"

Clarry laughed and said, "But are you old enough?"

"Probably, and I'm so tall I can look older if necessary!"

"That's cheating!"

"Everybody cheats!"

"What did your dad say about the war, Vanessa?"

"Easier to start than finish," said Vanessa, suddenly serious, "and definitely not over by Christmas, this year or next."

✢

Vanessa's father was right. Christmas came, with no Rupert returning. Vanessa was away training and Simon was with his mother and his great-aunt. However, on Christmas morning, Peter produced gifts for the first time in his life: a pencil box filled with pencils and a tiny knife to sharpen them with for Clarry, and a Christmas card for his father, a careful engraving of a big plain building surrounded by fields and beech trees.

"Er?" said his father, looking at it.

"It's school," said Peter helpfully. "The art master made Christmas cards to help raise money for the chapel roof. That's the chapel. That's my form room this year. That's the door for staff and visitors, but we have to go in at the side. You can't see where I sleep because the dorms are round the back. I thought you might be interested."

"Well, thank you," said his father. "Very ... er ... thoughtful. What's this, then, Clarry?"

Clarry, who had hurried forward with her own presents before Peter made any more pointed remarks, said, "Open it! Happy Christmas, Father! There's yours, Peter! Happy Christmas to you too!"

It was a scarf for each of them, knitted by herself, green for her father, striped dark and light blue for Peter.

"That's actually quite nice," said Peter, sounding very surprised indeed, and Clarry's father said, "So that's what you've been up to!" as if he had been worried about far worse, and then completely stunned them both by producing two small packages of his own.

In each was a watch, an actual silver watch, ticking.

Peter was so startled that he let down his guard enough to exclaim, "Gosh! Gosh!" while Clarry stared at hers with tears running down her cheeks. How often had she tiptoed down two flights of stairs from her room to check the time in the hall? Or raced across town, fearing she was late, pausing by shop windows, searching for clocks?

"Thank you," she said at last. "A watch will help with everything! Thank you, thank you, thank you!"

And so, despite no Rupert and no party, the extreme toughness of Clarry's roast chicken, and the oddness of her Christmas pudding, it was quite a happy day in the tall narrow house.

In the New Year they had news from Rupert that he was being posted to France. He sent a jubilant letter to Clarry.

Nothing could be better! *Bonjour, la belle France*, and good-bye, dusty old Oxford! Clarry, I rely on you and Peter to pass on all the gossip!

"Hurrah!" said Clarry. "The grandparents won't be able to get him now, however many people Grandfather goes to talk to in London!"

"Are you mad?" asked Peter. "*La belle France!* I bet he doesn't even know what he's fighting for."

"He's not fighting. He's not a proper soldier," said Clarry. "He wants some fun, that's all."

"There's wanting fun," said Peter, "and there's shooting people!"

"Rupert would never shoot anyone!"

Peter looked at the photograph that had arrived with the letter. It showed Rupert in uniform, holding a gun. He had signed it: *Au revoir, mes amis! À bientôt!*

"He thinks he's in France already," said Peter. "I suppose he won't have to shoot anyone if he can get close enough. That's a bayonet fitting on his gun."

"What's a bayonet fitting?" asked Clarry.

"It's a long, thin . . ." Peter suddenly stopped. What use, after all, to frighten Clarry? He tried to speak more flippantly. "Rupert had better watch out for German boys. They might want some fun too."

But it was hard to hide the despair he felt, for Clarry in this comfortless house, for ridiculous Rupert, for the summers that were so far away, for all the Ruperts and Clarrys caught up in this hardly understood war, and for himself, and his aching stiffened leg that would always hold him apart. Presently he reached out for Clarry's hand, and later he began to cry, and after a while Clarry whispered, "Does it hurt?" and he said, "Yes. Yes, it does. I'm sorry."

Fourteen

THE CHRISTMAS HOLIDAYS ENDED, PETER WENT away again, and Clarry took the Christmas cards off the mantelpiece. She kept the engraving of the school by the beech trees and looked at it often. Rupert used to complain that it was a very long wet walk from anywhere and she could completely see what he meant. And he wrote to her from France:

> *We are staying in an old farmhouse. There is an enormous hearth, you could stand six Clarrys in a line under the chimney! We light great fires there and roast chestnuts. A little cat comes to sit with us. Her name is Mina. We buy bags of chestnuts at the market*

and apple cider, and once, oh, Clarry, terrible shining
pink sausages made of TRIPE. Here comes Mina just
now with a mouse! Am I supposed to roast it with my
chestnuts?

It sounded safe enough, as far as Clarry could tell. At that time her life was almost blank when it came to news of the war. Her father never left his newspapers about. Whatever Peter knew he didn't communicate. Vanessa might have been useful, but she was suddenly busy in a hospital at Southampton that she had wheedled her way into through a friend of her mother's. Vanessa seemed to be constantly exhausted and constantly in love.

"Goodness, Clarry, it's glorious!" she told her. "Glorious and awful and exciting all together. So, so different from school! And I'm useful! I've never been useful before! I'm doing my patriotic duty! Hurrah!"

The war had brought new words and phrases and that was one of them. "Patriotic duty." Mrs. Morgan used it too. Mrs. Morgan said she no longer had time to waste with such things as cleaning the front steps, or queuing to buy lamb chops for Clarry's father's dinner. "I should be doing other things," she told him when, pinch-faced with temper, he sent away his lentil soup. "I could be doing my patriotic duty and packing shells for twice what I get paid here, and more thanks too!"

"Shells," that was another word that became more often

used. "Shells," and "shellfire." Always when Clarry heard it, her mind jumped to the fans and spirals and fragile treasures she had collected on the Cornish beaches, summer after summer. Pink and white and daffodil yellow. Pearl and indigo blue. "A rain of falling shells," Clarry caught the phrase one day as she hurried home from school. It sounded entrancing.

But the words that she heard most often were "Don't you know there's a war on?" Over and over, when the post was late, or the streets not swept, or when the school-dinner fish was even less appealing than usual. There was a war on, and Clarry made herself consider it: actual war, armies, nothing to do with a rainbow shower of seashells. Fighting.

How did an army fight?

On the other side of the river from Clarry's home the town was full of troops, but Clarry, closing the front door quietly in the early morning, or trudging home in the gray dusk laden with schoolwork, saw nothing of this. The only armies she had ever seen had been in the toy-shop window. Often she had paused to admire the soldiers there, armed to the teeth, arranged in patterns on a bright green cloth. Miniature horses, drummer boys, foot soldiers, and captains under flags, bright and neat as scarlet paint could make them, lined up in squares and diamonds against another army, equally delicious, in silver and blue.

"Charge!" Clarry expected someone would cry, when all

was arranged and the wind had caught the flags just right, and the horses were beginning to prance. Then there would be a great rushing forward and mingling of colors and the buglers would blow vivid encouraging notes and at the end the patterns would be completely rearranged on the bright green grass. The new patterns would show who had won and advanced, and who had lost and been pushed back, and that, Clarry supposed, was how a battle was fought, except with real people.

But even with real people, in Clarry's mind, the event was essentially the same. The armies rested at night. The horses were taken care of. The green grass was as clean and crisp at the end as it had been at the beginning. That was Clarry's understanding of a battle, and if someone had told her the soldiers did not fight on Wednesday afternoons and Sundays she would not have been surprised.

At school any war gossip was quickly subdued. Of course, in morning assembly they prayed for the army, except on Fridays, when, perhaps because it was fish for lunch, the navy had its turn. "'For those in peril on the sea!'" sang the girls, and of course the seas were perilous, that was well known from poetry.

The numbers included in Those in Our Thoughts Today were slightly increasing, and from time to time a girl's shoulders might shake when a particular name was read, but that was all. The no-fussing tradition was extremely useful in times of war. It was all very vague and distant. Rupert was in

France, and Peter did not approve, but so far as Clarry knew, the only certain awfulness that her cousin had had to bear was the shining pink sausages.

"What is tripe?" she asked Mrs. Morgan one evening.

"Very delicate," said Mrs. Morgan. "I do a tripe supper for Mr. Morgan on his birthday with milk sauce and onions."

"Rupert had it in sausages," Clarry told her.

"French?" asked Mrs. Morgan.

"Yes."

"Well, I daresay worse will come to him than tripe over there."

"What?" asked Clarry fearfully.

"Garlic," said Mrs. Morgan, slapping a dreadful gray dishcloth all over the table. "Frogs! Snails! Wait till he comes to a plateful of snails! Move your elbows, I can't wipe round you! There! I'll be off. I've done you and your father a pot of broth to hot up. Mutton. Should last two days. Can you stew some apples for after?"

"Of course," said Clarry.

"Then I'll be off and you stop worrying about your cousin. He's the sort who can take care of himself." That was true, and that was how, through the silence of the people around her, the stoicism at school, the absence of newspapers, and the terrible cooking of Mrs. Morgan, Clarry remained almost entirely ignorant of what was going on in France.

Fifteen

RUPERT WAS DEALING WITH HOMESICKNESS BY
writing letters. There were rules about this. They weren't
supposed to mention where they were, or details of what
they were doing or who was doing it with them. Or even
the weather, but everyone did write about the weather,
and it generally got through uncensored. After all, should
a German spy manage to get hold of the mailbag, would it
really surprise him to discover that it had been another rainy
day for the British? The armies were so close together that if
the British were getting rained on, then the Germans would
be equally soggy.

Sending letters was free, and everybody wrote them.

Rupert and his friends filled bagfuls every day. Rupert didn't very much mind not being able to describe what they were doing, because so far it hadn't felt like war. They'd been working on a new base camp, miles behind the front lines in Belgium and France.

So far Rupert had spent his time unpacking stores; building a cookhouse, a dining room, and a washroom; organizing a football team; and dismantling, cleaning, and putting back together the battery's new heavy guns. The guns would have been more exciting if they had had more ammunition. Then they could have practiced firing them more than once a week, not that he would have been allowed to write home about that.

Clarry's letters were the easiest. Chestnuts and the little cat Mina had been followed by his new skills at cooking, the eerie sounds of foxes in the middle of the night, and the difficulty of getting hold of banjo strings. Vanessa had different information, in case she and Clarry should happen to share. Vanessa had the sea journey (because her father was in the navy), the marketplace, and a good-bye in French (*Bonne chance, bonne nuit, ma belle amie*; he and Vanessa always did silly good-byes on their letters). The thin lovely girl he had met in Ireland had a mixture of Clarry's and Vanessa's letters, with Vanessa's ending. She was in England now, in London, where her grandparents lived. His own grandparents got a postcard telling them not to worry and sending his love to Lucy the pony. The girl with pink lipstick who had cheered him up at the station café got a postcard too, although he didn't know her name. He drew a picture of her smiling face above the name of the café, wrote the station and the town, and hoped it would reach her. He thought it probably would.

Peter and Simon got a joint message in the form of a map of the top floor of the school. If they followed the arrows and lifted the floorboard he had marked in the trunk room by the back stairs, they would find three bottles of beer and a key to the cricket pavilion that he and his fiery-headed Irish friend had hidden there last term. The cricket pavilion was a good place to sit out a long cross-country run. Simon might use it. Rupert himself had had many a comfy nap amongst the nets while others were slogging around four miles of cold field boundaries.

After this, Rupert could think of no one else for his letters. Not one person whom he could tell about the two field ambulances they'd unloaded that afternoon and reloaded onto the train for the coast and then home.

Poor devils, he had thought, but the men from the ambulances hadn't been sorry for themselves. One, pale as paper, flinching at every movement, gasped, "I got it in my guts. It's nothing. I'm out of this now." Another had grinned and grinned, with his left arm ending in a great lump of bandage at his elbow. Everyone who came from the front agreed that these were quiet days, hardly a pop from dawn to dusk, the cold was the worst, and the perpetual wet that did for your feet. Nothing like before Christmas, when things had been rough. Nothing like what was to come, best not think about that. So Rupert rolled himself in two blankets, and stretched out on his camp bed, picturing scenes from home to see him off to sleep. Lucy pushing her muzzle into his pockets for sugar. The run across the moorland to where the cliff dipped down to the sea. Pretty girls. That sort of thing.

Sixteen

EASTER CAME AROUND. EASTER 1915. ONE AFTERNOON,
Peter came home from school, with no warning to anyone and
Simon tagging on behind him. Clarry heard a sudden clatter
in the hall, voices, and the thump of bags being dropped, and
rushed down the stairs and there they both were.

"Peter! Simon! Oh, how good!"

"Hello, Clarry," said Simon.

"Hello! Oh, Peter, what's the matter?"

Peter had collapsed onto the old wooden chair at the foot
of the stairs, and sat rocking, his face crinkled with pain, rubbing his damaged left leg. "Couldn't get a cab," he said, from
between clenched teeth. "Walked."

"All the way from the station? With all those bags?"

"Don't fuss. Why's it so cold? This house is colder than outside."

"The kitchen's warm. Warmer, anyway. I've made some soup too. I thought I'd try. Come in there. Shall we help you get up?"

"No," said Peter, wincing as he got to his feet again. "You and Bonners could bring the bags, though. Don't want Father noticing them. When does he get home?"

"Father? Not for ages. Not till I've gone to bed some-times." Clarry held the kitchen door open for Peter and beckoned to Simon, now laden with a bag in each hand and another under each arm. "Come on, Simon! Come and get warm."

"Clarry," said Simon, hesitating for a moment and look-ing worriedly down at her. "Could I possibly stay?"

"Stay?"

"I've already said that you can," growled Peter from the kitchen. "There's no need to ask Clarry. She won't mind."

"Our house is shut up, you see," said Simon. "They're still at my great-aunt's, Vanessa and my mother. And she's not keen on me. My great-aunt."

"Oh, Simon, we'd love to have you!" exclaimed Clarry. "But there's Father, he's not very . . ."

"Friendly," finished Peter.

"Yes!" agreed Clarry. "I mean, no! But I don't know what he'd say. Why doesn't your great-aunt like—"

"Clarry!" interrupted Peter sternly. "Stop it!"

"Sorry! Sorry, Simon!"

"It's all right. I do seem to break things when I'm there. I don't know why." He paused and stared humbly at his big bony purple breaking-things hands. "She says I'm too tall."

"You are too tall!" said Peter, warming up and more cheerful. "There's nothing much to break here and Father doesn't matter."

"He might not even notice," said Clarry, taking heart. "I often don't see him all day. Come and try the soup I made. It's got barley in, and vegetables. And the fire's hot, we can make toast. Oh, it's lovely to have people!"

"I can sleep anywhere," said Simon, knocking over a chair or two as he sat down at the table. "Floor or a chair or a sofa, anywhere."

"There's a spare room with a bed," said Peter. "Rupe had it that Christmas."

Simon, who had been holding his face over his soup bowl, gratefully breathing in the warm steam, looked up and smiled.

"Thank you," he said.

He had a nice smile, like a great long-faced kindly giraffe. He was, Clarry thought, giraffelike altogether. She had seen one once, when a traveling menagerie had stopped on the outskirts of town and Peter had insisted to their father that the two of them must go, and most surprisingly, won. Clarry's heart had melted at the great, lanky, puzzled animal, so clearly much too far away from home. Now here was one at their kitchen table, eating their soup and toast.

"I'm glad you're here," she told him, and reached out a comforting hand. "How is your leg now, Peter? Does it still hurt?"

"Not much. It doesn't matter. Is there any more butter?"

"A bit. Save some for Father. It's harder to buy these days. You have to go and queue. I don't know what that room's like, Peter, I haven't been in it for ages and ages. Not since I got it ready for Rupe, and that was more than a year ago. I don't think Mrs. Morgan has either. She doesn't bother with bedrooms much."

"It will be fine," said Simon shyly.

"Freezing," said Clarry, "and I suppose the same sheets and things. I never thought of taking them off, I'd better go and look."

They all went to look. At the dead dusty ashes of the fire Clarry had lit for Rupert. At the rumpled bed, with the pillows still dented where Rupert's head had lain. At the damp that had got in around the window and turned into a patch of mildew. It was freezing, and it smelled fusty and abandoned.

Peter opened a window and let in a gale of wet cold spring air. Clarry said, "I'll light another fire and find some different sheets and dust. . . ."

"No, no!" protested Simon. "It's perfectly all right! Don't do anything! I didn't want to be extra work."

"Yes, don't fuss, Clarry," said Peter. "It just needed some fresh air. It's not any colder than your room, or mine. We don't have fires. Anyway, he can have one if he can be bothered to lug some coal up and light it himself."

"No, no, no," said Simon. "Please, no. Just perhaps a candle, for in the night?"

Clarry found a candle, soap, and a towel, searched for clean sheets and concluded Mrs. Morgan must hide them, took the pillow down to the kitchen to warm in front of the fire, and promised herself she'd sneak up with a hot-water bottle as soon as she had a chance. Simon paid her back for this hard work by sweeping the kitchen floor, scrubbing muddy potatoes to bake in the oven, and going shopping for onions and triumphal sausages, which he cooked in the big frying pan. The days that followed were just the same. He was far more useful than either Mrs. Morgan or Clarry at housework, scrubbing furiously at grime, mending loose doorknobs, window catches, and dripping taps, and cooking exotic foods, such as omelets and curry. It was the smell of curry that gave him away to Peter and Clarry's father, who tracked him down to the bench outside the kitchen door, where he was industriously polishing the household's boots, while Peter leaned against the doorframe, criticizing, and Clarry whacked dust from the kitchen hearthrug with an ancient tennis racket.

"Peter, Clarry?" he said. "Er . . ."

"Oh, Father, this is Bonners . . . Simon," said Peter, briskly unruffled. "He's at school with me. He's come to help us out for a few days. Simon, you remember my father?"

Simon smiled nervously, held out a polishy hand, changed his mind, and said apologetically, "Sorry, better not," half bowed instead over a boot, and added "I was here one Christmas. At the party. Me and my sister. I hope you don't mind."

"He's made Mrs. Morgan's end of mutton into wonderful curry!" said Clarry, hurrying over and standing protectively close to Simon. "Wait till you taste it! And he's cooking rice too. His father taught him, but he's away now and their house is closed up. That's why Simon is here."

"He's navy," murmured Simon. "Recalled. I needn't stay, really. I shouldn't. School's open, I think perhaps I'd better go back."

"No, no, Simon!" exclaimed Clarry. "Father's *nice*! He wouldn't want that, would you, Father?"

"I . . . er. No, of course not. No. Very welcome," said her

father, thus cornered into decency. "Do . . . er . . . stay. Well. We'll meet again at dinner, perhaps?"

So Simon the Bony One was accepted into the tall narrow house, not just then, but often afterward. When Clarry saw an especially long shadow through the frosted glass of the front door she knew he was back again, hovering uneasily before knocking, apologetic, kind. He liked to hear the latest news of her life, and to talk of Vanessa (still working in her hospital) and the braininess of Peter, and most of all, Rupert. They both had a good supply of Rupert stories—Simon from school, Clarry from her summers in Cornwall—and then there was always the chance that Clarry might have a letter to share.

"Let's send him a parcel," Simon suggested once, and showed Clarry how to make gingerbread. They cut it into careful squares, found a box, and posted it.

"All of it?" asked Peter, coming into the kitchen sniffing.

"Yes," said Clarry and Simon in unison. "Of course all of it!"

Clarry was knitting a scarf for Rupert too, and once, to her astonishment, Simon sat down with it at the kitchen table and added several rows to its length. "I learned to knit when I was very little," he said, smiling at Mrs. Morgan's astonishment. "I was stuck in bed with a bad chest and Mummy . . .

Mum taught me for something to do. My dad can do it too. Lots of sailors can knit."

"I daresay anyone can do it if they try," remarked Peter, who had been listening and watching. "You never let on you could knit at school, though."

"I'm not that much of a fool," said Simon.

"Mrs. Morgan can shoe horses," Clarry told them both. "That's more surprising still."

"Ah," said Mrs. Morgan, "I was a better lad than my brother ever was," but still she looked curiously at Simon, bent almost double over the wool, and when he had gone, suddenly clumsy, knocking over the hatstand on his way out, she said, "Soft!"

"He is not!" snapped Peter, before Clarry could speak.

"Well, to hear a lad as big as him call his mother that!" Mrs. Morgan was not daunted by Peter, nor ever had been. "*Mummy!* You can't deny it!"

"It's just the way their family talk," said Clarry, also indignant. "Vanessa says 'Mummy' too, when she forgets."

"It's a bit different coming from a girl," said Mrs. Morgan. "However, I'll say no more. Doesn't he get laughed at at that school of yours?"

"Yes, of course he does, and so do I," said Peter, still angry. "And so would Clarry and so would you, and so does anyone who isn't a silly, grinning, sports-playing, book-hating, first-year-tormenting, prefect-groveling, hair-parted-on-the-right—"

"Eh?" said Mrs. Morgan.

"I'm just telling you the *rules*!" said Peter. "So you don't get laughed at."

"Well, now, I'm sorry for what I said," said Mrs. Morgan. "I was wrong. I'm sure your friend is a nice enough lad. Folk can't help how they're brought up, nor how they turn out."

"No, they can't," growled Peter, and marched out of the kitchen, leaving Clarry and Mrs. Morgan to make peace together.

"All the same," said Mrs. Morgan, "you might just drop him a hint, Clarry, or mention it to his sister. About calling his mother what he does. No need for him to go around asking for trouble."

"I wonder what Peter and me would have called our mother," said Clarry, a little sadly.

"Ah," said Mrs. Morgan. "That was sad, how you lost her. It was a great pity she was so frail."

"Was she?"

"Well, of course she was. Not enough iron in her blood. Your father never accepted it, but there it was, anemia, and nothing to be done to help, from what that Miss Vane told me once. It was all left too late for treatment, not that they can do a great deal. And I'm guessing that's the first you've heard of it?" she added, seeing Clarry's shocked face and wide eyes.

Clarry nodded.

"White as paper, poor thing!"

"I didn't know you even knew her," said Clarry.

"I wouldn't say *knew*," said Mrs. Morgan. "I scrubbed this house out when they first moved in (last proper spring clean the place ever had!) and I'd see her in church now and then. Looked like the wind could blow her away but she hung on until you arrived. I used to think it was that kept her going, wanting to see her new baby."

"Mrs. Morgan!"

"Now what have I said wrong?"

"Nothing, nothing! But I always thought, and Peter did too, that it was because of me she died."

"Nothing of the sort! It was because of you she lived, my girl. Now, stop it! Don't take on like that! Now that's no use at all to us! No, don't use your sleeve! Nor that tea cloth neither! There's a handkerchief, blow! Dear goodness, if this kitchen wasn't damp enough without you adding floods to the mix! She was a very brave lady; you'd never have caught her dripping all over the kitchen table."

Clarry put her head on her arms and sobbed.

Peter, hearing the racket, stuck his head round the door and demanded, "What's the matter with her *now*?" as if she was forever doing such things.

"Nothing. Go away," said Clarry, without lifting her head, and when he had gone, closing the door rather hard, she said, "Don't tell him, please, Mrs. Morgan."

"Why ever shouldn't he know?"

"He should, but not now. It would change too much. I don't think he blames me anymore anyway, that was only when he was little."

"You're a funny girl, you are," said Mrs. Morgan, rather grumpily. "It wouldn't hurt your brother to hear he was wrong."

"It would," said Clarry. "It hurts people very much to know they're wrong. I'm better now anyway."

To prove she was better she got a cloth and washed her drips off the table and then peeled potatoes until Mrs. Morgan said, "Stop! They're getting scarce in the shops these days."

"What did they call it? An . . . something?"

"Anemia."

Clarry nodded. *Anemia, anemia,* she thought, to help her remember, and she found it in the dusty old dictionary in the living room. The pages were of tissue-thin paper, but it opened easily at the word, as if it had opened there many times before. "Pallor," it said, amongst other things, and, "Lack of vigor." Nothing about dying.

Clarry was still sitting on the floor gazing at it when her father came in.

"What's that you have?" he asked her, and when she replied, "Just the dictionary," he said, "I never knew we had one. Put it back when you've finished."

So it must have been her mother who had opened the dictionary so often that the pages remembered her touch. Clarry closed it carefully, but instead of putting it back, she took it upstairs to her room. Until now she had had no connection with her mother. There was nothing in the house to show she'd ever lived except Clarry and Peter. And now, this book. Gently Clarry fluttered through the pages and as she did so, she noticed that once again, the dictionary was choosing its own place to fall open.

Pushed tight against the stitched spine, on the first page of the *B*s, Clarry found the reason for this. An oval of cardboard, a little photograph. A round, young, smiling face, looking out at her.

JANEY PENROSE, 1901
(Mother)

read Clarry on the back.

Her mother's face.

Her mother's handwriting. There were no more pictures hidden in the pages. Clarry knew because she checked them, all 1,038.

Seventeen

I WISH, THOUGHT CLARRY, *I HAD SOMEONE TO TALK to about Mother. And that illness, anemia, that she looked up in the dictionary so often. Poor Mother.*

Who could it be? Peter was away. Mrs. Morgan had told her all she knew. Not Father, never. Not Miss Vane, who would fuss, or Simon, who Peter said had once fainted on glimpsing someone else's nose bleed. Vanessa. Sensible, loving, cheerful Vanessa, at present in Southampton, slaving in her hospital for wounded soldiers.

"How did you begin all this nursing?" Clarry had asked her friend once. "Everyone at school is so surprised they let you. They say you're not old enough."

"Oh, well, I always was too tall," Vanessa had replied very quickly and briskly. "It's rubbish for dancing but does make a difference for other things. I lied about my age, of course, and put up my hair and wore a dreary skirt and borrowed my great-aunt's ancient blue hat. And I talked a lot about first aid and nursing and the training I'd already—"

"Had you?" asked Clarry, surprised.

"And Dad being a naval doctor, and that helped enormously. Shut up! I know what you are going to say! Anyway, I'm good at it, and I work jolly hard!"

Vanessa was working hard the day that Clarry turned up in Southampton. She had to wait until her friend had a couple of hours free and they could scuttle away to a café.

"I'm sorry you had to hang around so long for me to get away," apologized Vanessa. "Did you nearly give up hope?"

"No, no, and there was lots to look at. I've never been here before. Lovely to be so close to the sea."

"I know. I come outside on windy days to blow away the carbolic smell. What's the matter, Clarry? It must be something worrying to bring you all this way."

So Clarry produced the photograph and the dictionary that remembered where to open, and related the brief minor tragedy that she'd heard from Mrs. Morgan. As she talked, Vanessa changed from her casual, flippant mood to the practical kindness that made her so useful in the hospital.

"Yes," she said steadily, as she looked at the little picture, so much like Clarry. "People do die of anemia. What bad luck for you all."

"Do you think she left the picture there for me or Peter to find?"

"I'm sure she did. A message for you, on the right page too. *B* for 'baby'! Maybe she guessed your father would never talk of her."

"Do you think perhaps Mrs. Morgan was right?" asked Clarry. "And it might not have been because of me that she died? Don't be kind, Vanessa, tell me the truth."

"It wasn't because of you," said Vanessa, reaching out for her hand. "It was never because of you. I'm telling the truth. You have to believe it. I'm sure that's what your mother would have wanted. You look so like her, Clarry!"

"There's nothing of her left anywhere in the house. We've searched and searched. Father got rid of it all. Nothing except this picture."

"You can get copies made of photographs, you know. I bet Peter would like one. I don't believe for a second he blames you either. He's much too decent." Vanessa yawned hugely. "Sorry, Clarry, I've been up all night. It's sitting down, and being warm that's sending me to sleep! Look after your photograph. She was beaut"—Vanessa yawned again—"iful."

With that Vanessa's head dropped, and she nodded forward and fell asleep on the table, scattering cups and saucers.

"Five minutes," she murmured unrepentantly, snuggling down.

"She's a nurse, she's been up all night," murmured Clarry to the waitress, as she helped her clear the fallen cups, and the waitress said, "Ah!" and the nearby tables also said, "Ah!" and the café became very quiet as people shushed each other, and nodded kindly at Clarry, who sat slowly allowing herself to believe what she had been told.

It wasn't her fault.

It was just bad luck.

She smiled at Vanessa when she woke up, rubbing her eyes and laughing at herself.

"Whatever were you doing last night?" asked the waitress, coming across with fresh tea.

"Dancing," Vanessa told her, airily rueful, but to Clarry she said later, "Actually, I was sitting with a poor bloke who was dying and needed a bit of company. I always seem to get that job."

Clarry could understand why. Vanessa, with her warmth and friendliness and glowing chestnut hair must be as comforting as a candle flame through such a night.

"I never can believe they're dying," went on Vanessa. "Never! I think, Well, you've got so far. Back to England. Safe in hospital, bandaged up. And they look too young, young hands and hair. No wrinkles. No gray. But still they go. Very unfair after all our hard work. How gloomy I sound! I'm not really. I'm tough. So are you, Clarry, stuck in that cold house alone with your father."

"I have Peter sometimes, and Simon almost every weekend."

"Good. Look after Simon for me, Clarry."

"I will," promised Clarry.

When students at Peter and Simon's school were over sixteen they were allowed to go home for Saturday and Sunday if they applied for a weekend pass. Peter did this only very rarely. Not only because he was studying hard for Oxford, but also because these days he had hardly any spare money, for train fares, or anything else. The year before, his godfather had died, and so Peter had lost the small private gold mine that had been so helpful in the past. It was different for Simon. He wasn't interested in studying, and he was never short of money. Almost every Friday evening he turned up on Clarry's doorstep, asking, "Is it all right? Do you mind?"

It was wonderful to see such a friendly face, and Clarry would pull him in at once. He always brought food: sausages or cheese or a pie.

"Vanessa said I should," he would explain, fishing apples from his pocket. "Because everything's so short in the shops.

Peter sent another book for you. Have you heard from Rupert?"

He always had a message from Vanessa and a book from Peter, and he always asked about Rupert the minute she opened the door.

"I don't want to be a nuisance," he said, one Friday evening, stumbling into the brass-topped table, dropping a parcel, and sending a vase flying. "Sorry, sorry! Is it broken? Gosh, I'm standing on the kippers!"

Clarry rescued the kippers, said they were meant to be flat, he wasn't a nuisance, she had been feeling so lonely, and the vase didn't matter.

"It was cracked anyway," she said. "It needed breaking. A letter came five minutes ago. I haven't read it yet."

Clarry, Clarry, send more gingerbread! And get your Miss Vane knitting socks. What's the use of being a family hero if you don't get constant luxuries in the post? I've got the grandparents onto it too. I am the golden boy in Cornwall these days, did you know? They say I have done the Right Thing and they couldn't be more proud. They've gone all patriotic. And mad.

Now, Clarry, I don't want you to worry, and please understand that where I am is all right. Perfectly adequate for football, although it'll soon be the cricket season and then we'll have problems finding a decent wicket. The ground's a bit bumpy round here.

BUT LUCY WOULDN'T LIKE IT!

Darling Clarry, make the grandparents see sense. Stop them sending Lucy here somehow. The fools. I'm shoving a few ten-bob notes in with this in case you need a train fare. . . .

Yours, with love and hope and faith,

Rupe

P.S. Don't worry about the cricket pitch either. Just post me the garden roller from behind the shed in Cornwall. Love to everyone, R

"He's all right," said Simon, sighing with relief. "Who's Lucy?"

Eighteen

NOBODY THAT RUPERT KNEW WROTE THE TRUTH
home. The days of roast chestnuts and the little cat Mina
were over, not that they had lasted very long. Not as long as
the letters describing them, which was a pity, because Clarry,
inspired by Miss Vane, a great cat lover herself, had sent a
small patchwork blanket for Mina.

I hope she likes it, Clarry had written. *Miss Vane told me
once that each of her cats has a blanket of their own to make
them feel secure.*

Rupert had written back that any cat would be proud of
such a mat and that it was the perfect color to show off Mina's
beautiful blackness. He was very much regretting his cheerful

early letters to home. Why, oh, why, he asked himself, had he told his grandparents that his unit had been busy building stables in France? How stupid had he been to describe the great care that he saw people taking of the horses?

Very stupid indeed, thought Rupert, furious with himself. Not that it wasn't true. The horses were looked after, as far as anyone could—rubbed down, watered, fed (although food was always short and sawdust was mixed in with their rations to make them go a bit further). He'd seen people hug them often. He hugged them himself, breathing in the comforting smell of horse. There were hundreds of horses working out there. They dragged supplies, camp equipment, heavy guns, sandbags, ambulances, and each other's dead bodies. There were corpses of horses rotting in spinneys, in ditches, and amongst the churned up remains of cabbage fields. If you got close enough you could see the pale bone around their eye sockets and along the length of their forelegs. Their teeth were always bared, as if their last thought had been to lunge in futile fury. Their barrel bodies were full of rats. Rupert, who had not prayed with any conviction since he was seven, now prayed, "Oh, God, not Lucy."

His grandfather had changed his mind completely about war.

He was no longer furious, he was proud, glad that Rupert was not skulking in Oxford, hiding behind books. He wrote that the patriotism of the young men of today was the finest thing he had witnessed in his entire lifetime. He wrote that if he could, he would be there too, but since he couldn't, well, perhaps Rupert could look out for a familiar bright brown pony coming up the lines! Of course, at fourteen hands, Lucy was a bit under what the army wanted, but she was a good sturdy pony and if she could not pull a gun, she could rattle along a canteen or a field ambulance, doing her bit. He was going to offer her anyway.

Your grandmother is not so keen, he had written. *She says at Lucy's age she is much too old, but I daresay Lucy and I will talk her round!*

Fool! thought Rupert viciously, but he did not mean his grandfather.

The horses, as well as being always hungry, were perpetually uneasy. After all, they had been rushed to this miserable new existence as fast as the men, and without a word of explanation. It was best not to catch the look in their eyes. It was best not to think about them with any emotion at all, if possible. Rupert wished he had not asked the reason for the evening firing from the gunners. Ammunition was so short they could fire for only a few minutes a day. So they waited until just before nightfall, in order to target the German horse transport. . . .

Rupert was thankful Clarry didn't know about that.

It was late spring now, nearly summer. The flies were dreadful. Along the front line the trenches were being reinforced with barbed wire and sandbag parapets, propped up with timber. The duckboards that made tracks were being repaired or replaced. Two hundred yards away, across the ruined landscape of no-man's-land, the Germans were doing the same. Something big was going to happen very soon, everyone knew, and everyone wondered where they would be when it began. Nobody stayed in the front-line trenches for long. The pattern varied, but at present it seemed to be a week at the front, and then a few days back in camp, where they cleaned kit and drilled and caught up on sleep. There wasn't much sleep at the front, even though there were bunkers now and then, dug into the sides of trenches. These were lantern-lit, earth-smelling caves, blue with the cigarette smoke that hung in the air. Everyone smoked. It was comforting and it covered a multitude of smells. There were unburied bodies in no-man's-land, too far out to collect, and too long dead. They were slowly sinking into the earth, and they had been there so long that they were no longer shocking.

This time last year, thought Rupert, *I was still at school, and now I don't find unburied corpses shocking. I use them as landmarks.*

He was still writing his letters home, with less and less to say.

He wrote to the thin girl (her name was Elizabeth):

I think of you every time someone's hat blows off and goes rolling away, and whenever I hear an out of tune piano, and whenever we have lemon curd tarts for tea. You will be pleased to hear that in the whole time that I have been here I have never seen a single spider, and so of course I am quite safe. . . .

Elizabeth thought, *He must be tired; he's gabbling. And what's more, he's mixing me up with someone else. I've never minded spiders. I wonder how many girls he writes to. Not that it matters.* She wrote back, with great compassion, *Stay safe, Rupert,* and sent him peppermints and chocolate.

Rupert wrote to Vanessa,

I meant to tell you about a place in a village we came through. We sold them tinned beef and tobacco and knobbly socks and they sold us red wine and very good sausages. "What's in the sausages?" I asked, and the woman said, "Garlic, rosemary, sage, and pepper, and vilain garçons allemands. Naughty German boys!"

Is that funny? wondered Vanessa. *I suppose it is; I'm just* in a mood. I think he's forgotten I'm working in a hospital full of men back from the front. I'll remind him.

Drlng Rp, today 32 bedpans sluiced and scrubbed, 12 Mackintosh sheets as above, 3 stockings left unladdered (all different shades of black unluckily), 2 slices of Victoria sponge—jam very thin and no cream at all, 1 fall on BTM—slipped on wet floor in sluice room, 26 dressings changed, 3 marriage proposals, 4 hours' sleep last night, 0 mention of spiders in your latest, thank gdness for that hd begun to dread opening. Simon and Clarry are up to something wicked. Gd nght, swt drms, may flghts of angls etc. VnSa xx

Last of all, Rupert wrote,

Wonderful Clarry, the rain here is wetter than English rain. I am getting severely trickled on. You might send me a small handkerchief for dabbing the drips from my neck. The other thing I would like, if you have a moment, is a magic carpet. Remember how you made one in Cornwall with the old landing rug, by stuffing the lining with feathers and flowers and setting fire to the corners? Baffling that it wouldn't fly but probably for the best since you constructed it on a cliff top. I realize now that if you had sprinkled it with eau de cologne and a very small amount of gunpowder you would have had better luck. I would try to make one here, but unluckily no access to either eau de cologne or the right kind of feathers. Don't let them send Lucy here, just don't. And love, Rupert

Nineteen

THIS SECOND LETTER ARRIVED ON SATURDAY morning. Two letters about Lucy in two days. Clarry became very still as she read.

Simon, who had taken upon himself the Saturday morning task of cleaning the fireplaces, saw something was wrong and asked, "What is it?"

"It's from Rupert," said Clarry, and her father overhead and asked, "Rupert? Quite the family hero, I gather, these days. Is he well?"

"I think so. He says it's raining. He mostly writes jokes."

"Ah," said her father, and hurried away, as if fearing he might have to listen to them.

"He's written about Lucy again," said Clarry, holding out her letter to Simon. "Look!"

"I've been doing the grates," he said, rubbing ashy smudges onto his trousers.

"Never mind that. Just read it!" Clarry pushed Rupert's letter into his red bony hands and noticed that they were suddenly trembling.

"He's not telling you a lot of things," said Simon, after a moment.

"I know. I know it's not as nice as he pretends."

"Nice," repeated Simon, shaking his head solemnly. "No."

"I think I'd better write back straightaway and say not to worry about Lucy. That would help."

"Then what?"

"I've got a sort of friend who knows about horses. At least, he must, because he's got a horse. Jester. I often see him about the streets. Mr. King, he drives a rag-and-bone cart."

"The one who told you how to clean a chimney!" said Simon suddenly. "I remember!"

"Yes, him. Perhaps he would help. Perhaps there would be room in Jester's stable for Lucy too. Then Jester could have some days off pulling. He's very old."

"But how would you get Lucy here?"

"Jester came from Devon in a horse box on a train."

"You'd have to steal her first!"

"Not steal! Never mind that just now. The first thing is to write to Rupert. Wait!"

Clarry found a pen and writing paper and began.

Dear Rupert, don't worry any more about Lucy. . . .

Clarry paused and looked up at Simon. "Are you helping?"

"Of course. Anything."

Simon and I are going to Cornwall today. By the time you get this Lucy will be safe somewhere else. I will send you the handkerchief for the rain trickles next time I write to you. . . .

She looked up into Simon's dark eyes. "That's just a jokey bit so he knows we can manage," she explained.

He nodded, understanding.

Simon sends his love. . . .

"You do, don't you?"

"Yes, I do."

And so do I,

Clarry

"Can I write my own name?" asked Simon.

"Yes, of course."

Simon C. Bonnington, wrote Simon carefully, and added *Bonners* in brackets.

"Give me the pen and I'll do the envelope. I've done it so often I know it by heart. Wait!" She put kisses at the end of her message. "I always do," she told Simon, offering him the pen.

"I'd better not," he said, smiling a little. "Now, listen. You post that, and then go and look for your friend with the horse. I'll go to the station and find out about tickets. Meet me back here as soon as you can."

"Rupert sent some money. I don't know if it will be enough."

"I've got some too, and just in case I'll . . . I'll pawn Dad's watch!" said Simon, and waited for Clarry to protest at such recklessness, but instead she said, "Oh, what a good idea! And I've got one too we could use."

"Not like this one," Simon said, fumbled in his pocket, and then held it out to show her, and Clarry saw that it was heavy and gold, a fat gold pocket watch on a brown plaited lace. "He gave it me to look after just before he went away."

"Would he mind?"

"I don't know. I wouldn't mind if I were him. I'll do it on the way to the station. Bring yours, though! We'll need it for the train times."

Clarry nodded, picked up her precious silver watch, and hurried after him out of the front door.

"Good luck!" she called, as he set off for the station, and she wasted a moment to watch him hurry away; great lanky clumsy strides, as if he wore badly fitting seven-league boots.

"Good luck," he called back, half turning, before walking

into a lamppost, staggering a little, and then vanishing around the corner.

Clarry didn't have good luck. It was easy enough to find Mr. King, but to persuade him to look after Lucy turned out to be impossible.

"No, no, no!" he said, walking backward with his hands in the air. "Not ever! Not on your life! Them Sunday school prizes is one thing! The books had your name in, I could see they were yours. But nothing else! Not after the piano and the brass table! How'd I be sure the horse wasn't stolen?"

"She would just be borrowed," pleaded Clarry.

"Borrowed my hind foot!" said Mr. King rudely.

"Wouldn't you like to have another horse to help Jester?"

"And have him standing idle with his hocks all swelled from nothing to do? Jester earns his keep on the streets, same as me, and that's that, so good day to you, missy, and mind you keep honest!"

"He was no help at all," Clarry told Simon, half angry, half tearful, when he arrived back at the house.

"Would a field do?" asked Simon. "I should have thought of it before but I was in such a hurry to get to the station. It's just a field, no stable or anything, but it's out at my great-aunt's, where my mum's staying. It belongs to the cottage."

"A field for Lucy? It would be perfect!"

"Come on, then," said Simon. "Shove some things in a bag and we'll get the tickets. I pawned Dad's watch, got another two pounds. The Cornwall train's in half an hour and the first one back with a horse box is Monday."

Nothing would have worked without Simon, Clarry wrote to Rupert two days later. *He thought of the field and when we got Lucy back here he unloaded her at the station and walked her all the way there. It was nine miles. We stayed in Cornwall on Saturday and Sunday nights and we pretended to Grandfather that Simon had just come with me to visit. But Grandmother knew the truth, and she was so pleased. She helped us get Lucy to the station early on Monday morning, and she said she would manage Grandfather.*

"Now perhaps I will be able to sleep at night," she said.

Before I left she did something she never had before, she kissed me and she said, "Dear Clarry." And she said that Simon was a wonderful friend, and he is. Will you write to Simon, please, Rupert? He pawned his father's watch so we had enough money, and I could see he was worrying about what his aunt would say. Vanessa told me that once his aunt said he was soft because he cried when his father went away.

Clarry had almost cried herself when the train left the little Cornish station, so early in the morning. She waved and waved to her grandmother, and Grandmother waved back, alone on the platform with the empty pony trap behind her, and if Clarry could have done one thing then, it would have been to stop the train and leap out and rush back into her arms.

"I liked it there," Simon said, when she finally retreated from the window and went to sit beside him. "That house and the moor and the sea." He had spent the weekend being as invisible as possible, but Grandmother had given him Rupert's room, and Clarry had taken him round the old treasured landmarks: the sunny hollow where Rupert had once found a baby adder, picked it up, and been promptly bitten. "He said it hardly hurt at all, and walked all the way home," Clarry told Simon. "But by the time he got back we had to cut his sleeve off his jacket to get his arm out and it was swollen for a week."

She showed him too where the swallows always nested, the spot where Peter had jumped from the train, the bathing place by the cliff path, and the shop where they bought ice creams.

"One day we should come back," said Simon, and Clarry said, "Yes, you and Vanessa, and Peter and me, and Rupert. All of us."

"And Lucy," said Simon. "Did Rupert love Lucy a lot?"

Clarry nodded, suddenly unable to speak. Simon sat twisting the empty watch lace in his big bony hands. His long giraffe face was patchy with shadows, and presently he closed his eyes.

Twenty

Thanks, I knew I could ask you.

R

That was all Clarry heard from Rupert, scrawled on a postcard. Peter told her that Simon had a postcard too. It had arrived at school, said Peter, and Simon had not shown it to anyone, just tucked it in his pocket and walked away.

For a long time after that no one heard anything from Rupert. Clarry turned thirteen with, for the first time ever, no acknowledgement from Rupert at all.

"Don't be angry with him," said Peter, unexpectedly.

"Of course not," said Clarry. She wrote to Rupert every

week, with news of Lucy, gleaned secondhand from Vanessa or Simon, and of the grandparents in Cornwall, who, her grandmother reported, were "managing very well with an elderly gray donkey." Without these things Clarry would have been stuck for much cheerfulness to put into her letters. There was no Cornish holiday that year, and it was a relief to Clarry when the new school term began in September. The war news was dark and there seemed nothing they could do to help. Miss Vane knitted feverishly, and when she wasn't knitting she was busy at a Red Cross center, packing parcels to go abroad. Mrs. Morgan found a job in a munitions factory, cooking in the canteen. She still appeared occasionally however: she turned up one afternoon when Vanessa happened to be visiting.

"Oh, what bliss to see you!" exclaimed Vanessa, whom Mrs. Morgan always filled with a hilarious joy. "How are you, Mrs. M.? Are you very busy?"

"I'll give you Mrs. M., my fine lady!" said Mrs. Morgan. "And yes, I'm busy, but in the wrong place. I'm not suited at all in that canteen. I'd rather be filling shells."

"Perhaps you soon will be," said Clarry comfortingly.

"I'd better be," said Mrs. Morgan. "And if it's not soon it will be never at all. If you ask me it's only a matter of weeks before the whole place goes bang!"

"Then you should stay safe where you are!" said Vanessa.

"If it goes, it goes," said Mrs. Morgan philosophically. "Canteen's attached, so it would make no difference. Mr. Morgan's in the thick of it, stacking and crating."

"Poor Mr. Morgan!"

"He's having a high old time," said Mrs. Morgan, sniffing. "All those young women that's there, it's one long party for him! And how's your blessed father, Clarry? Still full of the joys of spring?"

"He's very well, thank you," said Clarry cautiously. "I don't see him often. He mostly goes out for supper. I can't seem to cook the sort of food that he likes."

"None of us can cook the sort of food that we like these days," observed Mrs. Morgan severely. "And what about your own meals?"

"We have hot dinners at school," said Clarry, "so it doesn't matter so much about me."

"I thought so!" said Mrs. Morgan, diving into her shopping bag. "Sausage rolls!" she added triumphantly, producing a paper-wrapped bundle. "They was left over at the canteen, being a bit darker than people like. Now don't go wasting them! I daresay your friend gets fed at her hospital. . . ."

"I do, I do," agreed Vanessa. "Smoked salmon one day, roast beef the next, ice cream and trifle puddings . . ."

Mrs. Morgan gave her a look as if to say, *Just as I expected.*

"Well, then, you put them by, Clarry," she ordered, "and later on you can hot one up and have it with a cup of tea. If your young man turns up you should give him one too; he looks like he could do with a bit of meat on him. All bones, if you don't mind me saying! Now what?"

"My young man?" asked Clarry, outraged, while Vanessa spluttered with laughter.

"Now don't go all coy on me," said Mrs. Morgan briskly. "You're growing up, no use pretending! I was your age when I first met Mr. M. and I never looked back!"

"Juliet was only fourteen," agreed Vanessa, solemnly. "But who is Clarry's hungry young man? Do you mean Simon, Mrs. M.? Simon the Bony One? My brother, Simon? Clarry, you could have said!"

"I misremembered he was your brother," said Mrs. Morgan crossly. "Yes, him. What other young men do we ever see here? The one she took off to Cornwall, with never a word to her father! Not that I blame her there!"

"How did you know about that?" demanded Clarry, still recovering from "your young man" and "Clarry, you could have said!"

"Little bird told me," said Mrs. Morgan. "Scraggy old bird what lives opposite and watches every movement in the street! And what did your father say when you came back from your jaunt?"

"It wasn't a jaunt," said Clarry indignantly. "It was something I had to do for Rupert. Simon helped me. So did Grandmother. And I don't think Father even noticed I'd gone."

"He notices your young man, though," said Mrs. Morgan, "and he makes no effort to chase him away. My old dad was the same. Glad to get me off his hands. 'The sooner the better,' that was what my dad said, and if you ask me, yours'll be much the same!"

"Mine too!" said Vanessa cheerfully.

"I don't doubt it," said Mrs. Morgan, picking up her shopping bag and hitching it onto her elbow. "Well, I must be off. Should we not all be blown sky-high, I'll be back on Monday for the laundry, Clarry love."

For the sake of the "Clarry love," and just in case she was blown sky-high, Clarry forgave her and went with her to the front door.

"Thank you so much for the sausage rolls."

"You're welcome."

"I hope the factory stays safe!"

"What will be will be! There's your old dicky bird, twitching at her window again!"

Clarry waved to Miss Vane, hugged Mrs. Morgan, and went back inside to Vanessa, who said with unusual seriousness, "Are you really so fond of my bony brother, Clarry? If so, may I murmur a few words of gentle warning?"

"I don't need any gentle warnings, thank you very much!"

"All right, all right, we'll change the subject! Let's have something to eat before I go. Not the sacred sausage rolls! I brought cheese. Hospital cheese, very nutritious. We make it into sandwiches and fry 'em in the starving watches of the night."

"I thought you were all stuffed with salmon and beef and ice cream!"

"I wish. As it is, we are practically vegetarian. Come on, Clarry! Food, before I keel over. Then I must go. I only meant to stop for a minute to check you were all right. I haven't seen you since Southampton. Promise you're not falling in love with Simon!"

"Oh Vanessa! First Mrs. Morgan and now you! You needn't worry. Do you really think I've fallen in love with Simon? I just like him. I like him so much; he's so kind and he tries so hard. We're friends."

"Good," said Vanessa. "I love you liking him! He needs people to like him. He's hardly ever happy, poor Bony One."

"He was happy rescuing Lucy from under Grandfather's nose."

"Yes, he told me. He does tell me things sometimes. I'm sorry, Clarry. I was interfering with my gentle warnings! I was being like Matron when she tells me things for my own good, about nice girls not needing lipstick, and not getting fond of patients. And about my voice . . ."

"What about it?"

"It gets loud, she says. And loud is vulgar! Does it get loud?"

"Hardly ever."

"Ha!" said Vanessa. "You too! Never mind, tell me, how is darling school? Do they miss me? Have I been mentioned in Those in Our Thoughts Today?"

"Of course. 'Let us hold in our thoughts today Vanessa Bonnington. Loud and vulgar but very much missed.'"

Vanessa burst out laughing, and then said, "You love it, don't you, Clarry? School? More than I ever did."

"Yes, I do," said Clarry, her face suddenly bright. "I really do. It gets better and better and better!"

Twenty-One

IN CORNWALL, CLARRY HAD FOUND ONE WORLD OF freedom; at school she found another, equally exhilarating. It had the added advantage that she never had to leave it behind; she carried it around in armloads of books. Up in her room she would pile them onto her bed, and curl beside them to read. She slept with them within reach, comforting, solid companions that would see her through the night.

Nothing about school dismayed her. The cold classrooms and the constant demands for quietness which other girls complained about, did not bother her at all. Her home, with its clammy rooms and long silences, made school cheerful in comparison.

Best of all, she had found that she had a brain. A good, quick brain that could see patterns in math and links in history, was entranced by science, and was getting faster and faster at decoding Latin and French. When Peter came home at Christmas and inspected her work he nodded with satisfaction.

"It was you who started me off," said Clarry, and saw for a moment the secret, hidden Peter, eyes gleaming with pride in their joint success.

"Has Father said anything?" he asked.

"What about?"

"You. School. What you will do afterward."

"No," said Clarry, but something in the way she spoke made Peter say, "Somebody has!"

"Yes," admitted Clarry. "When I got moved up faster than the rest."

"Did you?"

"Twice, at the beginning. And last year I won a little shield for Student of the Year."

"Go on."

"Well, you know how the head invites people to her study?"

"No."

"For tea. And to talk. When I went I told her about you going to Oxford. . . ."

"If I get a scholarship!"

"You will. And she said that I should think about it too."

"Your Head thinks you could get an Oxford scholarship?" asked Peter, and then a moment later, he said slowly, "She's right. You could get an Oxford scholarship."

"Not for years, though."

"Well, you need years!" said Peter robustly. "You're nowhere near yet! And it would be worth it. It would get you out of this place one day, wouldn't it?" They were in the sitting room, every year more faded and unwelcoming.

"Father doesn't notice it, I don't think," said Clarry. "He's out so much I hardly see him. But if I didn't have school to go to, I don't think I could bear it here. I'll have to do something when I leave. I was thinking of Vanessa and her hospital but she pretended to be much older than she was to get in. I don't think I could do that. I don't look grown-up."

"You don't have to look grown-up to go to Oxford. You just have to have brains. Do you ever see Vanessa?"

"Yes, once I went to Southampton and she comes quite often if she's visiting the cottage. She's not supposed to do, but she borrows her dad's car. She makes Mrs. Morgan laugh, and even Father smiles sometimes."

"Does she ever . . ." Peter picked up a book and began turning the pages very rapidly. "Does she ever ask about . . . anyone?"

"She asks about everyone," Clarry told him sturdily. "You and me. Simon, if he's been here, Rupert, of course, and what he's doing . . . you know, in France."

"Belgium," said Peter.

"Is he?"

"Must be. I hate my leg. Don't say, 'Does it hurt?' It serves me right if it hurts. I'm a coward."

"Peter, you are not!"

"I tell people I fell. I don't tell them how!"

"It wasn't your fault!"

"Of course it was! I jumped off a train to get out of school. What would Vanessa say if she knew that?"

"You told Simon, so perhaps she already does. She wouldn't say you were a coward anyway! How could you have known there would be a war?"

"I wish I could do something to help."

"Vanessa helps. I think that's how she stays so happy. She talks about terrible things, awful injuries, and then she tells me about people who get better. And she has fun. She loves it."

"Dancing," said Peter gloomily, glaring at his leg.

"Lots of things. She's either terrifically busy or falling asleep and she smells all the time of carbolic soap. Last time she was here Father said, 'Good God, what is that appalling smell?' and Vanessa said, 'Darling, it's meeee!' and laughed and laughed."

"What did Father do?"

"Oh, he just went away as fast as he could."

"Typical," grunted Peter. "Clarry, is there any food? I'm starving! I should like bacon and sausages and grilled tomatoes! All right! You needn't laugh. I know it will just be toast!"

"It won't! We have sausage rolls!" said Clarry jubilantly. "From Mrs. Morgan's munitions canteen! She's been keeping me supplied with them, every time a batch gets burnt! She came yesterday and brought some more. Come into the kitchen! There are six. Shall we hot them up or eat them like they are?"

"One each as they are now, two more hotted up. I haven't had anything to eat all day, and then it was only porridge."

"One each hotted up," said Clarry firmly. "I'm keeping two for Father. Toast and apples afterward, and there's a pot of honey I've been saving. A patient gave it to Vanessa and she gave it to . . ."

"Me," Clarry had been about to say, but changed it to "us" and saw her brother's face brighten briefly and then grow somber again as he said, "I've got to plan what to do after school. I used to think if I could, I'd go to Oxford and study natural sciences, but how will that help anyone?" He got up from the table suddenly and began pacing and rubbing at his leg. "It cramps," he said apologetically. "It never mended properly. It was badly set."

Clarry had learned that saying "Poor old Peter" only

aggravated him, so instead she asked something she had been saving for a long time to talk about when they were safely alone.

"Can I show you a picture I found in the old dictionary?"

"What sort of picture?"

"A photograph. Wait!"

Ever since she had found the dictionary, Clarry had hardly let it out of her sight. Now she produced it from her schoolbag, carefully unwrapping it from a piece of brown paper. "I've been wanting to show you for ages," she said. "Only I've been so afraid it would make you sad. Look!"

Peter took the little picture, stared in disbelief, turned it over, read the back, and then, to Clarry's great relief, laughed in delight.

"That's her! I remember! That's just how I remember! How brilliant, Clarry! Doesn't she look like you?"

"That's what Vanessa said."

"You showed it to Vanessa?"

"Yes, that time I went to Southampton. Do you mind?"

"Of course not. But why?"

Rather hesitantly at first, Clarry told him about Mrs. Morgan, and her description of their mother's illness, and how afterward she, Clarry, had needed to talk to someone who would understand, because all her life it had been dreadful, believing—

"Listen, Clarry!" interrupted Peter at this point. "When I was a kid I believed that too. But I was stupid; I saw that years and years ago. It wasn't your fault; you didn't choose any of it. Vanessa should have told you that."

"She did. And she said she knew you didn't blame me. She said you were much too decent. I wish someone could have helped Mother, though, Peter. Wouldn't everything have been different now if they had?"

Peter nodded, picking up the little picture again.

"Vanessa says you can get copies of photographs," Clarry told him. "How much do you think it costs? Might there be somewhere in Oxford?"

"I'll find out," promised Peter. "And one day we'll do it, however much it costs."

"Take it with you, then. It'll be safer with you. Father might—"

She jumped suddenly at the sound of the front door, they glanced at each other, Peter stowed the picture back in the dictionary, the dictionary in his bag, and his bag under his arm, while Clarry hurried into the hall.

There he was, meticulously rolling his umbrella, taking off his hat.

"Hello, Father!" said Clarry brightly. "You're just in time. I've filled the kettle for tea and we saved you hot sausage rolls!"

"I've eaten, thank you, Clarry. Is Peter back again? I see his coat."

"I'm here," said Peter, appearing with his bag. "How are you, Father?"

"Quite well, rather too busy. All well with you?"

"Yes, thank you."

"I lit a little fire in the sitting room to make it comfortable for you," said Clarry.

"Thank you, very thoughtful," said her father, and went in and closed the door.

"I expect he's tired," said Clarry.

"What he is . . . ," began Peter, and then looked at Clarry, and shut up, a thing he would not have done a year before, but then, Peter was changing.

Twenty-Two

THE WINTER THAT FOLLOWED WAS VERY HARD TO bear. The war news was terrible. No one heard from Rupert. School helped Clarry through, the sane, cold classrooms, the friendly faces, the solid comfort of books.

In spring they said, "Well at least it's spring," but no one dared say "Over by Christmas." And then summer came around again, and to Clarry's complete surprise, her grandmother wrote to ask her and Peter to visit. Clarry and her father met at the foot of the stairs, each holding a letter, each smiling with delight.

"Very helpful, very helpful," said Clarry's father, rubbing

his hands together. "No more than they should do of course, but even so . . . er . . ."

Clarry looked at him in sudden apprehension, recognizing that something uncomfortable was coming.

"I have been wondering if it would be sensible for you to . . . be in Cornwall long-term."

"Long-term?"

"Out of danger. Air raids. I suppose you can't be expected to know, but there were air raids on London only a few weeks ago. Zeppelins. Very unpleasant."

"We had a talk about zeppelins at school from the geography teacher," said Clarry. "She said we were not to fuss about air raids because the prevailing winds from the Atlantic make it almost impossible that they will ever come this far west."

"Be that as it may," said her father impatiently, "I'm sure your grandparents would be glad to have you. There is no need for you to stay on at school once you are over fourteen."

"There is! There is!"

"The fact is, Clarry, well, this house. I've been thinking of giving it up for some time now. It seems hardly worth the cost, just for . . . er . . ."

He glanced away from Clarry's eyes. His face was quite expressionless, almost unconcerned.

"I have to go to school," said Clarry. "I'm sure Grandmother would say so too. And where would you live? And Peter, in the holidays?"

"Peter could go to Cornwall. Something could easily be arranged for myself. As a matter of fact there is a very pleasant set of rooms directly above the offices."

Clarry turned to the hall window and looked blindly into the street. After a while a movement across the road caught her eye. Miss Vane, gathering up a cat.

"Perhaps . . . ," she began, and then started again. "Perhaps I could live with someone else. They would have to be paid, of course, but maybe Grandmother would help."

"No, no, no!" exclaimed her father. "Whatever would people say? I assumed you would like to live in Cornwall. Please forget the suggestion. At any rate you will be there for the summer, which is something."

It was something. It was the summer that Clarry properly made friends with her grandmother. Peter, whose last year of school was coming up, spent most of his time studying. Clarry took schoolbooks with her too, but she also found time to garden with her grandmother in the long silky summer evenings, and to look through photograph albums of Victorian strangers who might, or might not, have been distant relations. Last of all came herself, Peter, and Rupert.

"Rupert is very like his mother used to be," said her grandmother. "Those golden good looks! We hardly hear from him, you know. I write to him weekly and his grandfather sends messages but there has been nothing back for months."

Clarry didn't reply. She had heard from Rupert, a few forlorn lines that she thought it best her grandmother didn't know.

I'm sorry Clarry. It's all a bit of a mess, isn't it? I try not to let myself think.

His friend was dead. His wild, mad, Latin-quoting, football-captain, red-haired Irish friend, Michael. Killed in no-man's-land, a mile or so from where Rupert was stationed, but word had come racing down the trenches to him. "He's out there. We can't fetch him in."

"I'll fetch him in," said Rupert, and went crawling out into the terrible summer night, through cracked swamps of mud and splintered metal and wire and stiffened bundles that were not men or trees or anything recognizable anymore. Miraculously, although the dark was splattered with gunfire, no sniper's bullet found him, and he came to his friend all broken in a shell hole, still alive but clammy cold. There were strange shapes where his boots should have been and his right arm ended too soon but he got one eye open and croaked, "Rosy," out of the good side of his mouth.

Rupert pulled flasks from his pockets and said, "Rum? Water? Come on, my mad Irish," but he couldn't swallow. So then Rupert lay beside him and put his arms round him and said, "We'll get out a stretcher party and have you back before the pubs shut," and his friend's good eye glared at him, the white showing bright. "Go to sleep, get your head down," said Rupert. "Busy day tomorrow, if we're to get you home before dark."

"Cold," whispered his friend, so Rupert dragged his own jacket off and tucked it round his chest. He thought his back was probably broken as well as everything else, because of the way his legs were sprawled like a puppet with the strings cut. Right overhead a flare popped, greenish silvery light. Rupert felt the eye on him again. It seemed to take a long time for the flare to fade, and then there was another, but not so close, and a crump of explosion farther down the line.

"Cleaning the chimney," said Rupert, which was an old school joke from the time of Clarry's great idea and Peter and Simon's rocket. He wished his friend would hurry up and die, but he was young and strong and so it took until morning. Then Rupert tried to pick him up but he couldn't, so he walked back empty-handed in his shirtsleeves, forgetting his jacket. He took no care walking back but strangely nothing happened to him.

The next day he wrote a letter to Ireland saying how lucky that his friend had died from a single bullet, instantaneously, never knowing a thing.

It was only two years since they both left school but it felt an awful lot longer.

Twenty-Three

IT TOOK A VERY LONG TIME FOR MISS VANE TO overcome her mistrust of the girls' high school, that racketing collection of the unfeminine and inky.

"I always notice their stockings," she told her tortoiseshell cat (having few humans to talk to, she very often turned to this animal), "and their deplorable hats. Clarry will be spoiled."

By this she meant that Clarry would become noisy, opinionated, and "rough," said Miss Vane to the tortoiseshell, who blinked in dismay.

When this did not happen, Miss Vane said Clarry would ruin her health with overwork.

This also turned out not to be true. In fact, away from the seeping carbon monoxide fumes from the Miss Pinkses' paraffin stoves, Clarry flourished. None of Miss Vane's other predictions came true either. Clarry didn't destroy her eyes with reading, or begin arguing with her father, or even take to eating buns in the street, as Miss Vane had observed high school girls doing in the past. Miss Vane, watching suspiciously from behind her curtains, and always ready to dash across with reproachful remarks and offers to broker a reconciliation with the spurned Miss Pinkses, detected none of these things. It made her sad. She missed having Clarry as her perpetual Good Deed. She also missed having a person who would appreciate her latest cat story, or admire her knitting, or chatter beside her on a walk along the front. And so one gray afternoon in early fall she was very thankful to see Clarry sneezing in the street as she fumbled for her door key.

"She will neglect that cold and it will turn to pneumonia!" the delighted Miss Vane told her tortoiseshell cat. "I have seen it happen time after time!"

With this untrue but energizing statement, Miss Vane turned to her kitchen cupboard, and an hour afterward Clarry answered a knock on the door, and there she was bearing onion soup, a strip of red flannel to wrap around her throat, a large tin of mustard powder, and such a smile of pure happiness that Clarry welcomed her as if the last two years of crossness had never happened at all.

"You should shake a little dry mustard into your stocking feet on very cold mornings," said Miss Vane, quite husky with joy at the warmth of her welcome.

"I should never ever have thought of that," said Clarry, hugging her again.

By these means, Clarry's sneeze was banished, and she and Miss Vane became friends once more. Clarry was, as Miss Vane told the tortoiseshell cat, the same dear girl as ever. Still writing letters to the boys, still painting her butterflies, still tiptoeing around her father. Rather too confident about the safety of zeppelin raids, and still hobnobbing with the rag-and-bone man. "But that is nothing," Miss Vane assured her cat, "compared to what I had feared." In her joy she unearthed a length of tightly woven blue striped cloth that she had put away for curtains, and made for Clarry a brand-new dress. It turned out to be her finest creation ever.

"You are kind!" said Clarry.

"It has a four-inch hem and the gathers will let out," said Miss Vane a little proudly. "It really is almost your color, you know. I don't see why it shouldn't last you for years."

Clarry didn't see why it shouldn't either, and encouraged by this new friendliness asked, "Miss Vane, have you ever thought of having a . . . another person to live with you?"

"Goodness, Clarry!"

"Not for very long. Just until I finish school. Because Father said he may . . . he talked of closing up this house and going to live in some rooms over the offices, and of course Peter and I couldn't go there too. Father thought that Peter might go to Cornwall in the holidays, and that I might live there all the time."

"Well, yes," said Miss Vane, in a smoothing, understanding voice. "He knows how pleased you have always been to visit. And I expect he thinks you would be safer there too. I should miss you, but it would be much less worry for him."

"But there's school . . . ," began Clarry.

Miss Vane waved away school as if it didn't exist, and continued, "I think that you are old enough to understand, Clarry dear, that your father has found parenthood difficult from the start. Why, after Peter was born, for instance, he was rarely at home, absent with his work, for weeks at a time."

"Weeks!" exclaimed Clarry.

"Naturally, as a neighbor, I took an interest. And your poor mother was plainly not well."

Clarry managed to steady her voice. "Did she tell you that?"

"No," said Miss Vane, straightening her shoulders. "She told me nothing, and it was not my place to ask. I tried . . . I simply tried to be . . ."

A tear rolled down her cheek, an honest, ungossiping, remembering tear.

"Kind," she said, blotting it. "Oh, dear. I hope I haven't said too much. Please don't repeat it, Clarry. It was a sad time. Little Peter and his mama, and your father so silent. It brings it all back, remembering."

Miss Vane paused to smooth the folds of the blue-striped frock. "Since then, of course," she said brightly, "he has soldiered on wonderfully! All the same, I do see what a help it would be for him to have you both in Cornwall, and I couldn't possibly, Clarry dear, interfere. Besides," she added, just as Clarry's father had, "whatever would people say?"

All that evening Clarry's mind was a tangle of the shadowy past, and the uneasy present. Her schoolbooks were some comfort, though, a little escape that perhaps might one day become bigger.

Peter, Clarry wrote, *when you said about university for me, did you really mean it, or were you being nice?*

Twenty-Four

I DON'T KNOW WHAT YOU MEAN, "BEING NICE," replied Peter, rather grumpily. *What's the point of pretending you haven't a brain when you have? Obviously you will have to work. Like I do. You can send me your math to correct, if you like, and any Latin translation you need looking at. Once you get there you can earn money tutoring during vacation, enough to pay for somewhere to live, I should think. If I'm there too we could share and it would be cheaper. Last week I took the picture you found into Oxford to get it copied and I ran into someone there who gave me an idea. . . .*

Vanessa said, "You're always inky!"

"Often, but not always," said Clarry, delighted to see her friend again. "How's Simon?"

"Bothered," said Vanessa, after considering the question. "Bothered, bony, doesn't speak much, goes and visits Rupert's Lucy, sits and draws her on the letters he sends . . ."

"Letters to Rupert?"

"Yes, letters to Rupert. And he reads about the war all the time. He collects those magazines in the *Times*—don't say, 'What magazines?' I can see you're just about to do!"

"We don't have a newspaper here anymore."

"They'll have the *Times* at school. They always did. Look in the library. Oh, Clarry, Clarry, Clarry, I hate this war but I sort of love it too. Is that awful? Yes!"

"It's because you're doing something useful," said Clarry.

"Wise Clarry! You're right. And I make them laugh—the boys, I mean. The boys in the beds, that's what I call them, I kiss them like this. . . ." Vanessa kissed two fingers and planted them lightly on Clarry's nose. "Dad's ship was in a battle. He was taken prisoner. Simon knows. Did you hear?"

"No!" Clarry exclaimed. "No, I didn't! Oh, Vanessa! Oh, I'm sorry! When? What do you know?"

"Now, now," said Vanessa. "Don't fuss! Are you or are you not a high school girl? We don't know anything except he's alive. Or was. Don't look like that! Make me weep, and

I'll slay you, Clarry! Do you notice I don't smell of carbolic today? French perfume, that's what!"

Clarry sniffed and asked, "Where did you get it from?"

"Clever Rupert brought it, last week when he was back. . . . Clarry, you didn't see him? Oh, stupid me and my big mouth . . ."

"Rupert was back?" croaked Clarry.

"Only for a few days. In a very odd mood. Couldn't get anything out of him except he'd spent a day in Cornwall and it had been awful. Clarry, don't stare at me like that."

"Grandmother writes, but she didn't tell me."

"Perhaps because it had been awful. He would hardly talk, just frantic rushing about on a motorbike with me hanging on the back for dear life. He looked wonderful, so don't worry."

"Oh, good."

"Clarry, they often can't be bothered with family much. The boys in the beds. Well, not can't be bothered, but they don't want the questions and the tears and . . ."

"Fuss," said Clarry.

"Yes. All right. Fuss. Can't bear it. Neither can I."

"Sorry."

"Don't talk about Rupe. Don't talk about Dad. How's Peter? I do love him. So steady on his wobbly leg. So gorgeous and glum. He and Simon will be leaving school soon. Will you come to the speech day with Mum and me? We'll have to clap hard, to make up for Dad. Oh, where is he? I went home and Mum was hugging the globe. Wailing. Fussing. She went to the wrong school, obviously. Now you've made me howl!"

Vanessa sobbed, drooping against the wall, tears splashing on the brass-topped table. Then she sniffed, wiped her nose on her sleeve, said, "Adore you, Clarry, got to go now. Sorry about Rupert. Love to Peter. Peter the rock. My lovely dad, prisoner, imagine! No, don't! I've found some beautiful new shoes for dancing! Four straps, two on the foot and two above the ankle, red patent leather, shall I teach you how to tango right now?"

"Yes, right now!" said Clarry immediately, and so they did, up and down the hall and into the musty cold dining room and out back to the front door, and then Vanessa was gone. "I'll write!" she cried, and she did, a picture of her new shoes drawn on a postcard. Clarry wrote painfully back, dragging the words from the air one at a time and wrenching them grimly onto the paper.

Your poor mother, worrying. And your dad. I'm glad you could cheer up Rupert. Those shoes, the heels are pretty. Miss Vane says to tell you to clean patent leather with old bread! I hope you smell nice today.

Yours unfussingly,

Clarry

Simon thought that if the only way of being in contact with someone was by words written on paper, then those words must be both worth reading and true. For this reason, as often as he could manage, he made the long weekend journey by bicycle and train from school to his great-aunt's cottage in order to check up on Lucy. After Lucy, it was a nine-mile cycle ride to see Clarry. Sometimes he stayed the night there, but often he went back to the cottage in the evening, caught a morning train north to Oxford, cycled from Oxford to school, and was back for five o'clock evensong. This weekend break was called an exeat. There were no exeats granted for those who missed evensong, but Simon never did. He would stand beside Peter in the choir, breathless, exhausted, but with something to write about that night.

> *Dear Rupert,*
>
> *Lucy is very well and has four sheep in with her for company. She does no work, but is only on grass so should be all right. I caught her on Saturday, brushed her down, and washed her face. She curled up her lip and jumped about a bit. She lost two shoes so we took off the others because she doesn't need them in the field. Clarry had Peter's old bike out when I got to her house. It had a low crossbar because of his stiff leg so when we*

got the chain on and the puncture fixed she could ride it quite well. Next time I go I'll get there early enough to take her up to see Lucy. The roads are quiet that way and I'll make sure she's safe. I took six eggs in my knapsack. Her father said, "Good man," when he saw them, and said I was welcome to stay the night. He asked about my dad, who was taken prisoner, and I told them we had had a card but only a few words: "All well around here in how-do-you-spell-it?" When Clarry heard she jumped and said, "Oh, that's where he is!"

I'd better not write the name, but very good to know and I didn't stay the night but went straight back to tell Mum and my aunt. I thought Clarry was very quick and clever to understand, but she said it was your grandfather's old riddle.

I wish you all the best,

Simon Bonnington (Bonners)

"'All well around here in how-do-you-spell-it?'" Clarry had repeated. "Oh! He's in Constantinople! Or near Constantinople. 'Around here,' I suppose that means 'somewhere near.' Turkey! Goodness!"

Simon had stared at her, astounded.

"It's Grandfather's joke! His riddle! He used to ask us every summer. 'Constantinople is a very long word, how do you spell it?' And then we'd try and try and get muddled and he would say, 'I-t. It!'"

"Constantinople," repeated Simon, shaking his head.

"I saw it on a map last week! It's not terribly far from Troy! Odysseus found his way home from there, Simon! Through the Greek islands."

"Dad's sailed all round the Greek islands," said Simon, brightening wonderfully. "He used to tell us about it when we were little. They would often see dolphins. I'm going straight back to let my mum know where he is. Thanks, Clarry! Thank you!"

"It wasn't me, it was Grandfather!"

"It was you," said Simon, smiling down at her.

It had been wonderful news for Simon to take back to his family. His mother had put down the globe and hauled out an atlas, and found herself in familiar lands, the Aegean Sea that she and her husband had sailed years before. "First Odysseus, now your father," she had said. "Now I know he'll come safe home."

I wish I knew Rupert would come safe home, thought Simon. He read over his letter. Was it boring? Would Rupert remember his grandfather's old riddle and understand? Would he care? Simon stared into the dark beyond the window, and in his mind he wrote the letter that he would like to send.

Stay safe. There is no border nor battlefield, no empire worth your hurt. I remember your hand on my shoulder those times we sang at school. I looked at the sea yesterday, and I felt I could step over it. It didn't look big, it looked small.

Only a few weeks now, and school would be finished for ever. Good.

Twenty-Five

FOR RUPERT, THE FIRST TIME BACK IN ENGLAND
had been terrible. A huge mistake to go to Cornwall; the
questions from his grandparents had been impossible. He'd
been so terrified he'd snap and answer them truthfully that
he'd fled after one hideous day. However, he quickly found
that everywhere he went afterward was pretty much the same.
The pale, ridiculous English, secondhand heroes, proud of
their silly ideals, proud of him too, patting him on the back.
Once he had bellowed, "Don't touch me!" and they'd leaped
like they'd been shot.

Not that shot people leaped.

More crumpled. Or blurted out prayers and wanted

their mothers. Or just plain fell apart.

Vanessa and her friends had been the best. They'd made very good jokes. He hadn't known girls could be so callous. If he came back again he'd stick entirely to girls, but he didn't think he'd come home anymore. He preferred France. (Or Belgium. He couldn't tell the difference.) He spent his odd days of leave in the towns and villages away from the front; he'd lost the banjo long before but he'd got hold of a motor-bike again.

Some people wrote diaries, or sketched, filling book after book. Some wrote poetry. Some had got up a newspaper. "Why?" he'd asked, truly baffled at all this papery toil, and they'd tried to explain that they thought this war needed recording, so people at home knew the truth.

Rupert didn't think this was right. Not the truth about the bad things, anyway. Not about the gas, for instance, or the way he'd seen people treated when they wouldn't stop crying. He didn't think people at home would want to read stuff like that. He wouldn't. He'd rather never know it. As it was, he blanked it out.

Rupert could blank things out almost as if they had never been, a trick he'd learned at boarding school. You faked it till it was true. Now in France (or it might have been Belgium) he'd managed his greatest blanking of all. He'd unacknowledged the war. He'd found a way to ignore it, and in achieving this he knew that he'd become safe.

Blissfully safe.

Disaster proof.

Nothing could hurt Rupert. Explosions rocked the ground around him and left him standing unruffled. Bullets veered away from his head. All the minor problems that beset the others—sickness, bad feet, trembling hands, lice, sleeplessness, panic, bewilderment, grief—all those things did not touch him. He never saw ghosts, he rarely saw rats, he was not bullied, he hated no one. He cheerfully accepted boredom, deep mud, irrational orders, and strange-tasting tea. He enjoyed cheap red wine, silver flare light, the heat from a mug, the smell of wool blankets, woodsmoke, rum, and comradeship. He liked these things in a detached kind of way, as if he were hardly there. He rarely read letters from home, and gave away his parcels unopened. He had completely forgotten how he had worried about Lucy the pony, and Mina the cat. He'd stopped counting back to the time he was at school. He never deliberately thought of anyone in England, although once or twice, very rarely, a memory would catch him like a kick in the stomach. Not often, though. He couldn't imagine the war ever ending, and he didn't know what he'd do if it did.

It was not something he thought about much.

He was more or less content.

Twenty-Six

EVERY NOW AND THEN, IN THE STAFF ROOM OF Clarry's school, someone would ask, "How's our DH getting on?"

"DH" stood for "Dark Horse."

The Dark Horse was Clarry.

From the very beginning of her days at the high school, Clarry had been watched, at first with amusement, and later with interest. Mysteriously, her family history had become known. Opinions were shared about her brother and her father. Even the Miss Pinkses were given a passing (uncomplimentary) thought.

These days Clarry was being watched extra carefully.

Cool, critical, intelligent eyes glanced at her, and glanced again. They thought she was rather a promising Dark Horse.

"Excellent stamina!" said someone. "Never gives up."

"Heard her explaining some chemistry to a couple of youngsters in the library. Very clear. No wasted words."

"Shy?" asked someone.

"Quiet, not shy. Thank goodness. A dreadful handicap, shyness."

"Do we fancy her chances?" asked a new mistress.

"Best in the stable!" said Miss Fairfax, Clarry's form teacher. "By a country mile!"

Not long after this, extra training started. "Read this! You must read around your subject!" "Here is an interesting article. I should like you to sum it up in two hundred words. No, one hundred and fifty! Less if you can manage it. I want all the relevant points, mind, and you can bring it to me at registration tomorrow!"

"Tomorrow?" asked Clarry, startled.

"You must learn not to be fazed by a deadline!"

In math she was constantly stretched. "The demonstration of that proof for us now, please, Clarry! Up at the front! Never turn your back on your audience! You must practice using a blackboard, it's a skill. That's quite nice. Could they hear you at the back?"

"Could you hear me at the back?" asked Clarry, and

when someone shook her head the math mistress said, "In that case, Clarry will show you once more!" and Clarry had to do it again, louder and clearer, juggling the difficult skills of blackboard writing, algebra, and noticing the people at the back of the class.

"Quite nice, thank you, you may sit down now," she was told at last, and immediately scolded, "Don't flump!"

For month after month it continued, "This essay really won't do, whatever is happening at home!"

"You must always quote your references! Always, without exception!"

"This piece of work is a fail. I asked for five hundred words, and you gave me six. I have simply ignored the last hundred which has left you with no conclusion!"

However, it wasn't always so negative.

"Clarry, on Saturday afternoon I'm taking you to a lecture that I think you'll find interesting."

"I should like to show you my old college very soon. And the town. I wish I could show you it as it was before this BLASTED war, but it will end, it will end, it will end. The university has been there for more than eight hundred years! Have you visited Oxford before?"

"No, but my brother has, often," said Clarry eagerly. "His school is nearby. If he gets a scholarship he'll go after the summer."

"And is your father happy about that?"

"Oh yes. He went. So did Grandfather."

"Always the boys," said Miss Fairfax with irritation. "However, it's the girls' colleges keeping things alive at the moment. So your brother won't be enlisting?"

"He broke his leg, years ago. It mended, but it doesn't bend very well. It's shorter than the other one too. He hates not being able to enlist."

"There are more productive things your brother could do than fight," said Miss Fairfax acidly, for she did not believe in war. "I hope something will occur to him before much longer."

"I think it already has. He borrowed a bicycle and went into Oxford. He bumped into a man there. . . ."

"*Bumped* into?"

"Yes, with his bike. And when he got off to see if he was all right, the man noticed his hoppy walk and they talked, and it gave Peter an idea."

"Well, Oxford is full of ideas, good and bad," said Miss Fairfax. "Was it any particular man that he bumped into?"

"He was a professor. Quite old."

"They all are. Which one?"

"Osler. Sir William. I think Peter said he was American."

Clarry's teacher, Miss Fairfax, looked at Clarry through narrowed, considering eyes, and said, "He's Canadian, and that was a very fortunate bump. Will you come with me to

Oxford, Clarry, and see who you bump into there? You look worried!"

"I'd love to," said Clarry, "but . . ."

"Do make an effort, Clarry!"

"Of course I'd love to come. Thank you, Miss Fairfax."

"Whatever is the matter, then?"

"Nothing at all," said Clarry, which was not true. What was the matter was clothes.

In her room that evening, Clarry went through her wardrobe. Her school skirt that had come from Vanessa. Her three school blouses, two of them also from Vanessa. Miss Vane's blue striped dress that was, as had been predicted, going on forever. *No, no, no,* thought Clarry, remembering how Peter had burst out laughing the first time she put it on.

What, then? She had a green velvet Sunday dress, bought by her grandmother two years before, no longer as green nor as velvety as it once had been, and very much shorter too. Two cotton summer frocks with flapping collars. Nothing at all suitable for either a visit to an Oxford college or (even harder to imagine) the speech day that was coming up at Peter's school quite soon.

"You needn't worry," said Peter, when Clarry asked about this event. "I've given up expecting Father to bring you along to clap. Don't look like that! I don't care!"

"I do, though," said Clarry, and the first chance she got

she stopped her father in the hall to ask, "Please could we go to Peter's speech day this year, Father?"

"Oh, I don't think so," he replied blandly. "What would be the point?"

"It's the last one ever and Peter should have someone there."

"Let's not sentimentalize things, Clarry."

"He's worked so hard. Aren't you proud of him?"

"Naturally I'm glad he's worked, and I'm sure he's done very well."

"He said you wouldn't bother," said Clarry rebelliously.

"It isn't a matter of bothering. It simply isn't practical."

"Well, I'm going!" said Clarry.

"I'm very glad to hear it," said her father, smiling his empty smile. "This should cover the train fare," he added, taking a ten-shilling note from his wallet. "And let's have no more fuss!"

Ten shillings, Clarry discovered, could hardly have been more accurate. It would pay for the train fare and leave four pennies to spare. Four pennies would not buy so much as a pair of stockings, never mind a new dress. . . .

Mr. King refused to buy her silver watch but asked, "What about that bicycle?"

"No!" exclaimed Clarry. "Never!"

"You managed without it before."

"I couldn't again."

Clarry's world had opened up since Simon had got her riding. She kept the bike in Jester's stable, away from critical eyes at home, and it had given her a new freedom. Now on weekends she could get out to the cottage to visit Lucy, and Vanessa too, if she was there. On weekday mornings she walked the ten minutes to the stable, strapped her books on the carrier, and was at school in a fraction of the time it had taken in the past.

"Anyway, it's my brother's bike," she told Mr. King. "Not mine, so I couldn't sell it."

"Never bothered you before! Still got that brass-topped table, have you? Easy money, that could be."

"I couldn't."

"Well, then," said Mr. King, who had left school at nine years old and worked for his living honestly (and less honestly) ever since, "if you don't want money got easy you'll have do as other folks do, won't you?"

"What do they do?"

"Get it the hard way!"

"What's the hard way?"

"And you a clever high school girl!" exclaimed Mr. King, and went away shaking his head.

Clarry consulted Vanessa, cycling out to the cottage when her friend was back for the night. Vanessa was more helpful than Mr. King, at least. "You needn't worry about catching a train to Oxford!" she said. "You can come with us. We're all going together to cheer on Simon. I'm driving Dad's car."

"*I'm* driving Dad's car!" corrected her mother, coming in from the kitchen. "It's much too far for you. Lovely to see you, Clarry! Have you said hello to Lucy?"

"Yes, she looks wonderful. Any news from Odysseus?"

"How clever you were about Constantinople! No, not a word, but I'm not worried at all. I imagine he's escaped. A boat over to Greece somehow, and then it'll just be a matter of time. . . ."

"And dodging Calypso," added Vanessa.

"Horrible girl, be quiet!"

"All right! I'm taking Clarry off for a gossip. Come up to my room, Clarry! Absolutely you have to be there at speech day. It's the last one ever for both of them. You can't leave sweet P. with no one to clap him."

"No, I can't," agreed Clarry. "Vanessa?"

"Mmmm?"

"What do people wear?"

"Posh as possible," said Vanessa, who at the moment was gnawing an apple down to its core in a very unposh manner indeed. "You can borrow something of mine. I've got a lovely cherry red thing I bought in a sale. It's too tight, I knew it would be, but I couldn't resist it. I fell for the swishy silk lining. We'll turn up the hem and if it bags at the side you can just keep your elbows tucked in. Try it on!"

Clarry tried it on, and although the silk lining was certainly lovely, it was much too big, whatever she did with her elbows. And also very red. Much redder than cherries . . .

"All right, I admit it's not you!" said Vanessa, when she had stopped laughing. "Especially with those stockings! By the way, I hope you won't mind, Clarry dear, if I talk to Your Braininess about stockings for a few minutes."

"If you must," agreed Clarry, hanging the red dress back on its padded silk hanger.

"I must, I've been meaning to for months. Think of it as a tutorial. Take notes if you like. And while you are listening, help yourself to anything that catches your eye in my wardrobe."

"Thank you," said Clarry, "but if you don't mind I'll just concentrate. I may close my eyes sometimes, like I do in Latin."

"Very well," said Vanessa. "But this is much more important than Latin. Now, prepare to be amazed!"

She was the kindest friend ever, thought Clarry, as she cycled home that night. And the funniest, and the most generous. And the most ridiculous. *If I wore that red dress I'd be the reddest person in the room! And imagine it at Oxford! I'd be the reddest in the city!*

All of a sudden she was tired of living in a patchwork mixture of Vanessa's donations, Miss Vane's contrivances, and her grandmother's often-stated belief that it didn't matter what you wore, so long as you behaved.

Grandmother is wrong, it matters a lot! thought Clarry.

It seemed, astonishingly, that it even mattered to Peter. A postcard from him was waiting when she got home. He had sent instructions:

Don't call out my name when you see me, he had written. *Don't look too pleased if I win anything. Or too interested. Don't go talking to everyone like you do. Don't fuss and don't wear anything that people will notice.*

Clarry looked regretfully at the brass-topped table, remembering the time that she had disposed of the family piano without a single pang of conscience. As she gazed, she suddenly understood what Mr. King, that industrious rag-and-bone-man, meant by the hard way to get money.

I need a job! thought Clarry.

"I would love to come to Oxford with you," Clarry told Miss Fairfax on Monday morning, "but first I'll have to find a way to earn some money."

Then Miss Fairfax replied, exactly as if she had been waiting for this moment. "The Grace twins in class one missed most of last term through measles and whooping cough. Their mother needs someone to help them catch up. Their father is away, and their mother hasn't time, she works for the post office now, and is never home before six. Two hours every day after school except Wednesdays, and Saturday mornings, nine till one. Twelve hours. There's a six-year-old too, who the twins will collect on their way home from school. The family happen to be my neighbors and their mother asked my advice. I thought of you at once. She is offering six shillings a week, which seems fair, although not generous. What do you think? Will you have to ask your father?"

"No," said Clarry. "I won't have to do that. Thank you, Miss Fairfax. When can I begin?"

Twenty-Seven

"HE WAS CALLED OSLER," PETER SAID TO SIMON. "Professor Osler. He walked right in front of me as I was riding down the street. He admitted it was his fault. I didn't hurt him; he thought he'd hurt me. I had to push my bike afterward, and he saw the way I walked. Then we got talking, and I found out he was a professor of medicine."

"A doctor? So is that what you'll be?"

"At least I'd be useful."

"And they'll let you?"

"He said so, and I've already passed the entrance exams."

"It's not what I thought you'd do."

"It's not what I thought I'd do," said Peter, "but now

there's a war and I can't stand doing nothing."

"Neither can I," said Simon.

They were standing at the library window looking out over the sports fields, the same fields that they'd stared at the day they met. The view was unchanged—the same mud, the same rain—but they were changed. Peter no longer looked like he was waiting to step off a train for a second time. Simon, although taller and bonier than ever, no longer looked as if he was about to fall apart at the joints.

"It's not been that bad," said Peter. "I thought I'd die here, when I first came. Clarry kept me alive with her letters and her butterflies."

"I remember," said Simon. "She used to paint you a new one every time things got bad. Have you still got them?"

"Of course. Five. All the rarest. She never sent a swallow-tail because things never got that terrible. Do you remember how we cleared the common-room chimney that time?"

"Yes, and Clarry's Christmas party. And Rupert climbing the chapel roof. And us singing 'Three Little Maids from School' at the concert. Practicing in secret. Rupert making us learn the actions with the fans. My dad laughing till he couldn't breathe, and everyone saying afterward, 'I thought you were supposed to be shy!'"

Rain splattered against the window then, suddenly hard.

"It's not much like summer," said Simon, gloomy. "Look

at those idiots out there with that ball! God, I hate outside! Do you ever hear from him?"

"Who? Professor Osler?"

"No! Rupert, of course!"

"Oh. No. Never."

"I wonder what he's doing right now. Right this minute. Right this second. Over there!"

He spoke so passionately that Peter looked at him in surprise.

"You must think about him!"

Peter shook his head.

"I do. Well. I suppose you think I'm a fool."

"I don't."

"What, then?" asked Simon, slumping into a chair and dropping his head onto a table.

Peter, with great effort, dragged himself into Simon the Bony One's elusive, aching world and said, "I'm really glad you didn't climb out of that window. I'm really glad you stayed." Then, although he didn't do human contact much, especially in school, he made a great effort and rubbed his friend between his hunched bony shoulders for forty-five seconds, which he timed by the library clock. He broke off to laugh.

"Do you remember when he left us three bottles of beer and his spare key to the cricket pavilion?"

"What happened to that key?"

"I've got it somewhere. I suppose it'll be our turn to pass

it soon. We're nearly done here. Have you noticed any miserable mud-hating first years who deserve it?"

"They all look the same to me. Bellowing and wrestling. I don't care about them. Let them find their own escapes."

"All right," said Peter. "Let them. Clarry will be at speech day, did I tell you? She's coming with your family."

"I don't know why my family want to bother," grumbled Simon. "I won't be collecting any prizes. Never have, never will. Anyway, they're only books! What kind of prize is a book?"

"Would you like a prize that wasn't a book?"

"Yes," said Simon, after some thought. "I'd like a prize for sticking it out! I'm not going to university. I haven't written any good essays. I'll probably never read a book again. I'll definitely never kick a football. But I have stuck it out!"

"Yes you have," agreed Peter, and later that night Simon found an envelope shoved under his pillow. It was labeled:

THE PENROSE BONNERS AWARD
FOR STICKING IT OUT, WITH SPECIAL
COMMENDATION FOR THAT TIME YOU
DIDN'T CLIMB OUT OF THE WINDOW

Inside, on a leather bootlace, was Rupert's spare key to the cricket pavilion.

Twenty-Eight

THE LINE OF BATTLE WAS CALLED THE WESTERN front. It stretched 440 miles, from the North Sea to the Swiss border. It began in the corner of Belgium, bulged into Ypres, crossed the Flanders fields where later the poppies grew, ran south through the Somme (that nightmare place), swept eastward in a great curve across the French countryside and then up into the mountains. It was made of trenches, dugouts, barbed wire, jam tins, boredom, broken woodland, rubble of homes, duckboards, lost socks, latrines, hastily dug graves, love letters, liquefied bodies, sandbags, poetry, nameless machinery, songs rewritten, tank tracks, and a thousand other things, the chief amongst them being mud.

No wonder that it hardly moved, through all the years of war.

It was populated by (amongst others) Britons, Germans, French, Canadians, West Indians, Prussians, Australians, Irish, Dutch, two cavalry divisions from India, horses, rats, dogs, lice, pigeons, and fleas. Birds flew over it. Cats had more sense than to go near it, except a few of the most curious and brave. They were very much loved by whatever nationality they found themselves amongst. The line was lit by flares, stars, the usual sun and moon, rockets, shells, bullet flashes, firebombs, and carefully shielded lucifer matches. It smelled of earth, rum, death, smoke, urine, tinned beef, and hot metal. Guns thumped like intermittent heartbeats, and the barbed wire rattled and jangled in the wind. There were other sounds that made their hearers stop their ears till they were over, but the echoes stayed in their memories for as long as they lived.

The line was the shape of a long, lopsided smile. A ravenous, expectant smile. A greedy, unreasonable smile, considering how very, very well it was fed.

On either side of the line were the armies. Neither was winning, although not because they didn't try. They tried very hard and when one way didn't work they tried another. The Germans were the first to use poison gas, and the British were the first to use tanks. Perfectly reasonable people, the sort who in their previous lives let wasps out of windows, read storybooks to children doing all the proper voices, flinched at flat notes, and hardly ever shouted, got drunk, or forgot their mums' birthdays—absolutely ordinary people made considerable efforts to kill other absolutely ordinary people whom they had never even met.

Things didn't get better; they got worse.

It was all quite normal to Rupert now. It was 1917, he'd been there from the start, he was one of the unshakables. He'd moved about a lot but now he was back almost where he'd begun, in Flanders, on the left-hand curl of the smile. There was a feeling in the air of a job well done, because the British had just managed to blow up nineteen huge mines, right under the German front lines. They had other plans in mind too, equally uncivilized. First, however, they had to prepare the ground. That meant Rupert had spent the hours of darkness (never long enough at the end of May) crawling around in front of the trenches, cutting barbed wire. Barbed wire was wicked stuff. It caught men like fish in a net. Both sides used it in great tangled coils, held up by fence posts, all along the trenches. In some places it was so thick you could hardly see through it. They didn't try and cut those dark masses; they went where it was thinner and looser. It was a horrible job. It rattled as you pulled it away. They'd tried cutting it with machine-gun fire, but it didn't really work. The coils would lift and bounce down again, more or less intact.

Rupert had survived the night, got back to the trench just before dawn broke, eaten a sustaining but indigestible breakfast of tinned beef, rust-colored tea, and a slice of somebody's birthday cake from home, found a dugout with an empty bunk, and crawled inside. When Simon had looked out of the rainy window and wondered where Rupert was, that was the place.

Fast asleep with his boots on.

Away from the front, where the supply lines ran, there were rest camps and first aid stations, and even patches of farmland. Often at that time of year you could hear skylarks over the fields. Soldiers remarked how strange it was that the birds should be there, but in fact the birds had been there for centuries.

The really strange thing was that the soldiers were there.

Another thing that people thought odd was that the skylarks sang in the language of their homes. In English for the English, in French for the French, and in Dutch for the Dutch.

More puzzling still, on the other side of the trenches, a few miles away, the skylarks were singing in German.

It was a war where absolutely nothing made sense.

Twenty-Nine

IT WAS THE WEEKEND, AND CLARRY HAD A LIST OF jobs she ought to do. They included, amongst other things, her weekly letters to Rupert and Peter, and somehow organizing proper food for the next day. Clarry's father, despite his weekday absences, expected Sunday lunch to appear in a well-dusted dining room at one o'clock promptly, no matter what was happening in the rest of the world.

Clarry could hardly spare the time for cooking and housework anymore. The twelve hours a week she spent being a mother's help could not have been happier, but they made an awful hole in her days.

Worth it, though, thought Clarry. It was not just the six

shillings, welcome as they were, it was the warm house waiting at the end of the day, the half-grown kitten sleeping in the armchair, the teapot standing beside the cups, the pot of jam and the plate piled with brown bread and butter, ready to be shared before they got down to work.

At first, Clarry had hesitated at joining in with tea.

"There are four cups, Miss Penrose," a kind twin had pointed out, "and four plates."

Miss Penrose. That was how Miss Fairfax had introduced her to the children. "Here is Miss Penrose, and you are extraordinarily lucky to have her!" she had said, and given Clarry a firm *Get on with it* nod as she left them at the gate.

Clarry had fought back the desire to say "Call me Clarry!" and got on with it.

It helped being Miss Penrose, much to her surprise. Miss Penrose could do things that Clarry would have found difficult. Miss Penrose could say, "Tell me what you can remember from yesterday," or, "Robbie, I think you need to wash your buttery hands." It made her feel grown-up and confident. And already she was really helping. Often now a twin cried out, "Oh yes, I understand!"

Clarry loved it when someone understood.

Six-year-old Robbie had joined in from the first day. "Teach me too!" he had begged, climbing up to the table. At first he simply toiled over copying pictures Clarry drew for him. Then she drew him a kitten reading a book, and suddenly he was reading too. He loved words that rhymed.

Kitten.

Mitten, he copied, breathing heavily over the paper.

Ritten, he added triumphantly, all by himself. "Look, Miss Penrose, I've written 'ritten'!"

"You really have!" exclaimed Clarry, equally proud.

"Last week he could only write 'Rob,'" observed a twin. "R-o-b. That was all."

"Last week I cried in math," said the other twin. "From fractions! Imagine crying at fractions now!"

Years before, Peter had taught Clarry fractions with apple slices at the kitchen table. Now she was teaching kitchen table fractions herself, this time with bread and butter, but just as successfully. For a whole week no slice of bread was eaten before it had been divided into halves, thirds, quarters, sixths, and twelfths Now the twins could juggle fraction sums with ease.

"Two thirds minus one quarter," they said, studying their plates with care. "That's eight twelfths minus three twelfths. Five twelfths! Easy! You almost don't need the bread and butter!"

"I hear you're coping very well," said Miss Fairfax, at school. "Are you enjoying it?"

"I love it," said Clarry, and it was true, but still it made an awful lot of late-night homework.

✢

On Saturdays, it was always Rupert's letter that came first.

Dear Rupert,

The moon last night was like a picture in a book, a silver crescent with a big star nearby that was the planet Venus. I made a wish.

I have got a job now, Rupe. I am a mother's help! I earned six shillings last week! It was very hard not to rush to the shops and spend it all—I did buy a bottle of silver ink in the stationer's. Unfold this little piece of black paper and you will see the moon and Venus shining over the chimney pots. I drew them for you. The silver cat is a real cat that belongs to the people I work for. His name is Mr. Paws.

Grandmother writes that Grandfather is not well. She says his chest is very wheezy, and he won't go out of the house anymore. She is quite well herself, though, and she says nothing changes in Cornwall. I am glad about that. I like to think that every day our train huffs into the station, and stops in a cloud of steam. And people come hurrying over the footbridge to meet it, and you can see the sea as soon as you jump out, blue and green, behind the red rooftops.

I have to go. Miss Vane has arrived with a cookery

> book. *She says it will help me take care of my poor father.*
>
> *With love and a hug from Clarry*

As well as the cookery book, Miss Vane had brought a flabby parcel of liver, wrapped up in brown paper.

"Liver needs an onion with it," she told Clarry. "Have you an onion?"

"No," said Clarry thankfully.

"I thought not, so I brought you one."

Clarry looked fearfully at the brown paper bundle and asked if Miss Vane had rather not keep it for her cats.

"Clarry dear, there's a war on," said Miss Vane, rather sternly. "My cats are managing on beast heart. I was very lucky to find this liver, and I thought of you straightaway. The only difficulty is that it needs cooking at once, and I have to be out at a Red Cross meeting so I won't be able to help."

"Couldn't it be cooked tomorrow?" pleaded Clarry.

"I'm afraid by then it will be *off*," said Miss Vane solemnly. "Which is why it was so cheap. I have bookmarked a simple recipe and I'm sure you will manage. Liver doesn't take long. You can have it tomorrow with a baked potato and that will be a very nice lunch."

"But you said it would be off!"

"Not cooked," said Miss Vane patiently, always remembering that Clarry hadn't a mother to teach her such things.

"Cooking will save it. I must hurry. We're packing parcels for the Italian front where they are having a dreadful time."

"I'm a coward," said Clarry remorsefully. "I'll cook it. Will you come to lunch if it works?"

"I should be delighted," said Miss Vane heroically, "and I will bring a rhubarb pudding. There's a rhubarb glut, and I bought a great bundle."

"Lovely," said Clarry. She detested rhubarb, and the thought of the liver appalled her, but she was determined to be brave and so she opened the cookery book, unwrapped the brown paper, blinked only for a moment, and then began steadily following instructions. It was a peacetime recipe, so she had to improvise a little, with snipped-up (churchyard) grass for thyme, and cough syrup for sherry. She nearly forgot the onion on which Miss Vane had encouraged her to believe the success of the whole enterprise depended. Still, when it was done, she had gained so much courage that she was able to think of her most difficult task of all.

Clothes.

Somehow, she had to buy clothes.

Clothes that would do for speech day (the poshest of the posh but nothing anyone would notice) and Oxford ("Do make an effort, Clarry!"). She had twelve shillings from Mrs. Grace, and the train fare she wouldn't need from her father, less one shilling and sixpence for silver ink.

One pound and sixpence.

Enough to make a start.

But where to start?

Stockings, she thought, remembering Vanessa, who had not been polite about her old woolly ones, darned by Clarry with lumpy black knots. Vanessa's stocking tutorial had been surprisingly useful. She had demonstrated with her own collection: silk stockings for best (five shillings and sixpence a pair), cream lace for second best (less expensive than silk), and black for everyday. ("Only two shillings! Have a pair! Have two, and some silk ones! Or lace, at least! Go on, Clarry, please!") But Clarry had shaken her head and said no.

I'll buy my own stockings! Clarry thought as she walked into town, and here was a haberdasher's, and there, by great good luck, was a box on the floor full of lace stockings—cream, white, and black—all jumbled together and smelling rather musty.

BARGAINS!

read the label on the box.

"I just this minute put them out," the shop assistant told her. "We had a pipe burst and the stock got damp. Three pairs for two shillings!"

"How much for one pair?"

"One pair!" sniffed the assistant. "You don't want just one

pair. You won't find a bargain like this in a hurry!"

"I suppose not."

"Once in a lifetime," said the assistant fervently. "You'll need to match them yourself, though!"

That was easier said than done, but at last Clarry untangled her way to three matching pairs, and the assistant rolled them up and put them in a bag, assuring her, "They'll wash!" when she sniffed them.

"Of course they will," said Clarry, and went skipping into the street, and there right opposite was the stationer's that had sold the silver ink, and before she knew it, she was opening the door, because ever since the silver ink, she had thought about gold, and now she had a pocket full of money, and the stockings had been such a bargain.

They not only had gold ink, they had purple scented with violets. Or so it said on the box.

"Does it really smell of violets?" she asked the bored shopgirl, who was watching her.

"'Course it does."

"Could I smell it?"

"I suppose."

"Goodness!" said Clarry, when the bottle had been opened. "It really does! How gorgeous!"

"We got a pink one too, smells of roses," offered the girl, and that bottle was opened too. Clarry was swept away with the thought of sending a letter to Rupert and him opening it up and smelling flowers. Roses, such as grew in the garden in Cornwall.

Or violets. Violets grew there too.

"I'll have both!" she said recklessly, handing over the money.

"What about the gold? I can let you have it for a shilling if you buy the other two."

Clarry hovered in agony.

"Or ninepence. Half price."

Half price was irresistible. Clarry nodded.

"I like them flower ones," said the girl chattily, once she had got Clarry's money safely in the till. "We sell 'em for love letters."

"Love letters!" exclaimed Clarry. "I wasn't going to . . ."

"I used the violet myself when I wrote to the front," continued the girl, ignoring her. "*When.* Not anymore."

"Oh no!" said Clarry.

"Oh yes."

"I'm very, very sorry."

"Found himself a French girl! A French mamzelle! After all those letters! And tobacco! And cake! I'm done with him! You be careful!"

"It's my cousin I write to."

"Makes no difference. What are you doing now?"

"I've got to buy clothes," said Clarry. "To wear to Oxford."

"Is it an interview?"

"Sort of."

"You need a hat!" said the girl. "A proper one. Not that school mushroom thing you're wearing now. Shall I come with you?"

"What about the shop?"

"I'll put 'Closed' on the door," said the girl. "It's my aunt's shop. She's round the back. She'll never notice, not for five minutes. I haven't bought a hat for ages! Come on! I'll show you my favorite place. They've got a sale in the basement."

"How do you know?"

"They always have!" said the girl, hurrying her out of the door. "What color d'you fancy? Blue?"

"Not really."

"Black? Black comes in for funerals."

For some reason this made them both stagger with laughter.

"Orange!" said Clarry, swinging her bags and suddenly enjoying herself very much.

"Gold, not orange," said the girl knowledgeably. "They call it gold in hats! You couldn't, though, not for an interview. Gray?"

"I might as well just wear my mushroom!"

They found a deep raspberry-pink velvet beret that Clarry thought was the most beautiful hat she'd ever seen. It fitted her perfectly.

"Twelve shillings!" said Clarry. "Is it worth twelve shillings?"

"It's ever so pretty. You could wear it with all sorts."

"All right," said Clarry recklessly, diving for her money. "I'm doing it! There!"

Five minutes later it was hers, two weeks' work in a black and white striped bag.

"Gosh, goodness, it doesn't leave much," said Clarry, inspecting the change in her purse.

"How much?"

"Two shillings and some pennies. But I'll get another six next week."

"Pennies?"

"Shillings."

"Oh, well, then," said the girl, as if Clarry had announced she was coming into a fortune next week. "Let's go and get a cake! What's your name? I'm Vi. Violet."

"Like the ink!"

"Like my nan," said Violet. "Forget the ink!"

"All right. I'm Clarry. Can we afford cakes?"

Violet gave her a quick glance then, but said good-temperedly, "I can if you can."

"I think I can," said Clarry, and so they bought jam tarts and some very odd lemonade in Clarry's first tea shop ever. It came to eightpence each, plus a penny for the waitress, which Violet insisted on paying.

"Have a pair of lace stockings!" offered Clarry impulsively. "Go on, I'll never need three!"

"Don't mind if I do!" said Violet. "Same time next week?"

"What? Shopping? I will if I can. I'll probably have to scrub out the kitchen next Saturday, though."

Violet stared at her in such surprise that Clarry was alarmed and asked, "What is it?"

"Scrubbing out the kitchen!"

"I only didn't do it today because Mrs. Morgan didn't come."

"I thought you were posh!"

"Me? Posh?"

"That hat! Twelve shillings! *Twelve shillings! Twelve!* All that ink! Giving away lace stockings!"

"Oh," said Clarry, very startled to find that she had not appeared as sensible and economical as she thought. "Was that a lot for that hat?"

"Just a bit!"

"I've never been shopping before."

"I can tell."

"Thank you very, very much for closing up the shop!"

"Oh, Lord, I forgot the shop!" cried Violet, and turned and ran.

Thirty

CLARRY'S LIVER, COMPLETE WITH CHURCHYARD grass snippings and cough syrup, was a great success.

"Very acceptable," said her father, after ungallantly letting Miss Vane try it first.

"Delicious!" agreed Miss Vane. "Well done, Clarry! Didn't I tell you that cooking would save it from going off?"

"Yes, you did," agreed Clarry cordially, content herself with baked potatoes and spring greens.

"I can't think why you won't try it yourself."

"I'm vegetarian now," explained Clarry.

"Since when?"

"Since yesterday," said Clarry.

She didn't manage to meet Violet the next week, and the following Saturday things were somehow different from that first wild glorious shop. Violet became very bossy, saying things like "You can't charge her that!" to perfectly reasonable shop assistants, and "You can't go in there!" to Clarry.

"Why can't I go in there?" asked Clarry.

"You've only got twelve shillings."

"But look at that dress!"

It was gray striped with cream, and had a cream muslin bodice laced with gray.

"It's plain as plain. It's nothing of a dress! It's been hanging in that window for weeks."

"Then they must want to sell it."

"I thought you'd want pink, like that hat."

"The hat's enough pinkness for one person to wear at a time!"

"And that dress is seventeen shillings!" said Violet disapprovingly. "You said you'd only got twelve. I can't lend you anything, you know!"

"I didn't ask you to!" said Clarry indignantly. "Do you think they'll let me try it on?"

Violet shrugged.

"Well, I'm going inside to look at it properly," said Clarry, and as soon as she stepped through the door she was pounced on, and urged into the dressing rooms, where it was discovered that it fitted her perfectly.

"It's been too long in the window, it's faded down one side," observed Violet, who had followed Clarry into the shop after all.

"Not very much," said Clarry, and then absolutely scandalized Violet by offering twelve shillings for it now, and another five in two weeks' time, and meanwhile they could have her little silver watch, as proof that she'd come back.

They must have wanted to sell it. Instead of chasing Clarry out of the door, as Violet half hoped they would, the manager came over, inspected the watch, and agreed. Then they wrapped the dress, took the twelve shillings, the watch, and Clarry's name and address, and handed her the box.

"You've got a nerve!" said Violet, when they finally emerged onto the street. "And you are posh, whatever you say! Where'd you get your money from? Your millionaire dad?"

"I work after school and Saturday mornings," replied Clarry, too happy with her dress to be offended by this. "I stay with three children till their mother gets home and teach them things for their homework."

"What sort of things?"

"Oh, anything they need. Math and French and Latin."

"What was all that about scrubbing kitchens, then?"

Clarry looked at Violet, and saw that somehow she had hurt her.

"You can do Latin and scrub kitchens," she said.

"Huh," said Violet.

"You can borrow the pink hat whenever you like."

"How many love letters have you written with that ink?"

"Two," said Clarry, "but they're not love letters. I'm sorry about that person you wrote to in France."

"Oh, him."

"Miss Vane organizes a Red Cross group in Saint Christopher's Church hall. Wednesday nights and Saturdays. Lots of girls knit socks and mittens and things. And they put little folded messages inside them before they send them off, to cheer up the soldiers. Often they get letters back."

"Oh."

"And they have tea and do games at the end. And make jokes. Like pretending they know who they're knitting for. They say, 'This is for Albert. Don't tell his mum!' and make up stories as if they know them."

"Do you go?"

"Sometimes. I'm knitting a scarf. I'm a bit slow, though. They always need more people. Shall I call for you, next time I'm going?"

"Don't know. If you like."

"Wednesday, then, at seven o'clock."

"I'll think about it," said Violet, and she didn't say another word all the way back to the shop, where, just before she opened the door, she hugged Clarry hard and said, "Sorry!"

So Clarry went home with a new friend, as well as a new dress, and the following week she wore it with the pink beret and the successfully washed lace stockings to Peter's speech day. There she watched as her brother limped onto the stage eight times to deafening applause, and collected prizes that included the gilt cup for Best Science Essay; the debating society's Voice of the Year Award; an enormous dictionary in two volumes, which was the traditional gift to the editor of the school magazine; and an Oxford scholarship.

"I tried to make Father come," whispered Clarry, when she had a moment with Peter.

"Never mind him," said Peter, not whispering at all. "I knew he wouldn't from the start."

"He . . ."

"Just for once, Clarry, could you not make any excuses for him? I like your hat!"

Clarry, who had been so anxious to get everything right that she had brought his postcard with her for reference, sighed with relief. "And my dress?" she asked. "It's new as well."

"Oh. Sorry. I didn't notice it. Yes. Good dress."

"Vanessa liked it too," said Clarry happily. "Did you hear

her whistle through her fingers when you went up onstage?"

"Was that Vanessa?" Peter grinned.

"Yes, she's over there with Simon, come and say hello."

Vanessa flung her arms around Peter the moment she caught sight of him. "You and Simon!" she cried. "What a pair! Let's take Clarry round the school now you've finished. She's never been here before. Where shall we show her first?"

"The chimney we cleared with her rocket," said Simon. He had collected nothing onstage but the leaver's certificate that everyone had been given.

"Is he all right?" Clarry asked Peter privately.

"Of course," Peter replied, knowing that Rupert's spare key to the cricket pavilion hung around his bony friend's neck.

Then, while other guests were in the library drinking sherry with the headmaster, Peter, Simon, and Vanessa raced Clarry around the common room, the quad, the stage on which the three little maids had sung together, and the chapel, inside and out, so she could marvel at the height of the pinnacled roof where Rupert had long ago stood in triumph, supported by nothing but sunlight and cheek.

"I wish he was here now," said Clarry, and found she was clutching Simon's hand.

"So do I," he said.

Thirty-One

SIMON BONNINGTON, BONNERS, THE BONY ONE, the one who hated outdoors, found football painful, detested mud, had secret bed socks all through boarding school, who once wrote a letter to the Old Fish, the headmaster, about the lack of soap in the school toilets, who could have had almost another year brushing down Lucy, writing bad poetry, staring into the mirror, tidying his bedroom, and annoying his relations, and during that year the war might have ended . . .

Instead of these things, enlisted in the army.

When they asked him his age, after weighing him (132 pounds), measuring him (6'3"), and doing various other checks to see if he was real, he said, "Nineteen."

The doctor peered up at Simon's great height and stubbled chin (he had shaved twice a day since he was fourteen but it was still never enough), and raised an eyebrow.

"All right, twenty-one," said Simon, grinning.

"What have you been up to, then?"

"I don't know, really," said Simon, truthfully enough. He had considered this question beforehand. Did Lucy count as farmwork? Did "Three Little Maids" count as stage?

"I live with my mum," he said, and then, having nothing to lose, "And my great-aunt! And my sister."

Simon sensed amusement in his audience, which he never could resist. Also nervousness made him reckless. What else could he offer?

"I can sing," he suggested. "I'm a . . . a . . . a . . . bloody good singer! Don't you want me?"

But it was all right, they did.

Start to finish, the whole thing, including medical and a short (but much applauded) rendering of "On a Tree by a River" ("I sing it with my mum"), took eight minutes.

"Keep your head down, dicky bird," they advised him as he left.

Thirty-Two

PETER'S FATHER SAID, "A DOCTOR! A MEDIC! A medical degree! Where on earth do you get your ideas from?"

Peter thought of his mother, whom no one had been able to help, of the soldiers returning with injuries that would be with them for life, of his own badly set leg. However, he had lived too long with his father's complete lack of interest to try to explain these things.

"Just thought I might," he said, and shrugged.

"And how do you propose to manage? You won't be earning for years!"

Peter said quite the opposite, he'd a job for the summer already, porter at the local military hospital, with a letter of introduction from Oxford asking if he could spend his free time observing on the wards.

"Well, it seems that I have no say in the matter," said his father peevishly. "I did hope you'd find something meaningful to do. We could have found a place for you in the office, in time. I hope it's not just another of your fads!"

Their conversations always seemed to end with one or the other of them slamming out of the room. This time it was Peter, who stomped upstairs and related the conversation to Clarry.

"I used to think you'd work in a museum," said Clarry. "Researching, and writing books. Perhaps Father did too."

"He didn't. He thought I'd work in his beastly office."

"Oh, well, he can't make you," said Clarry. "I expect you'll be a good doctor. I'm so glad you'll be here this summer. I'm glad you're here now! Miss Vane brought us a great bag of watercress this morning, and a poor little duck!"

"A poor little *what*?"

"Duck. A duck to cook. To celebrate you doing so well. It's still got all its feathers and beak and feet and everything. It still *is* a duck. Will you come and help me?"

"What do you want me to do?"

"Stand guard while I bury it in the churchyard."

"Oh, all right," said Peter.

The summer passed in dust, thunderstorms, food queues, short tempers, work, and trying not to think. Fear lurked in the undergrowth of the days, waiting for the moments when clamor died down. Then, while Peter kept watch in the nighttime corridors, or Vanessa paused between dances to ease her aching feet, or Clarry hung, pen poised over a blank sheet of letter paper, then the fear would come.

Where was Rupert? Clarry wished she had someone to talk to about him. Peter was no good; it only stirred up the old guilt that Rupert was enduring a life he had escaped. Vanessa was elusive whenever his name was mentioned.

Violet was the best. Violet asked, "Did he like the ink?"

"He didn't say."

"Have you got a picture of him?"

"Yes." Clarry reached automatically into her bag for the one she carried everywhere, cut small enough to fit in a little card frame.

"Coo, lovely," said Violet. "Why's he not in uniform?"

"It was before. In Cornwall."

"Was it cloudy in Cornwall?"

"No, it's steam from a train."

"Who's he looking at?"

"Me."

"Well!" said Violet. "Don't tell me you don't write him . . . oh, never mind! I liked that Red Cross thing you took me to.

I've done two pairs of socks already and stuffed them full of messages! And I heard there's girls needed on the trams and I've applied. I know I shouldn't say it but I quite like this war. There's more to do. Do you think it's really so bad over there as some people say?"

"Yes, I think it probably is," said Clarry. She had found the newspapers in the library now, and had no illusions left.

"Still, you have to carry on," said Violet cheerfully.

It was true. They kept on doing ordinary things. They coped with the endless shortages in the shops, treasure hunting in the backs of cupboards for things they had never known mattered before, a forgotten packet of tea, or sugar or rice. A triumphant box of lavender soap, just in time for Miss Vane's birthday.

"I hope she didn't give it to us," said Peter.

"She'll be glad to get it back if she did," said Clarry practically.

They were both busy that summer. The Grace children no longer needed extra coaching, but their mother had asked Clarry to stay on for the school holidays. Peter was at the hospital day and night, hobbling down the corridors pushing trolleys and wheelchairs, or shadowing the doctors and nurses. Sometimes, scrubbed up, he hovered at the back of an operating room. In between shifts he found a quiet corner and made his way through as much as he could of the reading list sent out from Oxford. He often woke with a jump over a pile of notes, or a textbook.

Clarry was thinking of Oxford too. She arranged a day off with Mrs. Grace, put on her gray-striped dress and her raspberry beret, and traveled there with Miss Fairfax.

Thirty-Three

"NOTHING IS THE SAME," MISS FAIRFAX WARNED Clarry. "There are soldiers billeted everywhere. My college is a hospital; I can't take you in. They put us up in a little corner of one of the men's places. I'm going to show you as much as I can, and introduce you to a great friend."

And so she did, introducing Clarry to the Principal of the College, saying, "Miss Penrose, meet Miss Penrose!"

The Miss Penroses looked at each other and laughed in surprise at their shared surname, and then Clarry was rushed around libraries and common rooms, in and out of a punt, and back to college for tea with students who had stayed behind to work through the summer. Nobody there thought it was odd to like Latin, her raspberry pink beret was much admired, and there was a lot of hopeful talk about after the war. Clarry noticed how, unlike at home, they talked about it as if it really would end, had to end, could do nothing else but end.

Then colleges would fill up again, and there would be good academic work to be done, by women as well as men. Especially by women, now it had been seen what they could do. Everyone spoke as if Clarry would quite naturally be coming to join them. "Bring your bike!" they advised. "And your lovely pink hat!"

"So," said Miss Fairfax on the train home, "two years, Clarry, and then it could be your turn. You'd better get down to some real work now! Can that brother of yours start you on Greek, or had it better be me?"

"Greek?"

"Oh yes! They'll examine you in Greek and Latin and math the moment you set a nose through the door! Always supposing you're invited to that door in the first place! Still, we've made a start. Everything your brother did easily through school, you will have to do the difficult way. Which will toughen you up wonderfully, so let us not lament. No more Grace children next term, I'm afraid."

"Mrs. Grace doesn't need me anyway," said Clarry, a little ruefully. "The twins are all caught up with work, and they can take care of Robbie after school too, I expect."

"Excellent," said Miss Fairfax. "Then you'd better make that dress last and hang on to your hat! Now, then, Greek, recite after me: alpha, beta, gamma, delta . . ."

For a little while they both of them had forgotten about the war.

Thirty-Four

HOWEVER, THE WAR WAS STILL THERE, THAT monstrous smile. Rupert, back in Flanders, had a fleeting few minutes of awful clear-eyed sanity, during which he wrote a letter to Clarry, the first one for months.

> *Were they real, those summers? There used to be skylarks. There used to be green waves. There used to be buns with raspberry jam. There used to be grass and quietness. Is anything left how it was before? So many things are gone. Are you still the Clarry who sent butterflies? Or have you vanished too?*

He knew now that he should have taken more notice of grass and quietness. Thick, wild grass, springy with life. The clean smell of it. And quietness. So quiet that you could hear a wasp, shredding wood for its paper nest; so quiet that bird-song could wake you from a dream, a pony's hooves sounded loud, and a steam train pulling into a sunlit station was a glorious clattering, hissing roar.

"Clarry," he said out loud, and for one moment the grass felt close enough to touch.

Peter was at home when Rupert's message arrived, which was a miracle, because he was usually in Oxford. He saw Clarry's face light up at the sight of Rupert's handwriting, and then he saw the lightness fade, as she read.

"I've always written to him every week," she said. "I don't know if he gets my letters, though. He doesn't write like he did. He hasn't replied for ages. I thought he'd forgotten us."

"Not forgotten," said Peter, his mind going back to his early weeks at boarding school when it had seemed to him that the only way of surviving was to numb the memory of any other life. "He perhaps just didn't let himself remember."

"He sounds so far away."

Peter hugged her, less awkwardly than in the past. "He's

still alive, anyway," he said, and did not add, as he once would have done, "or was."

"What shall I say? Help me, Peter."

Peter looked down at the letter again. "Tell him that those summers were real," he said at last. "Tell him how we think of him every day. Tell him you haven't vanished. Make him believe it. He wants to believe it."

Peter paused, and looked at Clarry's anxious face. She wrote every week, she had told him, but perhaps words were not enough. *A photograph?* he wondered. *Would she look the same Clarry in a photograph?*

"Send him a butterfly," he said.

"A butterfly? To France? A butterfly when things are so terrible?"

"You never sent a swallowtail."

"I was saving it for in case."

"Now is in case," said Peter.

The butterflies that Clarry had once sent to Peter at school were three-dimensional models, as close as she had been able to come to a real butterfly. Their bodies were made of carved matchsticks wound round with embroidery silk, their antennae and legs were varnished black cotton, their painted wings were colored on top and beneath. They had never been quick to make, even when Clarry had had all the materials to hand and plenty of time to do it. Peter was back at Oxford before she reached the painting-of-the-wings stage on Rupert's swallowtail.

"Dolls'-house games," said her father, disgusted at this apparent return to childhood, but for once Clarry did not try to explain.

Thirty-Five

SIMON THE BONY ONE REACHED FRANCE BY WAY OF a ship from Southampton in the fall of 1917.

I'm here, he wrote to Rupert the day he arrived, crouched on a crate of tinned beef that looked like it had been abandoned by the roadside for years. *I can see now why no one says much about it at home. I keep thinking I see you. It would be nice to bump into you soon.*

Had he said too much? Nothing was private in the army except the space inside your head. If you died they got your letters out of your pockets and read them. And these last few days he'd started talking in his sleep again, it seemed. "Who's Rupert?" they'd asked, but he got out of that, quick as a flash.

"My dog," he'd replied, "golden Lab." He'd turned the talk to dogs very successfully. Dog stories had come pouring out from a dozen listeners. You were allowed to love your dog.

"You were shouting for your dog again last night," his neighbor remarked a few days later.

"Sorry," he said, completely casual. "I dream about him a lot. I dream he's lost."

"I dream I'm lost," said his neighbor, and Simon nodded and said, "Yes, I do that too."

Back to the letter. How not to sound desperate.

France seems a bit busy, he wrote.

It was a bit busy, miles back from the lines the ground throbbed with the pounding of the guns at the front. It was terrible seeing the horses, knee-deep, toiling, their carts slipping sideways. They were moving back the wounded as fast as they could.

Never for one moment did the Bony One wonder why he'd come. Nor was it worse than he'd thought it would be. He'd guessed it would be very nearly unendurable, and it very nearly was. His feet were agony. They didn't seem to make boots his size. Already he'd seen things that he knew he'd never ever tell. A cartload of dead men. Loose limbed, turned blackish. He hadn't known that happened.

"They're all Australian," someone said, as if that explained anything.

He'd never thought of grave digging, but then, he'd never thought of rum. It was very helpful stuff, he decided. He was nearer to Rupert than he'd been for years.

It rained and rained.

Three days after landing they sent him to the front. He had a pack weighing nearly sixty pounds on his back, and a rifle that he'd fired only half a dozen times. Round his neck was Rupert's spare key to the cricket pavilion, along with his dog tags, so they'd know who he was when he died. The dog tags were made of asbestos, so they wouldn't burn if he burned. There was a red one to be taken off his body and a green one to be left on. Whenever he reached the point when he believed he could not stand the misery for an hour longer, he thought of Rupert, who had stuck it for more than two years.

Peter was now at Oxford studying biomedical sciences, the consequence of jumping off a moving train, an adaptable brain, and accidentally running into the regius professor of medicine while getting a photograph copied. He was so busy he hardly had time to look up from his work, but when the news came that Simon was going to France, he spared a moment to drop his head on his arms and remember his friend. A long letter came from Clarry, he could picture her writing it, in her room at the top of the narrow cold house.

He shouldn't have gone. He needn't have. What use would Simon be with a gun? He used to walk round ants, he was so kind. It isn't fair. Mrs. Morgan says if anything happens to him, it's for the best. She says life isn't easy for boys like him. I'm never speaking to her again.

Thirty-Six

IN CORNWALL, CLARRY'S GRANDFATHER'S CHEST had almost got the better of him at last. He had pneumonia; he was drifting in and out, awake and asleep, slowly drowning.

"Had enough," he said. "Still, could wish for one more summer. Skylark time, I used to think. Hear them singing over the moor. Know I'd soon be off to the station."

"Always late!" said his wife.

"Hardly ever! There they'd be . . . our own skylarks. Little Clarry and the boys."

"Grown-up now," said Clarry's grandmother. "How we used to complain about them coming, and now we wish them back."

"Never complained about them!"

"Oh, you did! The upheaval! The house full. The dramas! Clarry nearly drowning! Peter's leg."

"They were no trouble."

"You didn't say that when Rupert ran away to Ireland!"

"Well."

"Or when Clarry kidnapped Lucy!"

"She was right," he said, sighing. "Don't know what I was thinking of. Silly."

"Silly," she agreed, and bent and kissed his forehead.

"Had this chest a long time."

"You have."

"Got over it before. Many times."

"Many," she agreed.

"My love to our skylarks. All three."

"Of course."

Thirty-Seven

SIMON THE BONY ONE'S LETTER TO RUPERT ARRIVED when he was a few miles behind the front line on the last evening of a three-day break. He hardly read letters from home anymore, but this one wasn't from England. It was from just a few miles away, battered from being carried round in a pocket, slightly damp and thumbmarked with mud.

Rupert stared at it incredulously, recognizing the handwriting of the all-too-familiar Simon Bonnington, Bonners, the Bony One, that borderline pest from the past.

The past. School. That lost world. Peter, Simon. Mad Irish, whom he had carefully forgotten. Once, long ago, in a different life, he had saved the Bony One by means of his mad

Irish friend. *Don't start going back, don't start going,* Rupert begged his weeping memory. *Don't start, don't start, let's find a drink, let's find a bottle. Anything.*

But still, it started.

Long before, when the redheaded Irish boy Michael had been dispatched to school in England in order to lose his Irish accent and toughen up for the army, he had had to suffer a certain amount of agony, as all the new boys did. Each of them had their weak point, and his was his Irish accent, his Irishness in general, and his way of comparing his present dismal circumstances to his previous carefree life, and so they tormented him with Irish ballads.

They sang them behind him as he stood in front of the notice boards, reading every word over and over, as if, in his misery, he cared. They roared them in unison when he entered the common room. They howled them even as he flew at them, at first with blubbering nose and badly aimed kicks, later with head butts, and in time with hard, freckled, lightning-fast Irish fists. They were more wary when he moved on to fists. They began to say, "He's a lot stronger than he looks."

Even so, he was an irresistible target.

"*In Dublin's fair city . . . ,*" began the smirking inventor of this glorious game, incautiously, at the top of a staircase, and a minute later there he was, swiped down, heaved up, and dangling from the mad Irish one's grip, held only by one wrist, on the wrong side of the banister.

The crowd around immediately switched allegiance and began a chant of "Drop! Drop! Drop!" The hanging boy didn't help either.

"Let go! Let go!" he foolishly wailed, but luckily the Irish boy did not let go, although his face was now dead white, with orange freckles. It was Rupert who raced to grab the hanging boy's arms, and held on tight.

Even so, it was a job to get him back to safety.

"What do you say?" demanded Rupert, when the inventor was back on his quivering legs at last. "Thank you thank you sorry sorry thank you sorry thanks I'm sorry I'm sorry," he gibbered, and reeled away.

Then Rupert and the Irish boy looked at each other, and they were friends. They grew into the two most popular boys in the school. The Irish boy's accent remained unchanged and so did his reckless temper. They were legendary sportsmen and practical jokers. Rupert climbed the chapel roof one Saint Patrick's Day and dressed the weathercock in shamrock green.

There were no more Irish ballads.

Not for years, not until Simon the Bony One arrived on the scene.

Simon's wistful grin and perilous tendency to walk into walls when Rupert was about got worse and worse. One day it happened to attract the passing attention of Rupert's Irish friend, who remarked, "Watch out, Rosy! I spy a blushing swain!"

All in a moment Rupert understood what would happen next. What the Irish boy saw today, the rest of the school would see tomorrow. The destruction of the Bony One would be as inevitable as time, if he didn't think fast.

Rupert did think fast. "It's your lovely little maid from school," his Irish friend continued, and Rupert caught him in a swift and wicked headlock and crooned as he gripped him, "Don't be jealous, you mad Irish! He's nothing compared to you."

After this he took to singing Irish ballads now and then. "'When Irish eyes are smiling,'" he caroled to his raging friend, and, "'A little bit of heaven fell from out the sky one day.'"

It took the attention from the Bony One completely.

"'Oh, do you love, oh, say you love . . . you love the sham-rock green!'" he loudly serenaded his friend under his study window, with the first form in stitches, rolling round in the quad. And Michael leaped fifteen feet from the window and half killed him.

In these ways, he, Rupert, had saved Simon the Bony One from the ridicule of the rabble. And now apparently the silly kid was here in Flanders. How had that happened? Why had that happened?

Rupert didn't want to think about that so he spent the evening drinking red wine that tasted as if something extra added, like hair oil. It was raining, as it had rained all August,

September, and October, the world was half liquid, the front line trenches were knee-deep in mud; if it weren't for the submerged duckboards you'd just keep going down. You moved with the same speed that you ran in a nightmare. It was very bloody hot and then very bloody cold; the temperature regulation was a complete foreign mess. His head had the strangest floating feel, as if it might detach from his neck and sail away. In two hours time his unit would be marching back up to the front again. The next morning they would go over the top.

"'Oh, Danny boy,'" sang Rupert, "'the pipes, the pipes are calling from glen to glen . . .'" This song had been the best of all to rouse Michael. He turned scarlet with rage at the first syllable of "Danny"; you might as well have set fire to his bed to see him move. It had been a guaranteed crowd-pleaser; people used to come running to witness the redheaded Irish temper at its uncontrolled worst.

"'And down the mountain side,'" sang Rupert, quavering deliberately on the long notes, and was ordered from all round to "Shut it, just shut it." "Shut it you fool." "Rosy, you're drunk. Just shut it, now, all right?"

So he did. Michael hadn't come running anyway. First time it hadn't worked. Very odd.

"This is all a dream?" he asked a stranger he found standing by his shoulder as they set off toward the front, and was reassured to hear that he was right.

Thirty-Eight

RUPERT WOKE UP TO BRIGHT BLUE SKY, A FEELING OF warmth and comfort, and such a fuzzy head that for several minutes he could not imagine where he was.

And then, like light flashing into his delighted consciousness, he remembered.

Cornwall!

For a few minutes he lay quite still, dazzled by the wonder of it. He was free. No more idiots bossing him about. No more sniveling youngsters, tagging after him with frightened eyes, needing a hero to look out for them. No more mud, no more itchy uniform, no more of never a moment alone.

He was back in Cornwall at last.

The first day of the holidays; there'd be a train to meet in the afternoon, Clarry with her face all shining, jumping into his arms. There'd be Peter and Lucy and hugs and jokes and laughter, there'd be days and days and days of utter perfection.

He'd forgotten that skies could be so blue.

Not a cloud.

He'd go swimming.

The glorious race across the moor, the brambles that caught at your ankles, the gorse bushes you dodged, and the boggy patches you leaped—had he ever run it so fast before? Already he could hear the rush of waves against the cliff, and the screaming of the white gulls, and off went his jacket and shirt, and was that the key to the cricket pavilion dangling round his neck? Didn't need that, didn't need boots either, didn't need any of this stuff anymore, and even the sound of Clarry's bullocks, got loose again and lumbering up behind him, didn't frighten him in the least because here was the cliff dipping down to the sea.

Time to leap.

Over.

When you enlisted you had to give your next of kin, name and address. These were the people who would be given news of your death. Rupert had hesitated for a moment over this. His useless parents were in India, which left either his grandparents, or Clarry and Peter and their father. His grandparents, at the time he enlisted, had thought him a fool and told him so.

Penrose, Rupert had written, and then the address of the narrow stone house where his cousins lived. He had no intention of dying, so he didn't think it would matter much anyway.

Thirty-Nine

MISS VANE WAS THE ONLY PERSON WITH CLARRY when the telegram arrived. It was Miss Vane who took it from her hand, wrapped her in a blanket, brought her tea, clattering in its saucer because her hands were trembling, and stayed with her when her father, arriving home to the news, rubbed his neck, said not a word of either comfort or regret, stared out of the window, and disappeared.

Missing, said the telegram, and also, *Presumed dead.*

Snow-cold shock held Clarry motionless, silenced every sound, faded the colors to shades of gray, and diminished her to a fragment of nothingness, a small lost point, rocking in an endless darkness of space.

And then a sound penetrated, as if from another world, and it was Miss Vane's cracked, exhausted, quavering voice. "There may be hope, there may still be hope."

Clarry found that she could turn her head, and there was poor Miss Vane, looking utterly tear washed, her powder all streaked into mauve and gray, her hair a fallen heap, her eyes pink and alarmed as sugar mice, and yet she was saying again, "All hope is not lost, dear," and Clarry realized that all the time she had sat in her frozen immobility, Miss Vane had been talking, and she, it seemed, had been answering, because they appeared to be halfway through a conversation.

". . . home to my cats . . . then we will think. . . . Many wonderful and astonishing things happen when we least expect them. . . ."

If shock had been cold, hope was warm. Hope brought Clarry back to life, her blood running again, her courage returning. By the time Miss Vane returned from feeding her cats Clarry was back to herself again and a rhythm like a heartbeat was bumping through her mind: *Wonderful and astonishing, wonderful and astonishing, wonderful and astonishing.*

"'Missing,'" said Clarry to Miss Vane when she returned. "'That's all we know is true. 'Presumed dead' doesn't mean anything. Not if you don't presume it."

"Of course it doesn't," agreed Miss Vane. "We must be

patient and believe that one day the dear boy may—"

"No, we mustn't!" interrupted Clarry. "You said all hope wasn't lost, and perhaps it isn't. And that many wonderful and astonishing things happen and I think they sometimes do, but not in this house."

"No," agreed Miss Vane, startled, but understanding. "Not in this house."

"But somewhere else they might," said Clarry. "There are hospitals in France and in England. There are some in Southampton. That's where I'll begin. *'Presumed'!*" continued Clarry, looking fearlessly at the telegram. "It means they don't know. If I was writing it, I'd put, 'Missing, presumed alive'!"

"You would be quite right!" agreed Miss Vane, finding such bravery contagious.

"Peter had a train timetable in his room. I've been looking up trains. There's one in an hour. You needn't worry, Miss Vane. I'll be quite safe."

But Miss Vane lifted her head at this, and her eyes were no longer either pink or alarmed. They were as bright as Clarry's and she said that she wouldn't worry, and would be quite sure Clarry was safe, and the reason she gave was that she was coming as well, to deal with porters, or take care of luggage, even to speak French, if necessary, and she finished this declaration with a hug and "Please do not argue," and so Clarry hugged her back, and didn't.

There were bags to pack and money to find. Also messages to be written by Miss Vane to Mrs. Morgan, Clarry's father, and Violet, now a trusted member of the Red Cross group. These messages consisted of triplicate instructions for the care of Miss Vane's cats. Each included descriptions of how to deal with the beast heart in the icebox, the individual names of the cats, and a discreet but urgent reference to the "earth box" in the scullery. Mrs. Morgan and Violet were instructed to "obtain the door key entrusted to Mr. Penrose at number forty-six." The door key was carefully labeled. Mrs. Morgan's and Violet's letters were stamped and posted, along with Clarry's far briefer message to Peter:

> *R missing, am sure not dead. Take care of Father.*
> *Much love, C*

All these things Clarry and Miss Vane managed with miraculous speed. In less than an hour they were out in the street with their bags, and suddenly good luck was with them. Mr. King and his black and white horse Jester appeared round the corner.

One glance at their faces told him that this was no time for trading insults with Miss Vane. With the utmost gentleness and discretion he offered his assistance in any way they cared to name.

So their journey began as honored passengers in a rag-and-bone cart, Clarry in the back, and Miss Vane on the seat beside Mr. King, where she had a cheering view of Jester's black and white rump and intelligently swiveling ears.

"I fear I have misjudged you far too long, Mr. King," said Miss Vane earnestly. "I can only apologize and try to assure you that I only ever had Clarry's interests at heart."

"Say not a word," replied Mr. King, pulling off his hat and holding it to his chest. "I should have shown more respect. Now I can see that you are one in a million. I'm glad to do my bit to help and I wish it was more."

Then silently, and with great furtiveness and glances over his shoulder, he replaced his hat, drew an old black wallet from its snug pocket over his heart, took from it three warm and well folded notes, all the paper it contained, pushed them into Miss Vane's hands, and murmured once more, "Say not a word!"

Miss Vane could not speak at all, such were her sudden tears, but when they were over, her old distrust of Mr. King was completely gone. With no encouragement, she recklessly confided her great concern for her cats, which despite the three sets of instructions, she found already gnawed at her soul.

"The whole arrangement depends," explained Miss Vane earnestly, "on whether or not Mr. Penrose will be available to supply my key. Owing to his work, he is seldom at home. And even if he is, I cannot imagine either he or Violet coping with the beast heart properly, and none of them managing the . . . the . . . arrangement in the scullery on which my oldest cat depends."

Mr. King said that he well understood, that his old mother had never been without a cat in all her long years, and that he and Jester always had one, knocking about the stable.

"Company, like," said Mr. King.

"Indeed, yes," agreed Miss Vane, and by the end of the journey her spare back door key was in his pocket and he was helping her down, unloading the bags, and swinging Clarry over the back.

"Now, then, ladies, good luck and God bless!" he told them, and a moment later was up on the cart again.

"Lively, Jester!" they heard, and saw his hat wave as he turned the corner.

"Clarry, that is a very dear man," said Miss Vane, gazing after him.

"Yes," agreed Clarry. "It is."

Forty

SIMON AND VANESSA'S FATHER, WHOM CLARRY HAD named Odysseus, had not been a good prisoner. He found prison camp life uncomfortable and boring and he didn't enjoy eating rats. So he and some friends dug a tunnel beside the latrines, and one happy morning they allowed it to be discovered, and while it was being thoroughly and indignantly explored they rolled, one by one, under a section of loosened wire, whispered "Good luck!" to each other, and set off to see what would happen next.

Odysseus made it to the coast, and followed it west through the countryside, traveling mostly by night. In a few days he came to a fishing port, hid under a pile of nets in a boat, and was well on the way to Greece when they discovered him and dropped him over the side to swim. The stars were bright and lovely, and being a sailor, he was used to navigating at night, and so he set off across the Aegean, and presently the sun rose and he saw a long cloud, with a coastline below it, and knew he had nearly reached Greece.

Odysseus had been to Greece many times, sailed the coast and climbed the hills and danced at the festivals, so he paused there to dry out for a while. He was aided by the kindness of a family, who accepted his help with their grapes and olive trees, and in return gave him a home. They became such friends that it was hard to leave them. Still, he had to go and he promised to return, so one day they waved him good-bye on a fishing boat with a big red sail and a little boy and a man with a broken arm. The red-sailed boat ran so beautifully for him that he might have known her all his life. They fished for three days and three nights, and on the fourth day they took him farther west. They dropped him off at a harbor where the water was as clear as glass. Just as he arrived a very small boy went scampering along the harbor wall and tumbled off into the sea. Odysseus dived in after him and got him out and then sat him on his shoulder and carried him to his father. The boy's father took Odysseus home for a lot of dinner with grilled fish and bread and tomatoes and pale cheese and dark red wine. With these, and many other adventures, Odysseus passed through the pearly, light-dancing, sea-swirling land of Greece, and then over the Mediterranean in a cargo ship to Spain. Traveling through Spain was not easy, but still better than the prison camp where he might yet have been deciding whether the rat for dinner should be boiled or roasted. Eventually, with the help of some Gypsies who knew the same songs as him, Odysseus arrived in Gibraltar, which seemed practically next door to home. He would have written from there to England, but there happened to be a ship sailing that night whose captain had known him twenty years before, when they were both very young and often seasick. It was too good a chance to waste, so Odysseus didn't wait, but went aboard and shared the captain's cabin, all the way to Southampton.

Odysseus, after disembarking with two borrowed five-pound notes in his pockets and a promise to meet his friend again at the Duke of Wellington on Bugle Street as soon as the blasted war was over, thought, *I wonder if my Vanessa is still at that hospital?*

So he went to see, and she was.

Forty-One

THE RETURN OF ODYSSEUS TO HIS LOVING FAMILY could not have been better timed for Clarry and Miss Vane. When they arrived in Southampton they found Vanessa (who was very like him) in a mood to believe that anything was possible. Such was her elation that, unlike Clarry, she ignored the second half of the telegram from the start.

"Missing! Missing!" exclaimed Vanessa. "Rupert missing! Rubbish! What does that even mean? Hello, Miss Vane, I didn't see you there! How darling of you to come! Go on about Rupert! I've got news for you too, but it'll wait."

"I told you, we had a telegram, early this afternoon. I had to come away. You know what Father's like, and the house . . .

it's a hopeless house . . . anyway, I couldn't bear doing nothing and neither could Miss Vane."

"So you took to your heels? I would have done too."

"I thought straightaway of hospitals, and you."

"Does Peter know?"

"No yet. He will tomorrow; I wrote. You don't mind us coming, do you?"

"Of course I don't mind! Come to our little staff room! It's a hovel, but never mind. Tell me more, and tell it quickly because I have to be on duty very soon. Whoops! Don't sit on that cup, Miss Vane! No one has time to wash up."

"Vanessa, we'd have heard if he was taken prisoner, but could he be in hospital, and no one knowing his name?"

"Well . . ." Vanessa hesitated. "Well, Clarry darling, we usually do know their names at least, if not where they've come from. But . . . oh, Miss Vane, you don't have to do that! The sink's piled! There are dozens . . . well, you're an angel, that's all! 'Missing' is so vague, Clarry! But what do they really know? Remember when they told us my dad was a prisoner? That wasn't true for long!"

"Wasn't it? What have you heard, Vanessa?"

"He wasn't a prisoner for five minutes!" said Vanessa triumphantly. "I've been bursting to tell you! I saw him off on the train to Mummy this morning! Tiddly as a fish!"

"He's back? Oh, how wonderful!"

"Escaped, just like we knew he would. Came back through Greece and the Med. Had a wonderful time. So you see!"

"Yes, I do! Vanessa, listen! You know thousands of people in hospitals. . . ."

"Hundreds," said Vanessa modestly.

"Ask them, and ask them to ask their friends, and ask their friends to ask their friends two things. I've worked it out."

"Go on!"

"Have they ever, in say the last month, heard of anyone in a military hospital whose name isn't known? And, has anyone heard about Rupert? Rupert Penrose. I've written down the last address I had, and his regiment and number and anything I could think of that might be useful. He started off in a Devon battalion but then he changed a year or more ago."

"I'll ask people, Clarry."

"And I need a list of military hospitals where he might have been sent. But, Vanessa, what if he's still in France, too ill to move?"

"Well," said Vanessa sensibly. "He'll still be taken care of. And as soon as they can, he'll be sent over here."

Miss Vane, enterprisingly drying teacups on her handkerchief, looked around to say, "Families of very sick soldiers are invited over to France if they can travel. The Red Cross arranges it."

"But if he was in hospital anywhere you'd have been told,"

said Vanessa. "Unless he was too ill to talk and had lost his ID. I suppose in that case he might easily not have reached England yet. They have to be stable enough for the journey before they're sent back home."

"Then we need to ask the French hospitals too."

"Clarry, do you know how many hospitals there are in France and Belgium?"

"No."

"There must be a hundred. Base hospitals, where they're brought from the field stations, before they get here. You'd never manage it, you'd need a passport, and if you did, you'd never get round a tenth of them."

"I know, but I could write. And if I heard anything, work out a way to get there. And meanwhile there's still the hospitals here."

"I wish I could go overseas," said Vanessa. "I applied, as soon as Simon went. They won't let me, though. You have to be twenty-three and they check! Now, listen, Clarry, promise me something. You mustn't tell Simon about Rupert being missing!"

"I've been worrying about that too."

"He couldn't bear it. He'd believe the worst. I'll do anything I can to help you, as long as you don't tell Simon. Promise?"

"Promise. But he might hear anyway."

"Not yet. Perhaps not for ages. It's hell over there right now. You must make Peter promise too. He will; he'll understand."

"All right."

"Good! Here's Emma! Emma, this is my great friend Clarry and darling Miss Vane! They've lost lovely, lovely Rupert!"

"Good Lord, look at our teacups!" said Emma. "Not your lovely, lovely Rupert, Vanessa?"

"I borrowed him! He wasn't mine! I was just trying to cheer him up!"

Never, thought Vanessa remorsefully, must Clarry know the lengths to which she had gone, trying to cheer Rupert up. Or Peter. Peter must never know. It hadn't worked anyway.

"I know he wasn't really yours; he had lots of girlfriends, he told me," said Emma cheerfully. "From Ireland, London, all over the place! Anyway, what do you mean, 'lost'?"

"Stop talking rubbish and listen, Emma! Clarry is Rupert's cousin. She and her brother are his next of kin. They've just had a telegram."

"Oh, I'm sorry!" said Emma, looking absolutely stricken. "Oh, it happened to us, last year, my brother. . . ."

"Not the same, not the same!" said Vanessa impatiently. "Emma, will you look after Clarry and Miss Vane for me? I can't be late. I already owe Matron for this morning, seeing Dad off from the station. Clarry, where are you staying?"

"Anywhere. Somewhere cheap."

"I've an aunt who does rooms," said Emma. "If it helps."

Forty-Two

THAT WAS HOW THE GREAT SEARCH FOR RUPERT began. Practical things kept them busy. Clarry remembered how Peter had the picture of their mother reprinted, and she got out her photograph of Rupert. They had it turned into postcards, a hundred, for thirty shillings.

"Please give me one for old time's sake," begged Emma when she saw them.

By the end of the first week, Clarry had the addresses of sixty base hospitals in France and Belgium, and she and Miss Vane had written to every one of them. Also the Southampton hospitals had been checked, and a long chain of nurses, VADs, patients, ex-patients, and friends had been contacted by way of telegram and postcard, and asked to send back news. As well as all this, Violet, stalwart tram conductress and dedicated packer of gloves and socks, had been contacted and had reported back on the state of the cats. (*Stuffed, but your dad's in a shocking mood, Clarry! Let me know when you have to come home and face the music, and I'll come along with you to see fair play!*)

Miss Vane's energy seemed endless. In between everything else that had to be done, the little staff room at Vanessa's hospital had been polished to gleaming point, all the cupboards turned out, and the paintwork washed.

"Please stay forever!" many people begged her, and Miss Vane had to earnestly explain about her cats.

Peter wrote, *Yes, I'll go round the local hospitals, but I can't pretend that I don't think it's hopeless. How is Vanessa? Are you managing for money? What about your school, have you told them? I'm enclosing fourteen pounds, afraid I had to borrow most of it.* ("I love your brother!" said Vanessa when she read this.) *I don't see how anyone could lose his ID tags, whatever happened to him.*

Vanessa said that to an up-and-well-enough-for-light-duties patient and got a sideways look.

"What?" she asked.

"Well, you'd know if you'd ever been out there."

"Would I?"

"I don't want to upset you, but not everyone gets found."

"I know."

"Supposing, I'm not saying it happened, but supposing I was out after a charge or a lot of shellfire or something, and I came across . . . across some poor chap and I thought I should take his tag, let someone know."

"Yes."

"And it was raining, deep in mud, and I had maybe a minute to get back out of it. Probably dark coming on, or dark altogether, you wouldn't be out there if it wasn't. His tags are on a cord. You've got to get it out from under his jacket or whatever, pull it over his head, or cut it with something. Take one off, leave one behind, that's what you're supposed to do. And you're thinking all the time you need to get back, you need to get back!"

"Yes," said Vanessa compassionately, seeing the fright in his eyes. "Come on, sit down, you're out of it now. Thank you so much for telling me."

"I don't mind. It's in my head anyway. But you can see how things go wrong?"

"So easily now."

"Good! There's other ways too, things get mixed. You see chaps write a letter, give it to their friend. 'Send that home if I don't come back!' Then the wrong one cops it, and he's got a letter in his pocket that gets sent back to England. 'Good-bye, pat the dog for me, you were the best, sorry about all the swearing.' Only it's not his letter, it's his mate's, and his mate's not dead after all. Now I've upset you!"

"I am never upset," said Vanessa. "Never. How's the arm?"

"I can still feel it."

"Everyone says that."

"Always wanted to drive a car. Never be able to now."

"You absolutely will!" said Vanessa.

"Like to know how."

"Next time I get a weekend off I'll bring my dad's car back here and we'll take off in it for a ride. You driving."

"Oh yes?"

"Dare you!"

"You wouldn't!"

"Wait and see if I wouldn't," said Vanessa, back in her normal state, and prepared, as usual, to do anything, absolutely anything, to cheer someone up.

Later she related these examples of confused identity to Clarry, with some of the details omitted.

"You see!" said Clarry triumphantly. "We're going to London tomorrow. Miss Vane's got a map, and a list of possible hospitals, all marked on in different colored inks."

"She's wonderful; she's loving this."

"So many people have been wonderful. You and Emma

and Violet. Violet's going to brave my father and see if any letters have arrived."

"You'll hear more," Emma had told them. "When we lost Tristam, so many people wrote. His officer and a nurse who'd treated him for a day or two. His friends. A chaplain."

"Oh, Emma, how kind!" Clarry had exclaimed.

"It helped," Emma had said. "It helped us face it."

In the darkest parts of the night, when the blackout blotted the windows and Miss Vane was snoring gently on the other side of the room, Clarry faced it. Rupert dead. And she couldn't believe it. She thought (as Emma's mother had thought when she lost Tristam, as people had thought since the beginning of time), *If he were dead, I'd know.*

Forty-Three

TO LIE OUT STRAIGHT, WITH CLEAN SHEETS AND A solid roof, thought the young gunner in the French hospital. To know that for you it was over at last, and for nothing more than the cost of an eye and a broken shoulder. Worth it. Cheap at the price. The pretty nurses. He'd sent a message home. His family could stop worrying now.

But the chap in the next bed wouldn't shut up.

Droning.

Or singing. Very quietly, not moving his lips, a hardly changing note, the same phrase over and over.

Like a mosquito.

"*Three little maids who, all unwary . . .*"

"Could you say a word?" he asked a passing nurse.

"What? I'll be back in a minute."

She was back in ten, saying, "I'm sorry, we're terribly rushed. Is it your head? Are you in pain?"

"No. Yes. It's him in the next bed. Is he all right?"

She hurried as if it mattered then, bent over to look, checked a pulse, and asked, "Why did you worry?"

"He was sort of singing," he said, not liking to say, *He was driving me nuts.* "He's stopped now."

"Mr. Rose," he heard her say, very clearly. "Can you hear me, Mr. Rose? Squeeze my hand."

Mr. Rose lay immobile and silent.

"Why do you call him that?" he asked, but she frowned at him and shook her head and carried on holding Mr. Rose by his wrist, looking at her watch, and counting. As a matter of fact, she didn't know why he was called Mr. Rose. She'd arrived only two days before and she hadn't had time to speak to anyone properly. She didn't know that when he'd first arrived, before they'd done anything about his fractured skull, someone had asked, "Can you tell me your name?" and quite a while later he'd croaked, "Rosy."

The patient who'd called her over was pretty stable, she knew, but this one worried her. And puzzled her. And suddenly she realized why.

There was a postcard in the entrance hall with a label

above it asking, *Do you know this man?*

And she'd unpinned it that morning to read the back, a family plea for someone lost. How desperate had they been to write like that? she'd wondered, halfway through. And why choose here, out of all the hospitals in France and Belgium? And then she'd read the end and found a line that explained that they hadn't just chosen this one; they'd written to them all. Poor souls. And his name had been a Cornish name, just as her own name was. *Penrose.*

Rose.

Mr. Rose.

It was a five-minute walk back to the entrance hall, and there were only three staff on the ward and sixty beds, all full, but all the same she went, almost running.

The picture showed a tall, curly headed boy, smiling at someone, eyes squinting against the sun. The patient in the bed in front of her had a head wrapped up into a great white bundle, two black eyes swollen shut, and lips all cracked with fever from blood poisoning. He was immobilized from a broken pelvis too, and scattered with bits of shrapnel, but that was the least of his worries.

"Rupert Penrose," said the nurse, taking his hand again. "Rupert. There's a message for you here from Clarry."

Then she knew her guess had been right, because he smiled, and it was the smile that she'd seen in the picture.

Forty-Four

THE TELEGRAM CAME TO EMMA'S AUNT'S, BECAUSE that was the address on the postcard. Two travel passes followed, arranged by the Red Cross for relatives of patients who were critically ill. They were for in three days' time.

"Three days be damned!" roared Vanessa's father, as Vanessa had known he would when she telegrammed the news. He thought very highly of Clarry, not least because she had named him Odysseus and turned his exile into hope. "Three days be damned!" repeated Odysseus, and drove down in full naval uniform, commandeered a friend with a boat, and took them across himself; Clarry and Miss Vane, because Clarry, being under sixteen, needed a guardian. "You'll be the guardian?" he asked Miss Vane.

"I certainly will," she replied.

That was how, when Rupert opened his eyes at last, there was Clarry's face, drifting in and out of focus, but growing clearer all the time, through waves and waves of consciousness, as once, long ago, when he had fished her half-drowned from the sea.

"Hello, Rupert," said Clarry.

Forty-Five

CLARRY'S FATHER LOOKED AT HER FOR A LONG time and said finally, "Well."

Two months had passed and Clarry was back, facing the music, as Violet had put it, only it wasn't music, it was silence.

The whole house was eerily silent. The air was so still that when she moved it felt like she was disturbing something, like a puddle when it was stirred with a stick.

There was still a half-painted butterfly.

"We found Rupert," said Clarry, a bit unnecessarily because she could see perfectly well that on the mantelpiece was a neat stack of the letters she had posted home, the envelopes carefully slit.

"I don't know what I'm supposed to say to you," said her father.

"Have you been all right without me? I'm so sorry if you were worried."

"Worried?"

"I knew Rupert couldn't be dead," said Clarry. "If he'd been dead, we'd have known, wouldn't we?"

"In what way?"

"We'd . . . we'd have ached. I think. We'd have known somehow."

"Your grandfather's gone."

"Gone?"

"More than a week ago. Did you know somehow? Did you ache? I thought not. I'm just back from Cornwall. The funeral was yesterday."

Clarry stared at him, absolutely stunned.

"I'm sorry to have to tell you like this. Your grandmother is very much distressed. Since you've finished with school, I think you should go there. You might be some comfort, I don't know."

That was the worst moment, as bleak as when the telegram came.

But it passed, and Clarry was grown-up now.

She put her hand on her father's arm, and led him to a chair. She would have liked to hug him, but she knew that he would flinch away. Nevertheless she held his hand gently and said, "Poor Grandmother, poor Grandfather, poor, poor you, what an awful time you've had. Does Peter know?"

"Why should he? I have given up expecting anything from my children."

"I'll make tea, with sugar in, we had some sugar, I know. Something hot. And light the fire and warm the house up. Stay there. Please don't go."

He let her fetch a blanket, light the fire, and make tea. She lit the fire in the kitchen too. The kitchen cupboards had clearly been recently restocked by Mrs. Morgan. She found potatoes and a tin of ham and another of peas and made a sort of meal.

"It's much too cold in the dining room," she said, "but it's warming up in the kitchen now and I've pulled the table close to the range. Did Grandmother get my letter from France when I told her we'd found Rupert?"

"I presume so."

"Did . . . did Grandfather know?"

"I have no idea."

"Miss Vane was wonderful. She helped so much in France. She looked after the other families in the hostel who had come to see their sons, and she went shopping in the town for people, she speaks French much better than me, and she wrote letters home for patients. She's brought back another cat! A kitten, all the way from France in a basket!"

"And your cousin is well? It was all a fuss about nothing?"

"He has a fractured skull and a broken pelvis. He had blood poisoning. He was caught by shellfire, they think. They found him in a bomb crater; they didn't know how long he'd been there. Probably three or four days, at least. He hadn't any identification and he can't remember any of it. He said he was worrying about someone, and the next thing he knew he was in hospital."

Clarry looked up and saw her father wasn't listening, so she stopped.

Forty-Six

RUPERT WAS MOVED TO ENGLAND A WEEK AFTER
Clarry left France. By either luck or charm or a mixture of
both, he managed to get himself into one of the hospitals in
Clarry's own town.

"Thank goodness we're not getting him," said Vanessa
when she and Clarry met at the cottage.

"I thought you'd be disappointed," said Clarry. "You
could have cheered him up!"

"No, thank you," Vanessa replied. "I tried cheering him
up that time he came on leave. It didn't work out very well.
I don't think Rupert and I could cope with sponge baths
and bedpans and just-let-me-look-under-that-dressing.

Besides, I'm seriously thinking of giving it up."

"The bedpans and dressings?"

"No, no, the cheering! The last one I cheered up, that lovely dark boy who lost his arm (I taught him to drive, he was wonderful, he even managed the gears by the end), how was I to know he was engaged?"

"How did you find out?"

"She ambushed me. Very cross. I hate being shouted at."

"Poor you."

"I know. I felt like saying, *He kissed me first!* But I didn't want to show that I cared."

"Did you?"

"No more than usual. Never mind. The good news is that Simon is being moved back from the front for a bit. Oh, when will this blasted war be over, and what will I do when it is?"

"America will speed up the end, that's what everyone was saying in France."

"Perhaps, but I don't think the fast bit will be much fun. Talk about something else. What was it like facing the music?"

"Not very nice. A bit better now, though. Grandmother has come to stay so she can be close to Rupert."

"And Lucy!"

"Oh, what a good idea, Vanessa! She could see Lucy! How could I get her here? Perhaps Mr. King?"

"Don't be ridiculous, Clarry! You know my dad adores you! He'll come and fetch you both in the car, since he has unkindly reclaimed it again. Leave it to me, I'll sort it. Are you going? Give Rupert my love, and Peter. And everyone at school. You are still going to school? Are you happy, Clarry?"

"Yes," said Clarry, and she was. It was the spring of 1918 and she was unexpectedly content. Rupert and Simon were temporarily safe. Someone who was not Rupert was in love with Vanessa. Peter was happy in Oxford, transformed by finding something worth doing at last. Small cheerful things happened. Violet, who had recently been writing very highly scented letters indeed, had come to borrow the pink hat.

"For a photograph," she said. "He's had one in my tram conductor's uniform, and he's had one by the shop, and now I want something fancy by the lilacs in the park. If it's all right that I borrow it?"

"Of course! It's lovely! Didn't I say you could?" asked Clarry, running to fetch it. "But Violet, who is he?"

"It's Eddie from those first socks I sent that were all your idea! I've had eleven letters now and two postcards with the same picture and he's looking out for a shell case to make into a vase. The brass ones polish up lovely, he says. I've told them all at Red Cross about him. I'm surprised Miss Vane hasn't told you!"

Clarry was not surprised because recently Miss Vane had

developed a new interest of her own. When she had come back from France to find her cats stuffed to cushion size, the earth box scrubbed white, and her back door repainted a beautiful emerald green, she had naturally invited Mr. King to dinner. He in turn had produced a perfectly respectable little dogcart, polished Jester so he looked like a newly varnished black and white rocking horse, and taken her jaunting into the spring countryside. She had returned looking ten years younger and carrying a bunch of cowslips.

"Good Lord, Miss Vane!" exclaimed Clarry's father indignantly, as soon as Mr. King drove away. "The rag-and-bone man!"

"He is actually a very knowledgeable art and antiques dealer," said Miss Vane proudly, "who prefers to source his own stock."

"He sourced my piano," said Clarry's father, who never ever forgot or forgave.

"It was entirely wasted and being ruined by damp," replied Miss Vane with spirit.

"You've changed your tune!"

"Yes, I have, Mr. Penrose," agreed Miss Vane. "I am happy to say I have!"

Clarry's father was very much put out. In the past he had never bothered to treat Miss Vane much more considerately than he had Clarry, but at the same time, the option that it might prove useful to marry her and that she would be grateful if he did had always been at the back of his mind. Now he was suddenly alarmed and he stood dithering in the street, half inclined to ask her now and secure her before she did anything rash, half inclined to rudeness.

Rudeness won.

"You want to make sure he doesn't source you, Miss Vane!" he snapped, and to his dismay she laughed happily, said, "Oh, thank you, Mr. Penrose!" smelled her cowslips, and tossed her head.

"That silly woman Vane is scheming to marry the rag-and-bone man!" he told his family at dinner that night.

"Oh, good," exclaimed Clarry. "Violet and I can be bridesmaids!"

"I told you years ago that you should snap her up," Clarry's grandmother said calmly. "As usual you ignored me, and as always, I was correct. Instead you let this house get into a dreadful state, and left it to me to put right!"

"It was perfectly satisfactory," said Clarry's father grumpily.

"It was a disgrace," said Clarry's grandmother. She had always been a woman who liked her own way and as soon as she had arrived, she had set about getting it. She couldn't bear cold rooms, and she detested damp beds, and she didn't like to see the wallpaper peeling off the walls in the corners. She also liked three hot meals a day, flowers in the windows, clean rugs, and polished floors.

"You can't find people to scrub for love nor money these days," Mrs. Morgan told her, but Grandmother had found them. Within a week of her arrival she had the rooms turned out, all the chimneys swept, the paintwork washed, and the paper glued back up.

"I have ordered coal and wood and kindling and opened an account at the general store," she told Clarry's father, who was so torn between temper and sulking that he didn't know what to say. "Also Mrs. Morgan's neighbor's niece is coming in for two hours every morning to help with the fires and two hours every evening to help with the supper, and in between I will cope."

"Er," he said, sneezing at the smell of polish and glancing ungratefully at the daffodils glowing in the window. "As long as I'm not expected to pay for all this, I suppose I will have to agree."

"Of course you're expected to pay for it! What on earth is the matter with you?" demanded his mother, and so he said he had to go out and then fell over Miss Fairfax on the doorstep.

"I've come to see what's going on with Clarry," said Miss Fairfax.

"I haven't the faintest idea," said Clarry's father, and almost ran away.

Miss Fairfax did not waste time on idle gossip. It had not gone unnoticed at school that their Dark Horse had vanished, and she was determined to find out more.

"Quite a number of people went out of their way to help your granddaughter," she told Clarry's grandmother severely, "and naturally they have been disappointed to find that they were wasting their time."

"I did write to school!" said Clarry, who had come into the room at the sound of her voice. "I'm very sorry, Miss Fairfax. I had to find out what had happened to my cousin, you see."

Miss Fairfax did not seem to see. Nor was she much moved when she heard the tale of the loss of Rupert, his rediscovery in France, and how at last he had been brought back home.

"Quite enterprising," she said. "How fortunate he has been. And now he is recovering?"

"He's making wonderful progress," Clarry's grandmother told her. "Luckily he is quite near to us so I have been able to see him often, and every day Clarry visits on her bicycle."

"Every day?" asked Miss Fairfax, turning to look at Clarry. "Is that really necessary? Is it not, now he is so well, rather a *fuss*?"

At this terrible word Clarry blushed red with shame and could no longer look at Miss Fairfax.

Peter was even more direct, and he did it in front of

Rupert, now promoted to crutches and encouraged to try them outside.

"You've got too comfortable with Grandmother fussing over you," he said to Clarry. "And Rupert here, held captive, so you can have fun playing nurses."

"Shut up, Pete!" snapped Rupert, who had reached the getting-well stage of feeling like a tiger constantly prodded with a stick.

"No, I won't," said Peter. "Clarry was doing all right, except her Greek was rubbish and she could have worked on that. Now you've appeared she's let it all go. You're not going to stay here forever, and neither will Grandmother. So what will she do? Run around skivvying after our father while she waits for someone to marry her?"

"No, I WON'T!" snapped Clarry, with flaming cheeks, but that night she got out her school uniform and gazed at it. The mushroom hat looked less becoming than ever, but she found herself opening the books.

Rupert was improving every day. One final operation had removed the last of the shrapnel from his leg, and he hardly had a headache anymore. The last of the bandages could come off any day. His temper had improved since they started him on exercises. He could walk with just a stick.

"I shall take him down to Cornwall for some proper sea

air," his grandmother announced, but when Rupert heard this proposal he grinned.

"I'm not going to live with my granny!" he said.

"What, then?" asked Clarry. "You'd hate it with Father and me."

"Well," said Rupert, "there are other places. I promised old Irish I'd go and see his family."

"He died, didn't he?"

Rupert's face closed up, the way it did when the war was mentioned. He could not bear it. All the time he'd been ill he had never said a word about what had happened. However, between things the hospital in France had told her, and letters that had arrived when it was heard Rupert had been found, Clarry and her grandmother knew most of it. *He was wild the night before,* someone had written, *light-headed, singing Irish ballads, talking nonsense, burning with fever. He should have been sent back, but we were going over into an early morning attack. We drank a bit, wrote letters home, everyone was jittery. We marched to the front and tried to get some sleep in the couple of hours before dawn.*

That morning had come the first blue sky they had seen for weeks, the rain had vanished, and so had Rupert. *We know now,* wrote the friend, *that he must have pushed aside the chap on sentry duty. He probably caught him dozing. Of course, nothing was reported.*

"Of course not," said Clarry. The penalty for sleeping on sentry duty was death by firing squad. Even her grandmother knew that.

We went over the top ourselves minutes later, the letter had continued. *And after that everything was hell.*

And so Rupert's escape had gone unrecorded. As had his fevered race across the battlefields of Passchendaele, shedding everything that might have identified him, pushing through the wires and winding paths and bogs, ending not in a leap to green and blue sparkling water, but in a roar of shell-fire and a blast that lifted him into a crater where he stayed for three days, unconscious in the good times, singing in the bad, until someone crawled out and found him and managed to drag him back into the chaos of the trenches where there was no one left who knew his name.

He'd been so great for so long, he'd stuck out so much, he didn't deserve it to end like that, his friend had written.

No one deserves any of it, Clarry had written back.

Now Rupert was watching her face, and she knew, with ice-cold fear, that he was about to tell her something awful.

"Darling Clarry . . ."

"Don't call me darling!"

"Haven't I always called you darling?"

"Just say it, Rupert."

"After Ireland, as soon as they'll let me . . ."

"No!"

"Yes, I've got to. I'm going back."

"Who have you told?" whispered Clarry at last.

"No one," said Rupert. "I'm just telling you."

Forty-Seven

AFTER RUPERT WENT TO IRELAND, THEY DIDN'T SEE him again. He passed his medical in August; he wrote and told them that. Simon, Clarry's gentle giraffe, sent a message to say, "Tell him not to come."

But they couldn't.

Vanessa raged, "How could he do that to Clarry?"

"He could at least have told us himself," said his grandmother bitterly. She was more distressed than Clarry had ever seen her before.

"The coward," said Clarry's father.

Clarry said nothing. She had said it all to Rupert the day that he told her, and it had made no difference, except that they had parted angrily, hurt and hurting, instead of parting friends. Peter said nothing because he sort of understood, although he couldn't have listed the reasons as clearly as Rupert had.

Rupert's reasons, spoken aloud to no one, were these:

One: Clarry. He could still hear Peter's bitter comments: "Clarry was doing all right. . . . Now you've appeared she's let it all go." And Peter was telling the truth. Clarry had a chance to escape. He couldn't risk her losing it. Two: That silly kid, Simon Bonnington, who never should have been there, who wouldn't have been, if it weren't for him. But if Clarry had already had her place at Oxford, if Simon had been safe at home, Rupert knew that he would still go back. He couldn't see that he had any choice. His third reason, the one that drove him hardest, was this: It wasn't finished.

Rupert knew that he couldn't rest until it was finished. He had to go. He'd left friends there.

When Rupert left them, Clarry's grandmother went back to Cornwall. Clarry could have gone with her, but she didn't. She got out her books and the mushroom hat and worked and worked and worked, driven at first by a grim, hungry anguish that waited to clutch every time she paused to think. Even after the pain faded to just a gnawing presence she still went on.

Her books saved her. Miss Fairfax regarded her Dark Horse with pride. "She's come through," she said. "She'll make it now. She's on the final stretch."

The war was also on its final stretch, a great last peak of suffering for everyone involved. The smile of the western front had twisted and become jagged-toothed in places, but it was still as insatiable as ever. August passed, and September, and then in early October, just when they could bear no more, another telegram came.

Forty-Eight

GIRAFFES WERE NEVER DESIGNED FOR TRENCH warfare. Simon the Bony One died at the western front, on the last day of September 1918. A sniper shot him, straight through the head. *He wouldn't have known a thing,* wrote his commanding officer wearily, although, actually, at that final moment, a great understanding had blown through the elated Bony One. He had died with such a certainty of joy and freedom that if he could he would have shouted out to those who loved him, "Hey! It's going to be all right!"

But of course, they knew nothing about that.

Vanessa couldn't bear it. She ran from her pain, not to

Clarry or her family, but to Peter in Oxford, who had understood Simon first.

"It's not fair, it's not fair," she sobbed in Peter's arms. "Say something, don't just stand there!"

"It's not fair," said Peter.

"I can't bear it any longer! I've borne it right from the beginning, and I can't bear it anymore. Simon never should have been there. Why did he have to go? Bloody Rupert," wailed Vanessa, answering herself. "Bloody Rupert, that's why! Oh, why did he have to love Rupert?"

"He always did," said Peter. "Right from the beginning."

"I know, I know, he told me," sobbed Vanessa, weary with tears. "And now look what's happened because of it. We've got to manage without him. For ages and ages. For the rest of our lives. For always, and I can't. I can't be *bothered*."

In spite of everything, Peter grinned at that.

"Stop laughing! I've got to go soon. They only gave me eight hours free. Eight hours, and Simon dead. I've got to go back and do the night shift and not fuss and be cheerful. Do I smell of carbolic?"

"Yes, very strongly, but I'm used to it. I suppose you could go to your family for a bit."

"No, thank you! They'd cling and weep. Cling and weep and I'd never escape again. I can't live there anymore. When this horrible war is over I'm going to marry the first man who

asks me and live happily ever after. Or as close as I can manage. I'll give it a damn good try."

"Oh," said Peter glumly, not liking this plan, and then a
very good idea struck him and he asked, "Vanessa, will you
marry me?"

"Yes, of course I will, you idiot," said Vanessa. "I thought
you'd never ask!"

Forty-Nine

AND SO THEY REELED THROUGH OCTOBER, AND in November the war ended, and Vanessa, hearing rumors of what was coming, borrowed a motorbike and rode through the night to be with her family at the cottage on Armistice Day. Simon had missed it by less than two months, which was very hard to bear, and for an hour or two they didn't try bearing it at all. They had reached the cup-of-tea-and-moping up stage when Clarry arrived on Peter's bicycle, saying, "Oh, Vanessa! I didn't know you'd be here! I just came to give them a hug. How are they?"

"Heroes," said Vanessa, who had met her on the door-step. "But it's been very damp. You were wonderful to come,

Clarry, but don't go in just yet. It will start them off again."

"I brought some sugar for Lucy," said Clarry, so they went across the field to find her. Lucy took the sugar ungratefully, looking over Clarry's shoulder, and they both knew she was searching for Simon.

"Oh, BLAST!" said Vanessa. "Oh, come on, Clarry! There's no one about for a million miles. Let's lie on the grass and howl!"

"Yes, all right, good idea," said Clarry, but she didn't howl, she lay on her front with her fists in her eyes and presently she said, "Wouldn't it have been lovely if there hadn't been any war? And we were all . . ."

Then she broke off, and didn't say any more.

The November day became quiet again. Under the hedge, a blackbird turned over dead leaves like someone flicking through a book to find the illustrations. The grass was damp but overhead the sky was a thin crystal blue. At last Vanessa sighed and said, "The moment has passed. It seems that I can only howl spontaneously. Do you think there are spiders out here?"

"What? Oh, probably hundreds."

"I can't lie on spiders. I'm fetching the hearthrug."

"Don't, it'll worry your parents. And spoil the smell of the grass."

"Oh, all right," said Vanessa. "I can't really be bothered

anyway. Grass is such an old-fashioned smell! Did they ever smell grass in France?"

"Yes, yes, of course they did." Clarry sat up and took her friend's cold hand, and held it warm in her own. "Often, and it must have reminded them of home. It is old-fashioned, think how far back it goes. Shakespeare smelled it, flat on his face in the Avon meadows! Arthur, before he pulled his sword from that stone, under the oaks and beeches of the ancient forest . . ."

"Go on, go on!" said Vanessa, gripping her hand.

"The Romans at the end of a day on their Roman roads, setting up camp. Flatbread and cheese for supper, and raisins and onions."

"Lovely."

"The people who raised the henge stones, collapsed, exhausted, staring at what they'd done and wondering if it would last."

"Hoping the woolly mammoths wouldn't knock it over," said Vanessa, "or the dinosaurs. Was there grass in dinosaur days?"

"Not until the Cretaceous," said Clarry, so seriously that Vanessa really did howl a bit, with laughter, not tears. Then they checked each other's faces and went to the cottage, and were very brave and cheerful. Later, with Clarry's bicycle hanging out of the back, they all drove into town where they

found bonfires and singing crowds and the pubs full to over-
flowing.

Vanessa and Clarry leaned wearily on each other and
said, "I suppose we should feel wonderful," but mostly they
felt empty.

The years passed.

They heard nothing from Rupert, who as soon as he was
released from active service went straight to India to track
down the parents who had abandoned him at age three. And
when he found them, he realized he should never have bothered; but India was different. He traveled farther and farther
north, losing himself in the otherness of the world that he
found there.

Clarry went to Oxford, which she loved more even than
Miss Fairfax had guessed that she would. She got her MA and
her grandmother came proudly to see her graduation but her
father, when invited, said he'd really rather not.

The spare key to the cricket pavilion eventually found its
way back to England, along with a few other bits and pieces. It
absolutely baffled Simon's mother, who sat rocking and gazing at it for hours some days, until Peter happened to visit,
glimpsed it in her hands, and exclaimed, "I never thought I'd
see that again!"

"Do you know what it is?" she asked.

"It's the spare key to the cricket pavilion. I gave it to Simon at the end of our last term. It's the Penrose Bonners Award for Sticking It Out at School, with Special Commendation for That Time He Didn't Climb out of the Window!"

"Oh, Peter!"

"He wore it always," said Peter, taking it carefully into his hand. "He put it on as soon as . . ." For a moment, the memory of Simon's incredulous beaming smile as he saw what his friend had given him caused Peter to have to press his fists to his eyes.

"He put it on straightaway," he continued, after a minute. "As soon as he got it. He was the best. . . . It wasn't a joke. There were lots of jokes, but that wasn't one of them."

Then, still holding the key, he told Simon's mother about clearing the common-room chimney with the rocket, and the way they had sung together in chapel, and the beer bottles under the floorboard, and how Rupert had taught them the fan dance for "Three Little Maids from School," and the way Simon used to laugh until tears ran down his face. And how they had stuck out school together, and how Peter couldn't have done it without Simon at his side, and that's why he had been given the award.

"You should put it on a new string and wear it sometimes," he said, as he very gently gave the key back and stood up to go, and she said, "Yes, I will. I will do. I will."

After Peter had gone that day, Vanessa and Simon's mother and father (whom Clarry had named Odysseus) told each other how thankful they were that Vanessa was marrying Peter, and how good it would be to have him and Clarry in the family forever, and after that they began to get better.

There were lots of weddings. Violet borrowed Clarry's pink hat again. It was her "something borrowed."

"I looked washed out in white and I'm not wearing a veil!" she said, very jaunty in pink and high heels. Miss Vane, however, had snow white silk, with Clarry and Violet for bridesmaids and she invited Mrs. Morgan. Mrs. Morgan rose magnificently to this peace offering, and gave the bride a lucky horseshoe, one of the collection of those she had made herself.

She gave another one to Peter, when he and Vanessa married.

"I never thought I'd see the day!" she said as she handed it over, and Peter said neither had he. He and Vanessa nailed their horseshoe over the door of their small cheerful house in Oxford. There, they lived together very happily, with a room for Clarry in the attic whenever she wanted it, and a great many books, the most wonderful being the one that Peter and Clarry wrote together. It was called:

Origins of Nomenclature in the Animal Kingdom
Clarry Penrose, MA (Oxon) and Peter Penrose, D.Phil. (Oxon)

It was a book that they had planned to write together when Clarry was eleven.

Clarry was a teacher. She loved it, as she had done ever since the first Grace twin had exclaimed, "Now I understand!"

Peter eventually became a professor, which did not surprise anyone. His home was filled with children, as well as books—first Janey after Peter's mother, and then Beatrice after Vanessa's, and then, at last, little Simon, who came with a surprise twin brother. The moment Clarry heard of the second baby's arrival, which was about three minutes after he was born, she exclaimed, "You will have to call him Rupert!"

And Vanessa and Peter, still blinking with shock, recovered and agreed.

The arrival of a new Simon and Rupert for the world to enjoy caused Vanessa such pride and delight that she put a notice of their birth in the *Times* in the hope that Rupert might see it.

PENROSE, TO PETER AND VANESSA (NEE
BONNINGTON). TWIN BOYS, SIMON AND RUPERT
(CLARRY SAID WE HAD TO CALL HIM RUPERT).
JUNE 21, 1924.

Vanessa went to this expense in the hope that somehow the news would reach Rupert in India.

At this time Rupert was working on a tea plantation at the foothills of the Himalayas. It was very beautiful there and he thought how much Clarry would love it. He thought of Clarry often, more and more of the happy times, and less and less of their last dreadful day together when she had begged him not to go back to France and he had told her to stop clinging and walked away and left her.

In those days, for the British in India, a large amount of the news from home came via the the *Times* newspaper. It was read and passed around, ringed in pencil and under-lined, and scrutinized for familiar names by everyone from England who got hold of it.

So it wasn't surprising that someone said to Rupert, "Oi, is this you?" and there, circled in blue, was his name, with Peter and Vanessa, and Simon, who had loved him, and Clarry, who it seemed had forgiven him after all.

So he sent a telegram back to England saying,

> *Congratulations, and love to everyone.*
> *Re Simon and Rupert*
> *Perfect.*

Fifty

NOT LONG AFTER THE BIRTH OF THE LATEST Penrose baby (Charles, after Charles Darwin), Peter and Clarry's grandmother died. For the last few years she had lived in Oxford, within reach of Clarry and Peter and the children, and with Lucy, now age twenty-nine, in a small field close by. From the very beginning she had loved being a great-grandmother. She had named herself Great-Granny and adored her great-grandchildren so completely and uncritically that she had astonished herself. *I never used to be like this,* she thought sometimes. *I've mellowed!*

But now she was gone, and she had left the house in Cornwall to Clarry and Peter. It hadn't been lived in for years and years and it was still full of her things, not just furniture, but all the letters and clothes and old-lady belongings that she hadn't wanted to bring to Oxford.

"I shall have to go and sort them out," said Clarry unhappily to Vanessa. "And don't say Peter will help because he'd be useless, and anyway Great-Granny would hate him poking through her things. She was a very dignified old lady."

"I've never been to Cornwall; there was never time after the babies started arriving," remarked Vanessa. "Peter said you used to love your summers there."

"They were perfect," said Clarry, her voice a little unsteady. "Perfect, from the moment we arrived."

"What made them so wonderful?" asked Vanessa, who was always on the lookout for ideas to make life wonderful for her own children. "I hope whatever it was is still there. Perhaps one day we could . . . oh, I'm sorry, Clarry!"

For Clarry, quite suddenly, was rubbing tears away.

"I'm an insensitive hag," said Vanessa repentantly. "Poor Great-Granny. But she was very old, Clarry darling, and happy, right to the end."

"I know. It's not Great-Granny," said Clarry, sniffing damply. "I was just remembering. Everything. Everyone . . ."

Vanessa looked at her thoughtfully and, when Clarry did not continue, picked up a child from the floor and handed it to her to cuddle. Then she waited a tactful minute or two before asking kindly, "Is it Rupert?"

"No," said Clarry miserably, after glancing down to look. "It's darling Bea."

"Thank you very much, Clarry! I can actually tell my children apart. And you know quite well what I meant!"

"Yes, I do. Yes, it is. Rupert. All right there, Bea?"

Bea nodded. All Vanessa's children were used to cuddles, especially at times like this: the sleepy end of the day between supper and stories. Bea put her thumb in her mouth, and tucked herself comfortably under Clarry's chin. She was a warm, solid child, very comforting, and Clarry hugged her as she continued slowly, "Cornwall and Rupert are all mixed up together, and it was so long ago, and magical. It'll be all changed now, but it was the best place in the world. We longed for it all winter, the moorland and the sea and the little town, and the train pulling into the station."

"That will still be pretty much the same, Clarry."

"And Rupert, waiting there."

"Blooming Rupert!" said Vanessa.

Clarry did not argue, just dropped her head a little.

"Did he always matter so much?"

"Yes," said Clarry. It was very difficult to describe what Rupert's sunlit welcome had meant after the long unloved winters of her childhood, but nevertheless, she tried. "The grandparents were so remote, you see. Most of the time

Peter lived in his own world too. And Father . . ."

"Neglected you completely," said Vanessa calmly. "According to Peter."

"It wasn't that bad. But it was lonely, and then Rupert, every summer, so pleased to see us. Such a welcome. Laughing. Kind, and funny and fun. It was so blissful to be talked to, and teased, and hugged and bothered about. I was a bit invisible, I suppose, and Rupert made me visible. And it wasn't just being kind because he was sorry for me. We were proper friends."

"You were. I remember you both at that Christmas party. And afterward through so much. Girlfriends, war! Even me!"

Clarry laughed, lifting her face from Bea's red curls.

"That must have stung."

"A bit. Mostly for Peter."

"I'm sorry."

"It was nothing. Not compared to the day that telegram came. Or when I found him in France, so broken."

"But you got him home again, and he got better."

"I thought so, but I was wrong. Inside he wasn't better. He couldn't live with himself."

"There were a lot like that, Clarry," said Vanessa, who never had a day without thinking of the boys in the beds. "They felt guilty for surviving."

"He told me he was going back, and then we stopped being friends. We smashed it all up."

"How?"

"I didn't try to understand. I argued. I fought him. I cried. He said I clung. He shouted, 'Leave me alone! Leave me alone!' and shook me off and ran away, stumbled away, with that stick."

"Oh, Clarry!"

"So I did leave him alone. I helped Peter write to him, after Simon, but I didn't sign my name and we didn't hear back. Simon must have been very hard for him. Rupert knew why he was there."

"Simon was an idiot," said Vanessa crossly. "No, he wasn't. He was just terribly young. They all had to grow up too soon."

"Yes," said Clarry. "You must keep yours little forever and ever. And put books on their heads when they start to grow tall."

Bea looked up at her in surprise. Clarry slid her to the floor, reached for a book, and balanced it on her own head, to show her. Bea copied, with *Peter Rabbit*. Janey, who was her father all over again, said, "I don't think it will work," but all the same picked up a book herself and tried it, just in case.

Bea laughed and her book slid onto her lap.

"You have to not laugh," said Janey solemnly.

"No!" said Clarry, tipping her own book off at these words. "I was wrong. No books on heads! You have to laugh! You have to grow! And I have to go to Cornwall."

"What is Cornwall?" asked Janey, and so Clarry told her about the blue and green sea, and the house on the moors, and how she and Janey's daddy had traveled there every summer on a train, all by themselves, with no grown-ups.

"Can I go?" asked Janey.

"One day, perhaps."

"On a train with just Bea and no grown-ups?"

"Do you think you'd like that?"

"Yes!" said Janey, jumping up and down. "Who would meet us at the station?"

"That's the thing," said Clarry. "You have to have someone very special and wonderful to meet you at the station."

"Did you?"

"Yes," said Clarry. "I did."

Later Vanessa said, "Listen, Clarry, leave the sorting and things a little while longer, and when Charles is bigger I'll come with you and help."

"Would you really? It would be better with two."

"As soon as he's a bit less nocturnal," said Vanessa, looking across at Charles, tight asleep in his cradle, collecting his strength so that he would be able, explained his parents, to stay awake all night imperiously demanding milk, songs, walking up and down, trips to look at the moon out of the window, and as many people as possible to keep him company.

A month passed, and then another; Vanessa's parents agreed to come and babysit. Charles's nighttime revels grew no less wild (worse, according to his mother), but suddenly she gave up waiting for him to change and said, "Never mind, Peter will cope, he's brilliant with the children. It's amazing how he knows how to manage."

"It's not," said Peter. "I just think of my own father and do the exact opposite." (Peter's father, when invited to visit his grandchildren, always blanched and said, "Good Lord. Very kind. I don't think so.")

So it was arranged, and a date was chosen, and everything planned except that Vanessa changed her mind over and over between going by train ("Such bliss to just sit") and driving down because a car would be so useful when they got there. But at last she decided on the train, and their bags were packed and their tickets were bought, and the grandparents installed, and Peter drove them to the station. Clarry and Vanessa found an empty carriage and put their bags on the saggy string luggage rack overhead, and the doors began to slam all along the train, and the guard raised his whistle to his lips and Vanessa said suddenly, "You know, Clarry, I think I should drive after all!" and before Clarry could say a word, she'd jumped off, and a second later the train pulled out of the station.

Clarry sat quite stunned staring out of the window, and outside the half-familiar landscape went floating by, and she fought back tears as the memories came pouring in and filled the empty carriage with their clamor.

At first they overwhelmed her, but as the journey passed she untangled them one by one and held them in her thoughts.

Her father, handing her the sovereign, stepping back with relief into his solitary world.

Peter, white faced and enduring. Happy now at last.

Simon.

Dear, gallant Simon.

Rupert, the bravest and the kindest. Who all through her childhood had never failed her once. For years she'd believed she would never see him again, but since the arrival of the twins she had known he still thought of them. *Perhaps one day,* thought Clarry, remembering the telegram he had sent back to Oxford.

Congratulations, and love to everyone.

Love to everyone, love to everyone, love to everyone, echoed the train, and Clarry drifted into sleep.

"Got her off?" Peter asked, reappearing on the platform as soon as Clarry's train had disappeared.

"Yes, but her face! I had to leave it to the last half second in case she ran after me."

"I've just telegraphed that she's on time."

"This is easily the most difficult cheer-up yet! The lies

we've told about poor little Charles! For months he's been the best behaved of them all!"

"Doesn't matter. Worth it."

"Is it going to be all right, Peter?"

"Yes," said Peter. "It's going to be all right."

Clarry awoke with a start. They were nearly there. There were glimpses of sea, brighter even than she'd remembered, and red rooftops in the distance, coming closer, and the train was slowing with great gusts of steam, and despite all that had happened, the familiar joy was growing and growing, so she could hardly wait to tug down the window and open the door, and jump out at the little station.

And there was someone hurrying over the footbridge, and he reached the train in time to swing her down onto the platform. She could feel him laughing as he held her, and he said, "Clarry. Darling Clarry!"

And it was Rupert.

THE WORLD BEHIND THE STORY

Peter, Clarry, and Vanessa. Simon the Bony One. Rupert, Odysseus, Mrs. Morgan. Violet and Miss Vane. Mr. King the rag-and-bone man. They came so alive for me writing this book.

I think that was because their world was true. It gave them such a solid background that they could stand out against it as real people.

The time is the very beginning of the twentieth century: 1902. Queen Victoria has recently died, and her eldest son, Edward VII, is surprising everyone by turning out not quite as useless as his mother had predicted he would be. There are bicycles (nearly all for men and boys, though), steam trains, a very few cars, and a great many horses. There are no airplanes or antibiotics, Everest has not yet been climbed, and the South Pole has not been reached. There is no plastic. Einstein is beginning to have ideas about relativity, but hardly anyone knows about this yet. Probably a good thing; the general public is only just getting over Charles Darwin's theory of evolution. People are reading books (although not paperbacks yet), and education is no longer just for those who can pay for it. Poor children can still leave school at nine or ten, but now they often stay on until thirteen. After that, for most students, their formal education is over. But for some there are boarding schools, as there have been for centuries, and the new secondary schools are beginning to open. Once again, these are mostly for boys: there are three or four schools for boys to every one school for girls. Clarry and Vanessa are lucky.

Money is different. Money is real. The coins are made of copper, silver, and gold. Top quality silver and twenty-two karat gold! There are twelve big copper pennies to a shilling. Twenty silver shillings to a pound. A pound is a golden sovereign, a very beautiful coin. Clarry has one from her father for her birthday one summer. I don't think it is a planned present: I think Peter has just hissed at him, last minute, on the railway station platform, "Of course, you've forgotten her birthday *again*!"

The background to the second half of *The Skylarks' War* is World War I. This terrible war began in the summer of 1914 and carried on until late in 1918. The suffering of those fighting, the occupied countries, and the families left behind who sent the soldiers off to war is beyond my ability to describe. So I will stick to plain facts.

Where Simon and Rupert fight, on the western front, more than four million men and more than a million horses died. (Read Michael Morpurgo's superb *War Horse*!) Soldiers were supposed to be nineteen years old to serve overseas, but it was easy to get around that. Birth certificates were not required to sign up. Simon is eighteen when he goes to France, but some were much younger. There are records of thirteen- and fourteen-year-olds fighting in the trenches.

While so many men were abroad, workers were needed at home. For the first time girls and women were given a chance to show what they could achieve. They made weapons, drove trains and buses and trams, farmed the land, ran the hospitals, worked in factories and offices. Sally Nicholls has written a great book called *Things a Bright Girl Can Do*, which describes the growing freedom of young women at this time.

When I am working on a story it helps me to have some "real" things about me as I write. That is why on my desk I kept Clarry's gold sovereign, Peter's star book, and the key to the cricket pavilion. If you would like to see what they look like, and find out more about this fascinating period of time, log on to my website: hilarymckay.co.uk.

BIBLIOGRAPHY
(WITH THANKS TO JIM!)

I could not have written *The Skylarks' War* without these books:

Addington, Scott. *World War One: A Layman's Guide*. scottaddington.com, 2012.

Adie, Kate. *Fighting on the Home Front*. London: Hodder & Stoughton, 2013.

Adlington, Lucy. *Great War Fashion: Tales from the History Wardrobe*. Stroud, UK: History Press, 2013.

Brittain, Vera. *Testament of Youth*. London: Virago Press, 1978.

Clare, John D. *First World War (I Was There)*. London: Riverswift, 1994.

Dent, Olive. *A Volunteer Nurse on the Western Front*. London: Grant Richards, 1917.

Gilber, Adrian. *Going to War in World War One*. London: Franklin Watts, 2001.

Grant, D. F. *The History of "A" Battery 84th Army Brigade RFA, 1914–1918*. Brighton, UK: The Book Guild Publishing, 2013.

Hansen, Ole Steen. *The War in the Trenches*. Lewes, UK: White-Thomson Publishing, 2000.

Jones, Nigel. *Peace and War: Britain in 1914*. London: Head of Zeus, 2014.

Langbridge, R. H. *Edwardian Shopping*. Newton Abbot, Devon, UK: David & Charles (Publishers) Ltd.,1975.

Mayhew, Emily. *Wounded: From Battlefield to Blighty, 1914–1918*. London: Bodley Head, 2013.

Picture Taking with the Brownie Camera No. 2. Toronto, Canada: Canadian Kodak Co. Limited, [pre-1923]

SSAFA. *The Great War, 1914–18: SSAFA's Official Guide to World War 1*. London: CW Publishing Group, 2014.

Tait, Derek. *Plymouth in the Great War*. Barnsley, Yorkshire: Pen & Sword Military, 2104.

Williamson, Henry. *How Dear Is Life*. Stroud, Gloucestershire: Macdonald & Co., 1954.